Book Smarts

and

Tender Hearts

Shelley Pearson

ISBN: 978-1-7324082-0-3

Cover photograph by Shelley Pearson.
Cover and book design by Bradley Knox.

Printed by Ingram Spark in the United States of America.

First printing 2018.

www.shelleypearsonwrites.com

For Shirley Burt

What's a zine?

A zine (pronounced "zeen") is a self-published magazine that has a relatively small distribution and is often photocopied. Zines can be about any subject chosen by the maker, and can include text, photos, drawings, or anything else that will copy.

1

The last thing I expect to smell when my mother pulls open the front door of the Silver Wells Alzheimer's Care Center is freshly-baked cookies. But the scent is there, along with a sickly sweet air freshener and an antiseptic tang. I glance around the fancy, uncomfortable lobby. Hard little couches, vases of flowers everywhere, and a fireplace that has probably never been used. A plate of chocolate chip cookies, small and not-quite-done in the middle, sits on an abandoned reception desk.

Mom follows my gaze and gestures to the plate.

"Have a cookie."

They're on a paper doily, and a small circle of oil is spreading out around each cookie, making the paper transparent. I remember from freshman science that this is called capillary motion, where liquid soaks into something porous. Like the rainwater from the puddles outside slowly seeping up each leg of my jeans. My cuffs drag on the ground, leaving wet trails across the perfect carpet. It's possible that nothing has ever been as out of place as me right now, standing in this room.

I am not one to turn down free cookies, but the thought of eating a greasy cookie in this cramped, artificial waiting room makes me feel a little sick to my stomach. I press my thumbnail into a leaf on a nearby bouquet, but my nail doesn't pierce through. Plastic. I hug myself to keep from shivering. I want to go home.

Mom is still talking. "The residents make them. They use the tubes of premade cookie dough, but they get to scoop them out and put them in the oven. It reminds them of home."

"Yeah," I mutter, "I'm sure it's just like home."

I'm saved from one of her patented glares by a short Latina woman, hair pulled back in a neat ponytail, who bustles through the door in front of the reception desk. When she sees us, her face lights up.

"Georgia!" She beams at Mom and reaches out to hug her. My mother has a way of making everyone around her feel comfortable. She gets it from my grandma, people have always flocked to both of them. Either it develops later in life than sixteen, or it's skipping my generation.

"Leticia, this is my daughter Hannah." Mom pushes me forward firmly. She pronounces the name so it has four syllables - Leh-tee-see-uh. I shake the woman's hand, and Mom tells me that she's the activities director at Silver Wells. I glance back at the cookies. Her doing.

Leticia leads us through the locked door by punching a series of numbers into a keypad. "It's 6041, just like our street address," she tells me. "Same code gets you in or out of the main doors. If no one is at the desk when you come to visit, you can let yourself in." I watch the door swing closed behind us. There's another keypad on the wall, this one with a handwritten sign taped above it. "Keypad broken, please use other door," it reads, followed by a frowny face.

"Do we have to go out a different door?" I point to the sign.

"Oh, it's not really broken," Leticia says with a smile. "That sign makes the residents forget that they wanted to go through the door. Sometimes they need something to break their train of thought, and they start going another direction."

She acts like it's such a convenience, like the ease with which the most reliable person in my life can be deceived is such a wonderful quirk. I guess it does make her job easier. And then I realize something.

"They can't go outside?" I didn't know we were locking Gran up.

Leticia glances at my mom, who sighs and puts her hand on my shoulder.

"We can't risk Gran wandering out into traffic or getting lost."

I know it's not that far-fetched. A couple of weeks ago, we got a call late at night from the Salem Police. They pulled Gran over for driving without her lights on, way below the speed limit. She broke down in tears when they questioned her and said she didn't know how to get home. My mom had tucked a card into her billfold with our phone number on it, in case of emergencies. The police called and we went to pick her up.

That night, Mom took Gran's car keys away, and we stayed over at her house. We moved in the next afternoon. Mom slept in Gran's bed with her, and I slept in Mom's old bedroom upstairs. It was where I used to play when I was younger, where I slept whenever I spent the night. There are still shoeboxes under the bed filled with my little plastic animals and the paper dolls that I made by cutting people out of JC Penney catalogs.

We lived with Gran for a couple of months and tried to keep an eye on her, but Mom had to work and I had school. And then Gran fell while my mom was on the phone and I was spending the night at Liz's. Mom found her and drove her to the hospital, and called Liz from the payphone in the waiting room. Gran had a big cut above her eyebrow, and Mom said she'd had blood running all down the side of her face. We'd just gotten back from renting videos, but Liz drove me to the hospital right away. She sat in the waiting room while we went in with Gran. The nurse asked some questions to see if the fall had messed with Gran's brain. She couldn't give basic answers, and he looked at Mom questioningly.

"She has . . ." My mom paused, glancing at Gran, who stared up at us patiently. Mom was holding Gran's hand in both of hers. Gran got upset if we talked about her diagnosis, so we both tried to avoid it. Mom began to spell slowly.

"A - l - h - " She paused and looked at me. She's never been the best speller.

I started, "A -l - z - h - i - e - "

"It's e - i," the nurse corrected. I rolled my eyes.

"That," I said. "She's got that."

"Okay." He put down his clipboard and picked up his sewing supplies. He stitched her up and sent her home with a lecture to my mom about elder care laws. Mom started making calls the next morning to see about moving her somewhere. And last week, we got the call from Silver Wells. They had an opening! It was like Gran had gotten into Harvard or something, my mom was that excited.

Leticia leads us down hallways of white walls and white linoleum. It smells like pee and old people, almost masked by the sharp scent of disinfectant. There are armchairs positioned here and there, and a few people sit in wheelchairs like they were parked on the side of the road and left. Some stare at their hands and some watch silently as we go by. One woman cradles a plastic baby doll in her lap. I feel my throat tighten and drop my eyes to the floor.

We end in room 208, where my mom delivered Gran yesterday afternoon. Like most of the other doors we've passed, this one has an old photo of Gran hanging next to it, with a sign that says her name. Sharon Ward. Her doorway is free of the drawings and snapshots that decorate others, though, and I make a mental note to look for some to bring. I feel nervous, even though I just saw her yesterday. I pull at my t-shirt, which has ridden up under my perpetually damp hoodie. Leticia opens the door, and there she is, sitting in an armchair in lavender knit pants and a blue button-up sweater. She's wearing the same navy blue Keds she's always liked, rubber soles scrubbed bright white. Seeing them on her tiny feet makes me feel a little better.

Gran looks up when we enter, smiling a shy smile. Like me, her top teeth are large and slightly bucked. Mom keeps saying my face will grow into my teeth, but I guess Gran doesn't think hers did because she usually presses her lips tight together when she smiles. She only opens her mouth when she's not expecting to smile, like when something surprises her.

I hang back, but Mom walks forward and sits on the end of the bed, reaching out to take Gran's hand.

"Hi Mom." She's speaking too loudly. "How was your night?"

Gran nods and smiles politely again. "Very nice, thank you."

I recognize this response; it's what she says when she doesn't know the answer to the question but can tell what the asker wants to hear. Her doctor told Mom once that she's exceptionally skilled at hiding her Alzheimer's because she keeps herself neat and clean, and is polite and acts like she knows the answers to questions even when she doesn't. I felt oddly proud of her when Mom told me this, like she'd gotten a sticker or an A. Exceptionally skilled.

I wonder if she remembers yesterday. I helped her pack her suitcase, choosing which framed photos to take and which to leave at the house. I don't even know if she knew who was in the photos, but I labeled each one with her name. Everything she brought had to be labeled, Mom said, because people with Alzheimer's tend to wander and take things from other rooms.

Mom takes one hand from Gran's and reaches toward me, digging her fingers into the flesh of my arm as she pulls me forward.

"Hannah came to visit also."

I give a little wave, and Gran smiles again.

"It's nice to see you." This is another of her tricks. If she's not sure whether she's met someone before, she says "nice to *see* you," never "nice to meet you." That way, all of her bases are covered. Thinking about her not remembering me makes the tightness in my throat unbearable, and I feel tears burning behind my eyes.

"Where's the bathroom?" I manage.

Mom looks exasperated. "Right there." She points at a door across the room. I open it and find a sterile white bathroom. I lock the door behind me, push the toilet lid down, and sit.

Gran has always been there for me. I used to take the bus to her house after school and she would have homemade cookies ready, never the kind from a tube. She never said no to me. Of course, I was always easy with her too. I never fought with her, never protested when she told me it was bedtime or threatened to run away like I did with my mom when I didn't get my way. Mom can make me feel so crazy and angry inside, but never my Gran.

I reach over and turn on the faucet so Mom won't hear me cry. I'm such a baby. This is something that happens, a natural part of life. People get old, they get sick, they die. Liz never even knew any of her grandparents. I'm lucky to have a grandma in my life at all, especially such a good one. But I don't feel lucky.

There's a sharp knock on the bathroom door. I turn off the faucet. "Just a second!"

Mom calls back, "Can you come on a short walk with us?"

"Yeah, just a second!"

I look in the mirror. My eyes are a little red, but haven't reached full puffiness. I splash some icy water onto my face and run my hands through my hair to dry them. My muddy brown hair isn't curly, isn't straight, just mostly wants to frizz up all the time. I dig a hair tie from the pocket of my jeans and pull it back into a ponytail. I wipe my face with my sleeve and open the door to face the women who raised me.

2

Liz is already at our locker when I get to school in the morning. Gran's house is a shorter bike ride to school than our house, but it's still far enough that I'm always sweaty when I get there. I'm surprised that Liz beat me to school. Liz Palmer is the most relaxed person I have ever met. She's almost never on time, usually because something interesting catches her eye between point A and point B. It used to annoy me, but I can't stay mad at her. Everyone loves Liz. She's open and friendly and is effortlessly cool. She plays guitar and sings beautifully, runs track, is clever and funny, and is always up for anything. One of the great unsolved mysteries of the world is what made her choose me to be her best friend.

When she transferred into my fifth grade classroom, the teacher had her move into the empty desk next to me, which I had been using to store my extra library books. We started talking about books as I stacked them up, since it turned out that she loved to read too. We were off from there. When we hit middle school, we never joined any cliques, but Liz was friendly with everyone, and I stayed at her side.

"Hey," I say, coming up behind her. She turns and a grin lights up her face.

"Where were you yesterday? I tried calling."

I shake out my helmet hair and look at her. Her chin-length hair is messy, but it looks good that way. I helped her bleach it and dye it bright orange, our school color, for a pep rally at the beginning of the semester, and it's faded and grown into a decent imitation of her hero, Kurt Cobain. He died two years ago, but she's more committed to him than ever. She has a huge poster of him hanging over her bed, and today is wearing one of her many Nirvana t-shirts over her gray thermal with a red Dickies miniskirt.

her eyes are deep brown, the kind where you can't tell where the pupil begins. I tear myself away from them and bend down to unroll the ankles of my jeans, now that I'm no longer at risk of being sucked into the bike chain.

"Sorry," I mumble when I stand. "My grandma just moved to that place and we went to see her after her first night . . ." I trail off. Liz's eyes get big and her hand flies to her mouth.

"I totally forgot. How is she?" Liz loves Gran. She and I have spent enough time together after school that Gran started keeping Liz's favorite flavors of Gatorade on hand.

I shrug. I don't really want to get into it right when the bell is about to ring.

"She's fine," I say. "What were you calling about?"

"Oh yeah!" Her eyes sparkle with excitement. "Paula got us a show! A big one. We're opening for Huckle Cat!"

I raise my eyebrows. Huckle Cat is probably the best girl band in town. Not that Salem, Oregon has a lot of competition. But they recently returned from a cross-country tour, and are basically living Liz's dream by supporting themselves with music. Liz has been in a band for the past year with our friend Paula on bass and Paula's boyfriend Brian on drums. They're called Susan B. Dangerous, a name I suggested last fall when we were all hanging out in Liz's basement, watching *Saved by the Bell* reruns and throwing names around. We had just picked research topics in US History, and mine was the 19th Amendment.

"That's great," I say. "When is the show? And where?"

Liz smiles proudly. "At the Loyola in two weeks."

"That's awesome!"

The Loyola is an old theater downtown that was abandoned forever until a few guys took it over and fixed it up last year. Now it's cool, all dark with a real stage with lights, not a cleared-out space in the corner of a party like the usual Susan B. shows. Parties where I'm probably hanging out with the household pet while Liz makes a bunch of new friends.

The first bell rings, so I promise we'll talk about it more at lunch and run to calculus, which is on the other side of the school, located as far as possible from my locker.

I slide into my seat in the back of the room after the last bell, but I know Mr. Keller won't care. I've had him for two years in a row, and he loves anyone who likes math, which I do. I love how everything makes sense. There's a right and a wrong way to do things, no murky gray subjectivity or unsureness. I pull out my notebook and start copying down the formulas Mr. Keller is writing on the board.

At the end of class, Mr. Keller calls me up to the front. I see that Philip Lawson is also staying back. He and I are the only two juniors in the class, the highest level offered at our school. Philip has always been there, ever since our first day of kindergarten when he marched in carrying a briefcase. Physically, we're complete opposites. He's black, I'm white, he's short and thin, I'm neither. He's neat and compact, with his dark hair cut short and shirt always tucked in. Next to him, I'm like an explosion. Hair everywhere, papers falling out of my notebooks, sneakers untied and soaking wet. But I'm right after him in the alphabet, and we always tie for the best grades in our classes. Teachers post grades using our school ID numbers instead of our names, but I've memorized Philip's because I always see it right next to mine.

If we want, Mr. Keller tells us, we can leave school early twice a week next year to take math at the community college. I sometimes see the row of boys sitting on a bench in the parking lot, waiting for the bus to come and take them to advanced calc or computers for geniuses or whatever. I imagine sitting there, Philip next to me. I'd ride the bus with him, not knowing anyone else in class. Or I could take an easy elective like intro to guitar, which would be even easier because Liz would be thrilled to help. I picture her leaning over me, moving my fingers onto the right strings.

"I'll think about it," I say. I shove my books into my bag and duck out of the room before I can see Mr. Keller's smile fall.

After calc is gym, which I hate. I've always been the chubbiest one in class. No one has mentioned it to me since middle school, but I still get picked last for every team and always get the positions that have the smallest possibility of affecting the outcome of the game. Which is just fine with me because, really, the thought of being the fat girl running for the ball, shorts riding up into my crotch while everyone giggles, is hardly my idea of fun.

It's an unusually sunny day for January, so Coach Roberts set us loose on his favorite activity: running. I tug at the too-tight collar of the Sonic Youth t-shirt I wear for gym, a gift from Liz after she accidentally ordered the wrong size, and watch her track team buddies take off. They're probably glad for the extra practice.

"Waiting for an invitation, Miss Lewis?" Coach Roberts gestures after them. I roll my eyes and jog onto the track, but I slow to a walk after a few minutes. I personally think 2nd-period gym is completely unreasonable. They only give us seven minutes to change before the bell rings, and I've never in my life seen anyone take a shower in that time. It's like the school is just begging to reek of sweat by noon.

After gym I have English, then Spanish, then lunch. I mutter a quick "Hasta mañana" to the girl next to me and rush to the locker when the bell rings. Liz has advanced musical composition before lunch, which means that she and Paula and a couple of other music nerds sit around and jam and get to leave whenever they want. Sure enough, the narrow green binder labeled "MUSIC" is already sitting on top of the stack of textbooks in our locker. I drop off my Spanish book and dig around in the teal plastic Care Bears lunch box that we store on the top shelf. We deposit our change into it whenever we have some, and either of us can use it whenever we need an emergency snack or lunch.

Our school is built around a large open room called the Commons that's full of round tables and plastic chairs, not arranged in any discernible pattern. We're allowed to hang out there before and after school, or during free periods. At lunch, silver doors on the west wall roll open, and ladies in plastic gloves and white aprons appear to sell us pizza and spaghetti and patty melts.

School lunch used to feel really loaded to me. I was always sure everyone wanted to see what the fat girl was eating, to reassure themselves that they were eating less and wouldn't end up like me. In middle school, I'd get the flavorless iceberg lettuce and non-fat dressing that they offered in the salad bar. Then I'd sit there while Liz and her friends stuffed burgers and fries into their mouths. I finally decided that no one really cared what I was eating except for me. I've never been that into meat, especially the mystery meat that the cafeteria cranks out, but they can't mess up French fries. I get a large order and a bottle of lemonade, cover half the fries with ketchup from the huge red plastic pump, and weave through the tables full of different groups. Popular kids, hicks, brains, goths, band geeks, everyone gets a table or two. We sit near the middle of the room, on the side closest to the art and music wing. Liz likes to keep her options open. Sometimes she abandons our regular lunch crew for whatever boy she's dating, but she recently broke up with Michael Jarvis, the editor of the school paper, and is back to sitting with us full-time.

Liz and Paula are already there when I slide into the molded plastic chair next to Liz. Paula raises her chin in greeting, and I smile awkwardly. She's really Liz's friend, and even though we have a few classes together, we've never gotten close. The truth is that she intimidates the hell out of me. She has red hair that's frizzier than mine, but she doesn't fight it, just brushes it out and wears it big like a rocker on one of the t-shirts she always wears. Today's is Heart, the fabric worn thin from washing and age. She wears tight black jeans and black eyeliner so smudged that I sometimes wonder if she puts it on before bed each night.

Her boyfriend Brian drops into the chair next to her. He always looks so normal next to Paula, a plain boy with shaggy brown hair, jeans and a worn blue sweater. She definitely doesn't seem to mind, though. He leans over and they kiss.

"So you arranged the Susan B. show?" I ask Paula when she comes up for air.

She grins and nods, preening like she just cured cancer. "Kathy knows a guy who works at the Loyola, and he heard that Huckle Cat's opening act fell through. He saw us play a couple times, and he recommended us." Kathy is Paula's older sister, and the two look enough alike that Paula was able to use Kathy's ID last summer to get her tongue pierced, despite being only fifteen.

"So awesome," Liz says, and I nod.

"That's what it's all about, man," Brian says, "connecting to people who can connect you to other people."

The final member of our group, a guy named Colin who's been Brian's best friend longer than I've been Liz's, slumps into the last open chair. Colin was in my art class last year, and he's quiet but actually pretty nice and a great artist. Liz even got Michael to print a couple of Colin's comics in the paper before she gave him the boot.

Colin has drawing class right before lunch, and his fingers are still smudged with charcoal. He had his growth spurt early and is tall and broad, always hungry. He's one of the few people at school who makes me feel small.

"Um, aren't you going to wash your hands?" Paula asks, looking at his fingers with distaste.

He glances down at his hand, wipes it on his faded black Carharts, and picks up his plastic spoon, shoveling mashed potatoes and gravy into his mouth. Paula rolls her eyes. She's a vegan who hates most vegetables, so she usually brings peanut butter and jelly sandwiches, washing them down with Diet Cokes from the vending machine.

"We need to practice every night until the show," Liz is saying to Brian and Paula. They both nod, but Paula speaks quickly.

"Starting tomorrow. We can't tonight."

Brian looks confused at first, then nods.

"We can't today," he agrees.

Liz rolls her eyes. "Oh my God you guys, this show is serious. Your sex life is *not* a priority."

"For you, maybe," Brian mutters loud enough for us all to hear. Liz and Paula giggle and Colin and Brian exchange smirks. I feel my face heat up and focus on my fries. There are definitely times when I feel like I bring the cool factor in our group down a few notches.

"Fine," Liz says, "We'll start tomorrow. What song do you think we should open with?"

The band talk takes over, Brian pulling out a notebook to start a set list. They try to include Colin and me, asking our opinions of the order and how many Nirvana covers is too many. It's nice of them to ask us, but it's hard to not feel like an outsider.

3

Since practice is off the table, Liz invites me over after school. We load my bike into the back of her car and drive to her house. Shortly after her 16th birthday, Liz convinced her parents to buy her the forest green Subaru station wagon that she found in the classifieds. Susan B's equipment barely fit into Brian's Camry, forget about adding the members of the band. It's handy that my bike fits perfectly in the back too, since I haven't even gotten my learner's permit.

Liz's mom and stepdad stay at the nursery they own until it closes at seven, and her sister has cheerleading practice, so we have the house to ourselves. Liz unlocks the front door and I follow her into the kitchen. She opens the fridge and pulls out a clear glass bowl of homemade chocolate pudding, her speciality. She grabs two spoons and I fill a glass with water from the tap.

In her bedroom, Liz sits at her desk while I set my glass on the nightstand and stretch out on the bed. Instead of a bedspread, she uses this fuzzy blue blanket printed with a white unicorn that she's had forever. I trace the horn with my finger.

"What do you want to listen to?" Liz flips the power switch on the stereo on her desk. I shrug even though she's not looking at me.

"Whatever." I reach for my backpack and pull out my copy of *Frankenstein*, which we're reading for English.

She puts on a tape of Huckle Cat and spins in her chair to grin at me.

"It's so cool that you're going to open for them!" I say, and she giggles and stomps her feet. She kicks off her Chuck Taylors and flops down next to me. I shove my bag down toward my feet to make room.

"I was talking to Mr. Walters today," she says, serious now, "and he said he thinks I have a good chance to get a music scholarship at U Dub." Mr. Walters is the band director, and he teaches her composition class. "But maybe Evergreen would be better. Either place, Seattle or Olympia, has so many cool people making music. Have you decided where you're applying yet?"

I shake my head. I've been avoiding college decisions, planning on applying wherever Liz applies. I've been waiting for her to make up her mind between University of Washington and Evergreen, figuring I'll follow wherever she goes. To be honest, the only thing that matters to me is getting out of Salem, where nothing ever happens. I don't care where we go, as long as it's not here, and as long as we're there together.

"Oh my God," Liz says suddenly. "I haven't even asked you about Gran. How is she? How was your visit?"

I roll my eyes and groan. "It was really weird. The whole place smelled like old people, and she didn't know who I was, and . . ." I look down at the bed.

"I'm sorry, Han." Liz reaches her arm across my shoulder and pulls me toward her. I let her do it, wrapping my arm around her waist and pulling our bodies closer. We lay like that for a moment, and then she pushes herself up to sit.

"I'm sure she'll be okay," she continues, ever the optimist.

I roll onto my back. "I guess. I mean, I know." It feels wrong for her to seem so gone. I lean my head against Liz's knee, and she strokes my hair. Liz is the most physical person I've ever met. We always slept in the same bed when we had sleepovers, and we'd wake up with arms flung over each other or hips pressed together. When we walk, she puts her arm around me or loop hers through mine. She's always hugging or resting a hand on someone's shoulder. I keep my arms wrapped around myself as I navigate the hallways at school, holding books or just shielding my boobs. Liz parts the hallway with a soft touch on a cheerleader's back, a hand down the arm of a letterman jacket. She flirts without even trying. Then she doesn't understand why these guys are always falling all over themselves for her, after she laughs at their stupid jokes, touches their knees, smiles the way she does that makes you feel like the only person in the room.

I've known other girls like Liz, strong girls who crack jokes and speak their minds. But it always feels like Liz sees me in a way that other people don't, like she actually cares what's inside of me. I felt so proud to be chosen by her. Then one night when I was sleeping at her house, I dreamed we were kissing. I woke up and her butt was pressed low into my belly. I knew I should move, but I stayed there for a few minutes, the warmth of her body and the dream memory feeling delicious. When my mom picked me up, she asked how my night was and I told her it was fine. I didn't want her to see the heat that I still felt deep inside. When Liz and I are together, I feel like there's a string strung tight between my hipbones, like a guitar string that Liz would know just how to play.

She's had a bunch of boyfriends over the years, from band geeks to fellow members of the track team to, most recently, Michael. But she never seems all that attached to any of them. That gives me hope. I've been carrying my hope of Liz for years. We share a locker every year, we change clothes together, we've spent a billion hours curled up together on the couch in her basement or squeezed into the overstuffed chair in my grandma's living room, my arm wrapped around her so we fit. But that's it, we've never kissed or anything. It's probably never even crossed her mind. Sometimes I don't know how much longer I can keep it in, especially when we're together, alone in her room like this. But then what if she won't talk to me anymore? What if she's repulsed? I mean, even if she did like girls, what makes me think that perfect Liz would ever go for me?

The click of the tape turning over snaps me back to the present. Liz climbs off the bed and sits back at the desk, scoops a spoonful of pudding and slurps it up.

"Do you want to stay for dinner? Mom left money for pizza, and I'm starving."

"Yeah, I just have to call my mom."

Liz hands me her phone, clear plastic with visible wires and guts. I was so jealous when she found it on one of our thrift store trips, but it's not like I even need a phone of my own. She's the only person who ever calls me.

Mom agrees to pick me up after she visits Gran and runs some errands. I hand the phone back to Liz so she can order pizza. She balances it between her ear and shoulder and pulls her bottom desk drawer open, removes a plastic Batman lunch box. When we found the lunchboxes at Value Village, we rock-paper-scissored to see whose would go in the locker to hold our spare change. I won, so Wish Bear holds court in the locker. Batman eventually found his true purpose, though, in the bottom drawer, storing Liz's weed.

I get up and open the window, sitting on the floor in front of it. Liz rolls a joint and lights it, sucking hard. She offers it to me like she always does, not really expecting me to take it because I usually don't. But I feel guilty about my mom visiting Gran without me and I'm getting really sick of feelings, so I accept it and inhale, blowing the skunky smoke out the window.

4

Mom picks me up a little before seven. Liz and I are watching TV in the basement, and I see Mom's headlights shine through the little window high on the wall. Liz walks me out and I move my bike from the back of the Subaru to the rubbery prongs of the bike rack that my mom already has attached to the trunk of her car. I've been around my mom a few times after smoking with Liz, and she hasn't ever noticed that anything was up, but I still get nervous. One day last fall, I started panicking when I realized that my mom was on her way to pick me up and I was way too high. Liz grabbed my shoulders, stared into my eyes, and used her soothing voice to tell me, "You're fine. You're totally fine. You are an Academy Award-winning actress, and you're fine." And it worked. I repeated that to myself as I sat in the passenger seat, and all my mom did was tell me that I seemed quiet. I told her that I was thinking about a paper for school. Since my grades are her favorite thing about me, how could she argue?

"Thanks for picking me up," I say as I slide into the passenger seat. Mom has the heat cranked up, and I immediately regret putting my jacket on. "How's Gran?"

"She's fine," Mom says, backing out of the driveway. I can't help smiling, remembering Liz's pep talk. Mom pushes her hair out of her eyes, and I notice the gray at her temples. She usually keeps right on top of her hair appointments to dye it back to her usual dark blonde. "We walked around a little and I helped her get settled in for dinner."

"What do they eat there?" I ask. I'm still stuffed with mushroom-and-pineapple pizza.

"Mostly bland food. So many of the residents are on low-salt or low-fat diets."

"She must hate that." I picture Gran standing over the stove, tasting and seasoning. She was never afraid of salt.

"I don't know how much she notices."

"Oh."

For some reason, this strikes me as extra sad. Maybe because I like food, like Gran always did. I've always thought of it as how she showed her love, making special meals and always hosting big family dinners with everything made by her, from scratch. I realize that those meals will never happen again.

I reach over and turn the radio up, letting Billy Joel fill the silence so I don't have to.

When we get home, Mom kicks off her pumps and heads to Gran's room to change out of her work clothes. I go upstairs, saying I have more homework to finish. It's true; I didn't really get anything done at Liz's.

I shove the door to my room open and flop down on the bed. A minute later, I hear the soft meow of Olive, my black-and-gray cat. I found Olive in Gran's woodpile when I was eight, a little black ball that I named after the olives that I loved to stick on my fingers whenever Gran put them out at family meals. Mom and Gran let me take her home with me that night, and now she's back too.

She leaps onto the bed and burrows her face against my hand until I start petting her. I stroke her long fur and look up at the built-in bookshelves that cover the wall around the bed. My mom was so lucky to grow up in a bedroom with a giant bookshelf like a library. Some of the books on the shelves are mine, mostly from when I was younger, and there are Mom's old Nancy Drews, Gran's romance novels, years of yearbooks, a couple of volumes of an encyclopedia set. Everything in this room is a mix of my stuff and old stuff. My stereo and CDs sit on the desk with an ashtray that my mom made in elementary school and this wooden bowl that holds my grandpa's old marble collection. He used to play marbles when he was little, and he tried to explain the rules to me once, but I always preferred sorting them by color and style. Some are shiny, some scuffed, and some are solid while others have swirls of color reaching through clear glass.

Olive arranges her body against my side, and I lean into her, feeling her vibrate as she purrs. I think about my visit with Gran yesterday. Our walk around Silver Wells was short like Mom promised. Gran didn't talk much, just nodded as Mom blabbed on like we hadn't seen her the day before. She told Gran about the Little League game my cousins Jeremy and Taylor played on Saturday. Mom wasn't there, but Aunt Marion filled her in during one of their almost-daily phone calls. Jeremy's not good at sports like his twin brother, which has always made me secretly like him a little more. I hope he'll find his own thing when he gets older than seven, but for now, the boys are pretty much joined at the hip.

The hallways of Silver Wells are like a giant maze with little sitting areas tucked here and there, decorated with wooden dollhouses, stuffed animals, and framed posters of old-time movies like *Gone with the Wind*. We ended in the activity room, a large room in the middle of the building with vinyl recliners and big tables with jigsaw puzzles spread out on them. Puzzles are supposed to help delay the onset of Alzheimer's. The day after Gran was diagnosed, Mom started carrying a little book of crosswords in her purse. She pulls it out in waiting rooms or while watching TV at night.

Leticia stood in the corner, which was made up to look like a kitchen with a low breakfast bar. She had a plastic laundry basket on the counter, and a few old people sat across from her, matching up and folding socks. Leticia grinned and waved when she saw us. I wondered how she stays so cheerful. She must not have known any of these people before. She doesn't know what they've lost.

We settled down at a table with Gran, and I fiddled with a puzzle piece. The pieces were large, and the puzzles probably only had 20 pieces each. I used to love puzzles when I was younger. I felt a pang of guilt over never asking Gran to do them with me. What if I could have prevented this?

I stare at the ceiling in my room and sigh. Gran seemed like she was following the conversation okay yesterday. I wonder if Mom moved her to Silver Wells too soon. Maybe she should be back at home with us. But then I remember Mom's defeated expression when she was listening to that stupid nurse lecture her about *appropriate care*, and Mom saying Gran didn't mind bland hospital food, like she's not even the same person anymore.

I reach over and stroke Olivia's fur. She turns her round green eyes to me.

"Did we do the right thing?" I ask as I rub under her jaw.

As usual, she doesn't give up any answers.

5

Liz wants a new outfit for the show, so we decide to go to thrift stores on Saturday. I head downstairs when Liz is supposed to pick me up and find my mom in Gran's room, kneeling in front of the closet with a cardboard box next to her.

"What are you doing?" I look in the box. It's half-full of Gran's shoes, wedge sandals and high heels with delicate straps.

"I'm starting to clean out some of Gran's stuff."

"What do you mean, 'clean out'?"

"Well, she doesn't wear these kind of shoes anymore."

I know she's right, but it feels wrong to go through Gran's stuff like she's dead.

"I want to get a head start for when we put the house on the market," she continues.

"You're selling this house?"

I love this house.

"We have our house. We certainly don't need both."

"So sell our house! This house has history." I touch the door frame like I have fond memories of it in particular.

"That doesn't make any sense, honey. This house will make much more money, plus it costs more to maintain. And it's too big, especially since you'll be gone in a couple of years."

She pushes her hands against the ground to stand up, and I take a step back.

We both turn at the sound of the Subaru pulling into the driveway.

"I'm going shopping with Liz," I say, starting toward the door.

"For how long?" She follows me down the hall.

"I don't know, a few hours?"

"I was hoping you could visit Gran with me today, but we

should go before it gets dark. Sometimes Alzheimer's patients get more confused as it gets later."

I pause with my hand on the doorknob. "I don't know, Liz has a bunch of stuff she wants to shop for, so we might be out for a while."

She either accepts that or gives up.

"Do you have your house key?"

I pat my backpack and nod.

"Okay, well, have fun, and I love you." She's been saying this a lot more since Gran started declining.

"Love you too," I tell her.

Liz drives to the Veterans' thrift store on the edge of town, her favorite, and heads directly for the pants. With her narrow hips, she can wear either men's or women's pants easily, but I rarely find pants that fit me at thrift stores. Sometimes I feel like things that are for other girls just aren't for me. Like cute little Juniors clothes and makeup trends and the latest hairstyle to make him notice you! That's part of why I like Liz, because she could fit into that teenage magazine lifestyle no problem, but she chooses not to. She wears makeup sometimes and certainly knows how to get all the *hims* to notice her, but she doesn't seem to care as much as girls are supposed to. Especially pretty girls.

I flip through the sweatshirts, hoping to find another gem like my favorite shirt, a dark blue hoodie printed with iridescent hot air balloons that I once got here for only two dollars. I find a few tops to try on and weave my way back to Liz. She's in front of a mirror, holding a pair of torn jeans in front of herself.

"What do you think?" she says when she sees me in the mirror. The denim is really shredded.

"There's hardly even any fabric there," I say, and she snorts.

"That's the point, *Mom!*"

I laugh and drop my clothes on top of the ones she's piled

into her cart. She tosses the jeans in and flips through a few more hangers.

We always share the big corner dressing room, so we can see each other's clothes without coming out in the open. Liz kicks off her sneakers and unzips her jeans, letting them fall on the dusty linoleum. I hear another snort of laughter as she sees herself in the mirror.

"Oh my God Hannah, I forgot to tell you about this."

I turn and see that she's wearing lacy pink underwear and a matching bra.

"What's there to tell?"

"Michael gave me this. He was like, trying to make me into his fantasy woman or something."

She turns in the mirror, sucks in her almost-flat stomach as she examines herself. I don't want to stare at her, so I look at my reflection. Cheeks red, hair escaping my ponytail, shirt riding up my stomach. Back to Liz. She's watching me in the mirror, waiting for my response.

"You only dated like a month," I say.

She laughs. "Two and a *half*, thank you very much."

I bow my head in concession.

"It's kind of fun to wear shit like this under regular clothes." She nods at the pile of fabric on the floor. "Like no one knows what kind of secrets I've got going on underneath." She wiggles her eyebrows and I laugh. I look back at myself, thinking about the secret I'm keeping.

"I understand that feeling."

She goes on like I haven't spoken. "Michael was boring. So *normal*. I'm ready for something a little more exciting, you know?"

I nod, even though everything exciting I can think of looks like her. I turn back to the wall and start trying on my shirts.

We leave the store half an hour later, Liz with a bulging bag of clothes, including the shredded jeans, and me with one shirt. We drive to the Goodwill across town, and Liz sings along with her favorite driving mixtape. Nirvana, Hole, Pearl Jam, Soundgarden. Her voice is clear water running over gravel, sweet with just a touch of roughness.

"We *have* to move to Washington," she says.

"My mom isn't really into the idea of Evergreen or U Dub," I say. I tell her about the conversation Mom and I had about it. First, she stared at me like I said I wanted to go to college on Mars. Then she'd started in on how I can get better scholarships at private colleges, and I'm *certainly* smart enough to get in.

"There are fancy private schools in Seattle, Brainiac," Liz says with a smile. But I always imagine the two of us sharing a dorm room, popping popcorn and staying up late to study, holding hands as we venture into parties together. Snuggling on a twin bed. I blink to clear the image from my mind and join in with Liz, who's singing along to the chorus of "Alive." I know I'm a horrible singer, but she never mentions it.

I flip through the t-shirts briefly at the Goodwill, but I don't feel like struggling into more too-tight clothes in the dressing room. I wander to the books, and scan the titles on the battered spines. A familiar title catches my eye, and I grab the copy of *Annie on My Mind*. When I realized how I felt about Liz, I went to the place I've always gone for information: the Salem Library. I went to the teen section, marked with a cheesy neon sign and some brightly-colored bean bag chairs, a few shelves of young adult novels, and a computer to search the catalog. I sat and searched for boring crap until no one was behind me. Then, in the subject line, I typed: Lesbian. Gay. Homosexual.

To my surprise, several pages of results came up, and even a bunch of YA novels. In the past few years, I've read all of them. Stories about boys getting beat up for being gay, girls getting raped because of it, different and the same coming out stories over and over. I have, however, not come out to anyone in my life. It feels too raw, too secret to tell anyone. Too embarrassing to admit that I want someone who is so clearly not interested in me.

I drop the book into my basket. It's one I've checked out more than once at the library. I love the dorky sword fights and chivalry that the main characters act out. Not exactly my thing, but maybe someday I'll find someone to match my own dorkiness, someone who likes numbers and animals and solving puzzles. I toss a few other books in my basket in case Liz decides to examine my purchases, and find my way back to her.

She's in line for the dressing room, in front of a man with two kids. The boy is probably fourteen, old enough to be watching Liz as she waits for an open room, one hip stuck out, a finger twirling a strand of hair. I'm more interested in the other kid, though, a little girl who's younger, maybe ten. She's hanging from the man's hand with both hands, smile wide as she tells him some story. He listens like it's so interesting.

Seeing girls and fathers in public always makes me feel kind of uncomfortable. I never knew mine. He and my mom got divorced when I was a baby, then he moved away and we haven't heard from him since. I hate talking about it, because it always leads to all these questions or comments, like people asking why I'm not in touch with him, as if I could tell them. One Thanksgiving a few years ago, I was looking at an old family photo hanging on the wall. I was a baby in my mom's arms, and my dad was standing between her and my grandpa. Aunt Marion came up behind me and said, "You know it wasn't your fault, don't you, Hannah Banana?"

I looked up, embarrassed to be caught.

"What wasn't?"

"Your dad taking off." She drank deeply from her wine glass.

"I know."

But I wondered. I've read plenty of books about divorce, and I know that none of it is technically my fault. But I also know that there's something in me that's different, something missing. Other fathers want to stay with their kids and take care of them. Marion was never even married to the twins' dad, but he still takes them every other weekend and for two weeks in the summer. Mine never did. And every time someone asks me what happened to my dad, why there's just my mom, it's like a reminder that I wasn't worth sticking around for.

6

"Want to stop at Island on the way home?" Liz asks as she starts the car after we complete our Goodwill purchases.

"Sure," I say. Island is the only record store in town that's not inside of a mall. With a salon on one side and a hot dog restaurant on the other, it's basically a wide hallway with shelves of CDs lining the walls, records in the back, and t-shirt racks squeezed in the middle. They have a display window on the sidewalk with one chipped mannequin who today is wearing red leather pants, a black shirt that reads ISLAND across the chest, and a green wig. She's holding a cardboard sign that announces: "Next Friday, January 19, at the Loyola, check out local favorites Huckle Cat and Susan B. Dangerous!"

"Awesome!" Liz giggles. "I wasn't sure if it would be up yet!"

"How'd you score that?" I'm impressed.

She smiles proudly. "Larry offered! I told him about the show and he was all 'I'll have Monica hold a sign.' He's really into supporting young musicians and all that." Larry is the owner, a guy probably Mom's age with curly gray hair who loves to talk music, any genre, although his favorite is jazz. I'm not really into the jazz talk, but Liz thinks he's fascinating, and he seems to think she is too. And he always remembers me because of her. Story of my life.

We go in, but Larry isn't working today. Instead a guy with messy brown hair is leaning on the stool behind the cash register, wearing an open flannel over a black t-shirt for some band I've never heard of. Liz makes a beeline for him.

"Hannah, do you know Joel?" she asks, but her eyes don't leave his. I shake my head, although he does look sort of familiar from school. He smiles and holds his hand out to me. I take it, and he squeezes hard. I grip harder, and he pulls back.

"We're in guitar together," Joel says. "I work here on the weekends and after school." I nod.

"Cool," I mutter. I step to the wall of CDs and start scanning the titles.

Liz's voice gets high as she asks, "You're coming to my show on Friday, *right?*"

"Yeah, definitely. I'll head over after I get done closing up here." He pauses, glances over to see how far I've gotten from the register. I step toward the rack of magazines in the back corner.

"Maybe after the show, you and I could go somewhere," Joel continues, and I hear Liz giggle. I roll my eyes and pick up the first magazine I see. *Maximumrocknroll*. It's printed on newsprint, and the almost-entirely black cover lists the bands highlighted inside. I only know one of them, The Donnas, from a tape Liz made for me.

I turn to the interview with The Donnas and skim it, then flip through the rest of the pages. In the back are calls for bandmates, little personal ads for people looking for pen pals, and ads for zines. One of them catches my eye.

"Tiny Specks in Space. A small-town teenage dyke ponders the meaning of life. Send $1 cash to Corey, PO Box 983, Eureka, CA 95502"

The word "dyke" gives me a little shiver of excitement. I look up, sure Liz and Joel can see it glowing off the page like I can, as if this magazine has a light shining out of it like in a cartoon or something. But they're oblivious to everything but each other, smiling with their heads leaning together across the sales counter as they talk. I might as well not even be here.

I've read about zines in *Spin Magazine*, but never actually ordered one before. Sending just a dollar in the mail doesn't seem too risky, and it would be good to get to know another girl who likes girls. Another *dyke*. I shake my head, unable to really make the word fit. I feel all shy and rubbery inside, not confident enough for all those consonants to apply to me. Will the zine be about motorcycles or leather jackets or something? I decide there's only one way to find out, and keep the magazine in my hand while I step back over to scan the titles of the CDs on the wall.

7

Aunt Marion and the twins come over for dinner Sunday night. She makes a salad while Mom boils water for spaghetti and browns meat in a pan. I set the table lazily, half listening to the argument the boys are having in the living room over their video game. They're both very insistent that the other is the bigger fart-face.

Gran and Grandpa, before he died, used to always have everyone over for Sunday dinner. Grandpa and my uncle Richard would sit in the living room and drink scotch and complain about their patients while my cousins fought over the Nintendo controller and Gran cooked. Grandpa was a dentist, and he dreamed of all of his kids joining him in the family business, but the only one who actually went to dental school was Uncle Richard. Mom is the office manager at a clinic downtown, so she could join in the work talk sometimes, but she usually stayed in the kitchen with Gran and Aunt Marion. I hid out upstairs with my toys and books until it was time to eat. Mom is between Uncle Richard and Aunt Marion in age, but she's never been as close to her brother as her sister. They're like best friends, which seems so strange to me when I think about my no-nonsense mom and new agey, flighty Aunt Marion. It makes me wish I had a sister, someone to understand me and be there for me like Mom is for Marion, no matter what.

"So Georgie," Aunt Marion says, glancing up from the lettuce she's tearing apart, "my lease is up for renewal this month, and the boys are really starting to outgrow the apartment. And since there are so many empty rooms here, I was thinking we could move in."

She looks from me to my mom quickly, but Mom shrugs.

"I think we should sell the house."

"What?" Marion asks, shocked.

"An excellent question!" I say.

Mom stirs the water and turns away from the stove to face the two of us.

"The property taxes on this place are really high," she says, "and it's a lot to maintain."

"But we grew up here," Marion says.

"I know that, Marion."

"You should sell our house," I say, "and use the money to pay the property taxes here."

"It's not that easy." She shuts my logic down as quickly as her sister's attempt to tug at her heartstrings. "Richard thinks we should sell the house," she continues. Uncle Richard moved to Washington years ago, but he and Mom talk on the phone at least once a week.

"Why is it his decision?" Aunt Marion demands.

"Well it's hardly fair for us to just move in and take over. The house would go to all three of us."

"Moving in and taking over sure sounds like what you did!"

"Someone has to sort through all of Mom's stuff and deal with everything," Mom hisses. She turns back to the stove.

My cousins' chatter went silent when the voices in the kitchen started rising, and suddenly the sound of silverware clinking in my hand is the loudest thing I hear. After a moment, Mom breaks a handful of spaghetti in two with a loud crack.

"Breaking pasta is bad luck," Aunt Marion says in a low voice.

"Maybe *that's* what we've been doing wrong this whole time," I say, making my eyes round.

Aunt Marion smiles, but Mom just says, "I don't believe in bad luck."

"Well, the boys and I can stay here until we decide what to do next," Aunt Marion says as she digs around in the drawer for the salad tongs.

"Fine," Mom says. "It's going to take a long time to clean this place out, and I can definitely use the help. But we're putting it on the market when we're done."

After Aunt Marion and the boys leave for the night, Mom follows me upstairs to look at the sewing room. It used to be Uncle Richard's bedroom, but Gran took it over when he went away to college. Aunt Marion explained that she plans to move back into her old bedroom, and to move the twins' bunk bed into the sewing room. It's the biggest of the upstairs bedrooms, and it has a walk-in closet crammed full of boxes.

Mom lifts the first box she finds to the floor and unfolds the flaps. It's full of books. I take a step toward it.

"Take it," Mom says, pushing it toward me with her foot. "I'm sure you're the only one who wants any of these. Keep what you want and we'll take the rest to Goodwill." I shove the box down the hall to my room. When I come back, Mom has cleared a path for herself deep into the closet. I pass boxes of crushed Christmas bows, scraps of fabric and spools of thread, stuffed animals, old issues of National Geographic, and find her in the back of the closet, removing the lid from a banker's box.

"What's that?" I ask.

She pulls out a suit jacket, shakes some wrinkles out, then presses it to her nose. "It was Dad's. My dad. Your grandpa."

"Yeah, I get the connection."

Mom shakes her head.

"She told me that she gave his clothes away. She said that the veterans came and picked them up." She hands me the open box and takes the lid off the one below. More clothes. "She must have moved all these boxes up here by herself." She blows her breath out slowly and stares at the stack of boxes.

My grandpa died of lung cancer when I was ten. Mom and Gran took care of him together at the end. They moved a hospital bed into the family room and gave him oxygen and sponge baths. I played with my paper dolls in Mom's old room, an oblivious little kid.

"I can't even imagine what else we're going to find up here," she says. She pushes her bangs out of her face and shakes her head, looking lost.

I don't really know what to do or say, so I retreat from the closet, set the box of suits on the floor, and open another box. More books, large with textured covers.

"Salem High School yearbook," I read aloud, pulling out the top volume.

"That must be Mom's or Dad's," she calls from inside the closet. "By the time we started school, they had renamed Salem High to South Salem and opened North and East."

I flip to the index and there she is, Sharon Ward, page 39. I turn to the page, and she's in the middle of the top row. Her hair is smooth and curled, her smile restrained but still happy. She has that dreamy look that old school pictures always have. I touch the picture, then put it back into the box and haul the whole thing to my room. There's one shelf in the case behind the bed that's not full of books, but these will fill it up soon enough. I put the yearbook on the shelf, next to my light blue-green Care Bear, Wish Bear, a yellow star shooting across her stomach. I got her for Christmas when I was five or six. Uncle Richard still lived in town, Grandpa was alive, and the whole family was here. There had been a big storm, and the incline of the driveway was like a solid sheet of ice. Uncle Richard's three kids, all older than me, spent the morning sliding down the driveway on the plastic sled they'd found in the garage. I was terrified that I'd slide into the street and get hit by a car, so I was content to watch, but then David, the oldest of my cousins, started calling me a baby. His sisters joined in gleefully. Finally, in tears, I ran into the warmth of the kitchen, where Gran was opening the oven to check on the Christmas ham. Mom and Aunt Marion sat at the kitchen table, sipping champagne and munching on salted peanuts.

"What's wrong, Sweetie Pie?" Gran asked, closing the oven and reaching down to pick me up. I was still wearing my snow boots and I'm sure I got her holiday sweatshirt wet, but she still squeezed me tight. I buried my face in her shoulder and inhaled her perfume. I remember the edges of the puff paint on her sweatshirt poking my legs through my leggings.

"They're being mean to me," I said through my tears.

She rubbed my back, then deposited me into a chair by Aunt Marion and turned to pull a clean dishcloth from the drawer. She turned on the tap, then waited for the water to warm up before dampening the cloth. She gently wiped the tears from my cheeks.

"You have to toughen up," Aunt Marion said, already tipsy on champagne. "There are always going to be assholes. You can't be so sensitive and let them get to you."

"Marion!" Mom admonished.

"It's good to be a little sensitive," Gran said, turning to stir a pot on the stove. "It's good that you care, Hannah. Don't let the world take that out of you."

We opened presents after we ate, and Gran got me exactly what I wanted, like always. I removed Wish Bear from her box as carefully as I could and hugged her to me, her fur still soft from the factory. I looked up, past my cousins running around shrieking, their sweaters and hair covered in stick-on bows, to where Gran sat on the couch with Grandpa.

"Thank you!" I called across the noise. She met my eye, smiled, and winked.

8

The Huckle Cat show is all we talk about at lunch for most of the week, and the band practices every night after school. Liz and I make copies of the tape of their six original songs, and I spend an afternoon sitting in Brian's garage during practice, cutting and folding the liners for the tapes. Colin drew the cover, a little picture of the three of them on a stage. He stays after school to silkscreen some thrift-store t-shirts with "Susan B. Dangerous" written in curly cursive, like on the edge of the tape. His art teacher lets him use it as extra credit.

On Friday, Liz is unusually quiet as she drives me home.

"Are you looking forward to tonight?" I ask.

She nods, but then exhales deeply.

"It'll be good, right?" she says. She's staring at the road, but I can see the nervous furrow in her eyebrows. "I mean, I won't totally fuck everything up and screw up my chance to get in good with Huckle Cat and show everyone that we're not just messing around?"

I nod. "Of course! You'll do great, Liz. You always do."

She glances over like she's not sure if she believes me.

"You're an amazing guitar player," I continue. "And tonight, everyone will see that."

She pulls into Gran's driveway and shifts the car into park. I start to give her a reassuring pat on the shoulder, but she reaches across the emergency brake and hugs me hard.

"Thanks, Hannah," she says into my hair, then pulls back. "I've never played this big of a show. I really want it to go well."

"It will."

I can smell her on my hoodie when I get out of the car, clean sweat and and the lavender laundry soap that her mom uses.

Liz is picking me back up for the show at seven, so I finish reading *Frankenstein* and start on a book from one of the boxes I moved into my room. It's a teen novel from the sixties, girls in plaid skirts and sweaters hoping the boys on the basketball team will notice them. They remind me of the girls at school, falling all over themselves for the jocks. So much for progress.

About twenty minutes before Liz is supposed to come get me, I start getting ready. I settle on my current favorite jeans and a baby blue tank top with my green zip-up hoodie. I wrap my hair into a loose bun on either side of my head. I don't know how to get my hair to be smooth without products, and I don't know anything about products, so I go for a messy-on-purpose look.

"What do you think?" I ask Olive, who sits on the bed watching me. I spin for her, and she closes her eyes in what I can only assume is disapproval.

9

The Loyola's stage door is in the alley where Liz hides to smoke weed when we go to shows. She pulls her car up like she owns the place, and we haul everything backstage. I find Colin when the bands start their sound checks. The owners of the Loyola took out most of the theater seats, but they left a few rows in the back. We sit and watch while Liz and Paula strum and call over to the sound guy in the corner. I feel a little shiver of excitement. I've never been to a real sound check before. I glance over at Colin, to see if he feels it too, but his head is tipped against the back of his chair and his eyes are closed.

People start trickling in around 8:30. Some wear bright orange wristbands and drink cups of beer from the bar in the lobby, but there are a lot of groups of teenagers. I recognize some people from East, including Joel. He jumps onto the stage like he's done it a ton of times and pushes through the closed curtains; looking for Liz, I assume. As the room fills, Colin stands, says he's going to the bathroom, and disappears.

A thin redhead bounces up to me, and I recognize Paula's sister Kathy. She's wearing a crocheted tank top and jeans, without a trace of her sister's rocker style. With her are two girls I don't know. All three of them are wearing orange wristbands. One girl is thin and Asian, her lips deep red and her long straight black hair streaked with bright blue. The other girl is white, with short blonde hair, and I have to do a double-take when I see her. I'm almost always the fattest person in the room, especially when I'm around other people my age. Sometimes, when I was younger and kids at school would make fun of me, call me fatty or swing their arm like an elephant's trunk, I would think that maybe my purpose in life was to always be the fattest person, so no one else had to be. Everyone else could look at me and think, "Well at least I'm not as fat as *her*." But this girl is fatter than me, and is wearing a short pink plaid skirt that I would never wear, showing off dimpled thighs. She has a black scoop-neck t-shirt on too, stretching across her large breasts and showing off a ton of cleavage. She smiles warmly and her cheeks dimple too. I smile shyly back.

"Hannah!" Kathy exclaims. She hugs me like we're best friends, and points at the girls behind her. "These are my friends Heather and Miya." Heather is the blonde. "They're in school with me."

"Oh yeah," I say, "Paula said you were in cosmetology school. How is it?"

"It's really good," she starts, but before she can continue, I feel a tap on my shoulder, and Kathy's eyes are drawn to my left. I turn and find Joel.

"Liz needs you," he says without acknowledging the other girls.

I want to ask when he became Liz's errand boy, but instead I smile apologetically to Kathy and her friends, and follow him backstage.

Liz is holding the cardboard merch box I hauled in earlier.

"Hey Han," she says, "I thought the Huckle Cat roadie would sell our stuff along with theirs, but they said no. Can you sit at the table and sell stuff?"

The merch tables are always in the lobby, which means that I won't be able to see the show. I frown. "The whole night?"

Liz scrunches up her nose. "Maybe Colin can help? Where is he?"

"I don't know, he went to the bathroom like half an hour ago." I accept the box she deposits into my arms. "Can you take over after your set?"

She looks stricken. "But I have to watch Huckle Cat. I don't want them to think I'm not interested in them after they hooked us up with the show."

"What about . . ." I glance over at Joel, but Liz's eyes get big and she shakes her head emphatically. "He's never seen us play before! Or Huckle Cat! Come on, Han, you've seen us like a million times."

I sigh. "Fine. What do I have to do?"

She grins, looking relieved. "You're the best. You just have to stand there. The tapes are five dollars and the shirts are seven. Probably no one will buy anything anyway."

I heft the box down the stairs at the edge of the stage and out to the lobby, where an empty folding table sits near the bar. Another table is next to it, covered with Huckle Cat albums and shirts.

"Hey," I say to the guy hunched in a folding chair behind the Huckle Cat table. He's unshaven, in a flannel and jeans.

"Hey," he responds without looking up from the little notebook he's writing in.

I unpack a few tapes and t-shirts, try to arrange them attractively on the tabletop. There are Huckle Cat shirts hanging on the wall behind their table, but I don't have anything to hang mine up with. I also don't have any paper to make a price sign, or any change in case anyone wants to buy anything. I hope no one buys anything.

The lights in the theater dim, and a few people clap as Liz says into the mic, "Hello! We are Susan B. Dangerous!" The lobby crowd thins as people go to check out the band.

"We used to sell other people's stuff, no problem," the Huckle Cat roadie says like we've been talking about it. He's still looking down at his notebook. "But then one time the other band accused me of stealing some money, so we said no more. Fuck that."

"Yeah, totally," I say. "That makes sense." I nod, letting him know that I don't mind being out in the lobby and missing the whole show. After all, he does it.

"They're not bad," he says. He flicks his head toward the curtained door separating us from the theater. Someone pushes through the thick curtain, and I hear Liz's voice, clear and strong. I nod. "Yeah, they're pretty good." I pause, then ask, "So, is this like, your job?"

"When there are shows," he says.

"How long have you been doing it?"

He thinks for a second. "Maybe a year."

"How is it?" I wonder if he feels like I do sometimes, like part of the group but also not.

He stretches. "It's cool. We went all over the country in a van, did stuff I never would have done on my own."

"Cool." I definitely do things with Liz and Susan B. that I wouldn't do on my own, but I'm still not actually part of the group. There should be another choice, right? Between being alone or being the one out in the lobby?

10

Susan B. ends their set with Liz's favorite Nirvana cover, "Come As You Are," and then people start streaming out to the lobby. Several people come to check out the Huckle Cat merchandise, and a few people actually come to my table. I have to ask my fellow salesman to break a twenty for me, and he's nice about it. I've sold two tapes and a shirt when I see Colin ambling down the stairs. Maybe he has been in the bathroom this whole time; that's all there is up there.

"Colin," I yell across the lobby. He looks up, surprised, his dark brown curls falling in his eyes. He cuts through the crowd and joins me behind the table.

"Hey, what's up?" he asks. I'm never totally sure if that's a real question or just a generic greeting, so I don't answer, but then he repeats himself like he thinks I didn't hear. I feel my face heating up.

"I'm selling this stuff," I say, gesturing to the table.

"Johnny couldn't do it?" he asks, glancing over at the Huckle Cat roadie. He's digging around in a box under the table for a particular size of shirt and doesn't seem to have heard.

"A band accused him of stealing one time," I explain, "so he said fuck that."

"Ahhh." Colin looks ready to take off again, and I speak before he can.

"Where did you go? You missed the whole performance." I know immediately that performance isn't the right word, too big and too formal. *The whole set,* I say in my head, remembering the time I called a show a concert and how hard Paula and Brian laughed. "It's not Carnegie Hall," Brian had said, "It's just a *show,* you know?"

"Nah, man, I saw it."

"From upstairs? I thought the balcony was closed off." There are plywood sheets over the entrances to the balcony seats, covered in graffiti, to keep people out.

"Brian showed me a way to get in. It's cool up there. All the extra chairs from downstairs are piled up like a jungle gym."

"Please tell me you didn't climb them."

He laughs. "No, Mom, I was a good boy. All those people, man, all those shrieking girls, it's too much downstairs."

"So why even come?"

He looks surprised. "I'm not going to skip out on my friends!"

That's nice of him, I guess, but I'm annoyed that he did skip out on the merch sales.

"Well, you can avoid the crowds for the rest of the show by sitting with the Susan B. stuff so I can go watch," I tell him.

He rubs his face, then pushes his hand back up through his hair, making it stand up.

"Yeah, sure, I mean, of course. What do I do?"

Right then, Kathy appears in front of the table, face red and sweaty, a fresh beer in her hand.

"The cavalry is here!" she announces, slamming her cup down on the table. I push a shirt out of slosh range and look at her, confused.

"Paula said you wanted to watch the cat band, so I told her I'd push this stuff and give you a break." She gestures to the t-shirts and tapes, then notices Colin.

"Hey buddy, how are you?"

"Hey Kathy," he answers, not meeting her eye. I notice that the edges of his ears turn red. Is he into her? I look over at her. Even drunk and sweaty, she's still objectively hot. He's definitely into her.

"You working too?" she asks Colin, and I realize that we've gone from no one wanting to sell the merch to three possible salespeople.

I hear the house music stop, and people start heading back into the theater. I decide to take advantage of the situation and step out from behind the table.

"So, it seems like the two of you can handle things," I say. "Do you mind if I go in and watch Huckle Cat?"

Kathy puts her arm around my shoulders and leans against me heavily, breathing beer breath into my face.

"Hannah, you go have fun. We've got this shit under control."

"That's great. Thanks." Hopefully she won't completely mess it up, but really, what damage can she do with some t-shirts, tapes, and $17 in a shoebox? Colin stays, which doesn't surprise me, considering his dislike for crowds and the appeal of Kathy Connor.

I find my friends near the front of the room, and Liz hugs me like we haven't seen each other in weeks. We jump around and cheer for Huckle Cat. There are four women in the band, and their songs are energetic, fast and fun to dance to. When the singer thanks the Loyola for having them and Susan B. Dangerous for opening, Miya, Heather and I scream and clap. Paula, Brian, and Liz smile and wave. I wonder if Kathy's friends mind that she's out in the lobby, but they seem happy to hang out with the rest of us. I can't help but notice how much Heather's boobs bounce when she dances. Her short skirt flips around, probably showing her underwear to the whole room, but she doesn't seem to care. Joel stands behind Liz, his arms wrapped around her and the two of them swaying like Huckle Cat is playing slow jams.

The band does an encore, and then the lights turn back on and a pop song starts playing over the speakers. I glance around, and am surprised to see that Joel and Liz are kissing.

"I'm going to go check on Kathy and Colin," I say, mostly to get away.

Kathy and Colin, it turns out, are doing just fine. Colin sits in a folding chair while Kathy smiles at everyone who passes. I hear her tell someone, "I have the perfect color for you," as she holds up a royal blue Susan B. shirt.

"How did it go?" I ask after the customer leaves, shirt in hand. I squeeze behind the table. She winks and points at the shoebox so I can see the pile of bills inside.

"Nice!" I say. "I guess people appreciate good customer service."

"Well, yeah," she says like it's obvious. The three of us box up the remaining merchandise and Kathy asks, "You're coming over, right, Hannah?"

Earlier in the week, Paula invited Liz and me over for an all-girl slumber party after the show. I shoved some pajama pants and a change of clothes into my backpack before I left the house, but since Joel asked Liz out after the show, I wasn't sure if it was still happening.

"I don't know," I say. "I think Liz has a date."

"So what? You can't do anything if she's not there?"

"No," I say, too defensively.

Colin carries the box and we walk back toward the stage. The curtains are open, and I can see Brian chatting with the Huckle Cat singer while they pack things up to haul out to the cars.

We walk out into the cold night and hear Paula shriek.

"You're ditching us?"

Liz puts her hands up. "God, Paula, don't have a hissy. I'll come over later." She keeps her voice low and glances over at Joel while she speaks. He's loading amps into the back of the Subaru and and doesn't seem to notice.

Paula turns to me. "You're still coming over, right?"

"Sure, but I don't know if I have a ride." I look at Liz, who glares at me.

"Okay." Paula seems relieved that at least I'm coming over. It's kind of sweet, actually. "You can come with me and Brian," she says.

"We're already giving Colin a ride," Brian says, coming out the door. "Plus we have to make *a stop* before I drop you off, remember?"

I roll my eyes. Do they actually think that no one realizes that they're talking about sex?

"Oh, right," Paula says. "Maybe Miya can give you a ride? She and Heather are coming too."

I end up in Miya's Volkswagen, crammed into the backseat with Kathy. I discover that Volkswagen Beetles have maybe three inches of legroom in the backseat. Why even put seats in the back if a real human leg isn't going to fit between the backseat and the front? Kathy folds herself into a little pretzel and seems happy. I manage to sit cross-legged like in kindergarten, but I don't even try to fasten my seatbelt.

"Our parents go away this weekend every year," Kathy explains while we drive. "It's their anniversary."

"That's sweet," I say. I'm always surprised to hear about happily married couples, but when I do, it makes me feel hopeful. Like that could happen to me one day too, even though it didn't for my mom or aunt.

II

The front door of the Connors' house opens to two sets of stairs. One leads down to the bedrooms, and the other leads upstairs, which is where we go. Miya, Heather, and I drop our stuff in the living room, then follow Kathy into the kitchen.

"Want a drink?" Kathy asks, opening the fridge and pulling a beer out for herself. She opens the freezer and hands Heather an ice cube tray. Miya sets a backpack on the kitchen table and I hear bottles clink inside.

"What do you have?" I ask. I almost never drink, mostly because Liz is way more likely to smoke weed. Since we're sixteen, they're both illegal, but weed is easier to get, since it's not like you get carded.

"It's Heather's special," says Miya, handing me a white bottle to inspect. Her nails are the same bright blue as the streaks in her hair. "Malibu, pineapple juice, and club soda."

"Coconut rum, 80 proof," I read to myself like it means something. Coconut and pineapple sound good, so I nod and hand the bottle back to Miya.

"I don't know how you can drink that," Kathy complains. I look over at her. She flops down on the couch and slurps from her can.

"Why?" I ask.

"All that pineapple juice has too much acid. It hurts my stomach."

"Okay, whatever, Grandma," Heather begins as she starts pouring. "I'm sure it doesn't have anything to do with the time you drank a whole bottle of Malibu and barfed in my closet."

"I couldn't find the bathroom. If you're going to invite people over, it's only polite to have a bathroom nearby!"

"It was right next to the closet!" Heather laughs. She stirs the drink with a butter knife and hands it to me with a flourish. I take a sip. It just tastes like juice and coconut, so she must not have added much alcohol. I could get into this.

"Oh man, Liz is so fucking boring," Paula snorts, nestling into the couch cushions and sipping from her cup. She showed up about half an hour after we arrived, and immediately poured herself a drink. "I mean, look at me," she continues. "I have a boyfriend, and I love him very much, but I understand that it's important to give time to the ladies."

"Excuse me, but weren't you mounting your dear boyfriend in his car twenty minutes ago?" Kathy asks with a laugh. I giggle.

"Okay, but still," Paula concedes. "Tonight, her best friend," she points at me, "and her bandmate-slash-creative-partner," she points at herself, "asked for one night, just one night for a little classic female bonding. Is that so much to ask?"

"She's not that bad," I say with a laugh.

"Of course *you* say that!" she says.

"What do you mean?" I feel my face redden.

Miya and Heather's conversation comes to a lull, and they turn to look when I speak. I gulp from my drink, my second, and wait for Paula to answer.

"Do you need me to say it?" she says, half of her mouth stretching up almost into a sneer. I shrug in a way that I hope looks tough, and she proclaims, "You're totally in love with her!" My cheeks flush hotter than before, if possible, and her expression softens.

"I'm sorry, is it a secret? I know Liz is totally clueless, but it's not hard to see."

Miya and Heather glance at each other, eyebrows raised. Great, now they think I'm some stupid moony fat girl too, like Paula clearly thinks.

"It's fine, Hannah," Kathy says, and reaches over to put her hand on my knee. "We don't need to get all serious, it's not a big deal."

"But it *is*," I say, feeling the thickness in the back of my throat that means tears are coming. "She's obviously not into girls, and even if she was. . ."

"Wait a second," Heather interjects. "That other girl in your band?" Paula nods. "*She's* not into girls?"

Miya and Kathy crack up.

"But you are?" Miya asks when she regains her composure, and I nod slowly. I've never actually talked about it out loud.

"And Liz is into *guys*?" Heather repeats like she still can't believe it. "With *that* hair?"

Something between a laugh and a sob escapes my throat. "I helped her dye her hair."

"There have to be other girls out there for you, Hannah," Paula says, ignoring Heather. "Liz isn't just into guys, she makes every conversation about herself, and she's a fucking *bore*. Look at tonight, she totally blew us off to go fuck Joel Shithead."

"Do you really think he's a shithead?" I ask. Are they really having sex right now?

"Oh, he's one of those guys who thinks he knows more about music than any girl, just because he has a dick. Like those assholes in guitar stores who are all, 'Looking for a gift for your boyfriend, Little Lady?'"

"Ugh, men," Kathy groans. "The worst." She pushes herself up off the couch and toward the kitchen. "Are you guys hungry? Mom left a lasagna in the fridge. And a cheeseless little baby one for my little baby vegan." She ruffles Paula's hair as she passes. I look at the clock on the stove. Almost one, but I'm starving.

Kathy turns the oven on and takes two silver pans from the fridge. I get up to make myself another drink. The pineapple juice is gone, but Kathy hands me a can of RC Cola. I pour some of the coconut liquor into my glass with the soda. It smells like sunscreen and summer.

"I mean it, Hannah, you can do better than Liz," Paula says when I sit back down. She's apparently not planning on letting this go. I feel like it's about ten thousand degrees in here. I'm pretty sure my friends would be okay with me liking girls. They're not conservative assholes. But it's so tied into my feelings for Liz, into me being a pathetic girl with a crush, following Liz around like a dog desperate for attention. Could Paula be right, that I could do better? Who's better than Liz?

"Do you know any gay girls at East?" I ask.

She only has to think for a second before shaking her head. "I've heard that the drummer of Huckle Cat is gay. I should have introduced you. I can probably get her number."

I laugh. "Isn't she like, 25?"

Paula shrugs. "It can be good to be with someone older. And more experienced. Especially your first time."

My eyebrows shoot up. "Were you?" These cocktails are definitely loosening my tongue. Paula has been dating Brian as long as I've known her, but that's only a couple of years.

"Only Brian," she says. "But he *is* older!"

"Like six months!"

"And he was more experienced."

"Oh yeah? Who did he do it with before you?"

"Some girl he met at marching band camp," she says with a wave of her hand. "She goes to a different school. It was before we really knew each other, summer before sophomore year."

"Yeah sure," Kathy says. She raises her fingers into air quotes. "Someone at 'camp.'"

"What," Paula challenges, "you think he's lying?"

Kathy shrugs. "Guys always want to seem more experienced than they are."

Across the room, Heather nods.

"Tell me about it," she says. "I went out with this guy who was so confident in his skills in the sack, and he obviously had no clue what he was doing. It was like he'd never even seen a vagina before!" She and Miya shriek with laughter, and I try to sink further into the cushions. I always feel so transparent when people talk about sex, like just one look at me will tell them that I have absolutely no clue. I've read a lot, but I don't think that counts. Heather continues, "I finally had to take his hand and show him what to do."

"Aw, you can't blame them though," Miya says, still laughing. "It's not like guys get a manual. And pornos are no help, the girls just pretend to get off in a second. There's nothing *instructional*."

This makes Kathy and Heather make fun of her for expecting pornos to be instructional.

Paula turns to me, waving away the other girls' laughter. "The drummer from Huckle Cat is named Holly. She's got great style."

"Come on, Paula," I protest. "It's not like some professional musician is going to be into a high school student. Especially me."

"What do you mean, especially you? What's wrong with you?" Paula looks confused.

"Do you need me to say it?" I echo her sentence from earlier. I gesture to my stomach, my thighs.

Paula snorts. "Fuck that. You're awesome, Hannah. You're funny and cool and smart-"

"And I have *such* a pretty face," I finish for her.

From the other couch, Heather groans. "I hate when people say that! It's such a backhanded compliment. Like your face is okay, but as for the rest of you . . ." She wrinkles up her nose in an expression of disgust. "As if I even need their stupid approval about my appearance." She looks directly at me, and I feel my face burn. "Don't let assholes make you feel bad about yourself. You're totally hot. As long as you know it, it doesn't even matter if other people think so."

"That's the thing about life," Kathy says like a wise old sage.

"It's chock-full of assholes who want to make you feel like you're not doing shit right. And you have to keep being yourself because they're just jealous." She winks at me. "When you're old like me, you'll understand."

We're still laughing about that one when the oven timer goes off.

12

When I wake up the next morning, my head is pounding and the sunlight streaming directly onto my face doesn't help at all. My mouth tastes like a dried-up old sponge. I raise my head slowly and look around. It's definitely daytime, but everyone is still asleep. Miya and Heather are stretched out on the couches that line the walls, and Paula is in a sleeping bag next to me. Kathy said it was ridiculous to sleep in the living room when her bed was so close, so she went downstairs a little after three. Paula rented special female-bonding movies, and I fell asleep near the middle of *Thelma and Louise*. I reach over to my backpack and pull out my digital watch. Eight-thirty. Too early.

I'm kind of surprised that Liz never showed up, but I have to admit I knew it was a possibility. She acts like she doesn't care about impressing guys, but this isn't the first time she's blown me off for one.

I take my backpack into the bathroom so I can brush my teeth and get dressed. I gulp down handfuls of water from the sink to bring some moisture to my tongue. Dressed and slightly more hydrated, I lay back down on my sleeping bag with a book. I'm debating whether it's rude to dig through the medicine cabinet for some ibuprofen when Kathy emerges up the stairs.

"Good morning," she whispers. She shuffles into the kitchen and starts making coffee. I get up and ask her for the ibuprofen, then help make pancakes from a recipe in a vegan cookbook with pages warped from moisture and spotted with spills. The noise and the smell of the coffee rouses Paula, and she's sitting at the table sipping from a giant mug when Miya and Heather awake. Kathy carries over a stack of plates, the top one piled with pancakes, and we eat quietly. Everyone else seems to feel like I do, which I guess is hung over. I can't wait to get home and crawl into bed.

Miya offers to give me a ride home, which I accept after extracting promises from everyone that all the Liz talk from the night before will not leave the room. They all agree, Kathy making a big show of zipping her lips and throwing away the key.

I settle into the back of the Volkswagen, watching the backs of Miya's and Heather's heads as Miya follows my directions to Gran's house.

"So, do you two do each other's hair, or what?" I ask.

Miya smiles at me in the rearview mirror.

"I dyed mine myself," she says.

"Someone else in class did mine," Heather says, fluffing up her blonde curls. "I wish it had been Miya, though. She's the best." She pauses. "I mean, except for *me*, of course. Kathy told you we can do really cheap haircuts, right?"

Miya's eyes flick to me again in the rearview mirror, and I pull up the hood of my sweatshirt, suddenly self-conscious of the rat's nest I call my hair. She chuckles.

"It's the next driveway," I say. Miya pulls to the sidewalk, and Heather climbs out so I can extract myself from the backseat.

"Wait," she says before I can get very far. She digs around in her purse, and finally emerges with a battered pink business card.

"My card," she says triumphantly, handing it to me. It has "Salem School of Cosmetology" printed on the front in gold, and the phone number and address printed on the back, with "Heather Sokoloff" written in blue ballpoint pen.

"You can make an appointment with me at the same number!" Miya calls from the driver's seat.

"Ok," I say, pocketing the card. "Thanks for the ride. And it was nice to meet you both."

"You too!" Heather says, getting back in the car. She rolls down the window and sticks her arm out, waving as Miya drives off.

13

Luckily, Mom doesn't object when I find her in the sewing room and tell her I'm tired and want to lay in bed and rest.

"How late did you girls stay up last night?" she asks with an indulgent smile. She's sitting on the floor, sorting through a box of old greeting cards, photographs, and other pieces of paper. I groan.

"Too late."

She laughs.

"Do you have homework?" she asks, as if I ever don't have homework.

"Yeah, but nothing too big. I can do it tomorrow."

"Sounds good. I'll let you know when dinner is ready."

"Thanks," I tell her, and drag myself to my room. I wrap myself up in the comforter and make clicks with my tongue until Olive peers in and hops on the bed to join me. I think about Heather. She makes me feel so frumpy, hiding in too-big clothes like if I cover up my body, no one will notice it. Heather definitely wasn't hiding last night at the show. She seemed so confident. And she talked about sex and dating like anyone else, not like her body is a problem or a barrier. How do people get to feel like that? Everyone else always seems more confident than me, more sure of themselves, and I've kind of thought it was because most of the people I know are thin. They don't have people telling them over and over how bad their bodies are, how ugly and worthless. When we were learning adjectives in seventh grade Spanish class, the teacher read us descriptions of people and we were supposed to make little drawings in our notebooks, to show we knew the words. One of the descriptions was "una mujer gorda y bella." A fat and pretty woman. I remember stupid Josh Cramer piping up after Señora McKenzie said that, "But that doesn't happen. You can't be both fat and pretty!" And all the magazines and TV and movies, everything agrees with Josh. Fat is ugly, and fat isn't sexy. But Heather is sexy. She's confident and seems like she's just living her life how she wants to, and she obviously finds people who want to be with her. Does that mean I could too?

I roll on my side and rub Olive under her chin, her favorite spot. I've read that cats like this because it's where they secrete scent, and they like getting their scent all over their people. I can't tell any difference in how I smell, but it does make Olive want to hop onto my hip and get comfortable. In a minute, she's snoring gently. I wrap my arms around my pillow and nestle my head against it, close my eyes and wait for sleep to pull me in, too.

When Mom calls me for dinner, I'm reading a book that, admittedly, isn't for school. I have a copy of *Great Expectations* waiting on my desk, but there's something about being required to read a book for school that makes it so much less appealing. Even if it's a book that I would otherwise love, if it's assigned for school, I'm probably not going to love it. School turns reading into such a painful experience, dissecting a story to within an inch of its life and spreading its guts across ten pages and a thesis statement. It's just such a mean thing to do to a book.

"You got some mail," Mom tells me when I come to the table. "It looks kind of dark."

A thin white package sits next to my plate. Mom made tacos, one of her go-to meals, with shredded lettuce, ground beef, beans, and grilled peppers and onions. The kitchen smells delicious.

I sit and pick up my mail. It looks like a folded-in-half stack of paper, two purple staples shining from the folded edge, and Scotch tape holding the other sides closed. It's kind of beat up from the mail, addressed to Hannah, no last name. The return address is in Eureka, California. The zine I ordered. I turn it over and see why Mom called it dark. "Tiny Specks in Space," the other side proclaims above a grainy photocopied image. A cemetery at night, but the black sky is too full of stars, more like a photo taken by an astronaut than an actual sky we could see from Earth. I flip back to the address side. Several stamps are affixed to the corner, and there are stickers around my name, glittery stars and little pink-and-white Hello Kitty heads.

"It's a zine," I tell her, putting it on the empty chair next to me.

"What's that?" she asks, handing me the bag of tortillas. I take one and sprinkle cheese on it.

"It's . . . like a magazine, but a regular person makes it. And it can be about whatever you want."

"That sounds fun," she says. She nods her chin toward the chair where I've hidden my new zine. "Did a friend of yours make that?"

I shake my head. "No, you can put ads in other magazines. I thought this one sounded interesting, so I ordered it."

"Because of Gran?"

"What? No, it didn't have anything to do with her."

"Oh, I thought maybe it was, because of the graves on the cover."

"Gran's not dead," I say. "Obviously."

"I know, but Alzheimer's is still a big loss. They call it the Long Goodbye. It's natural to feel grief during this time."

"Did you read that in a pamphlet or something?"

She sighs, but manages not to snap back. She must be really trying tonight.

"You can always talk to me, you know, Han," she says gently.

"I know." I still don't look at her.

"It's really hard watching her go through this. No one knows that better than me."

I nod again.

"They offer support groups at Silver Wells," she continues. "Leticia told me about one for people supporting their parents through Alzheimer's, and I was thinking about going next week. Do you want to come with me?"

I hate it when she tries to be all sensitive and nice. Because how can I tell her that, if I did want to talk about things, about Gran or anything, it wouldn't be to her? There's always the chance that I'll say something that's too mean or too bad, not the nice, good girl I'm supposed to be. I'm supposed to get good grades and be polite and help out around the house, and I do that. Isn't that enough?

"No, my parents don't have Alzheimer's," I say.

"I know, but it might be good to hear about other people's experiences."

I shrug.

"Is that . . . *zine* about losing someone?" she asks. She puts emphasis on the word "zine," trying it out like a new word she's just learning.

"I don't know, I haven't read it yet," I mutter. Why doesn't she understand that sometimes I just want things that don't have to do with her, that are my own? "Don't worry about it."

"Okay," she says. "But please let me know if you ever want to talk."

"Yeah, okay."

14

After dinner, I take the zine up to my room and stab a ballpoint pen through the tape that holds it closed, carefully separating the pages. A letter, some stickers, and a few scraps of paper fall out. The papers, each about two or three inches square, are zine ads. A few are for this zine, but there are ads for others too. Some are handwritten, some typed, some are colored in or decorated with stickers, some are just black-and-white copies. They're all a dollar or two, and sending cash through the mail seems like the standard. I stack them up with the loose stickers and set them on my desk to look through later. I unfold the letter. It's brief, written on a sheet of Wonder Woman stationery in messy print.

Hi Hannah,

Thanks for ordering my zine. I'm glad my ad in MRR worked. You're the first person who's told me they saw it. I hope you like my zine - let me know what you think!

Corey

I re-fold the letter and open the zine. The first page is an intro:

Hello! My name is Corey. I'm seventeen and in my last year of high school in Humboldt County, California. I like Humboldt. I've lived here all my life, and I find all the stoners and aging hippies to be very comforting. I can't wait to be done with high school, though, and I'm trying to stay hopeful about college. Maybe people will actually care about learning there, not just about getting through classes to get a grade and climb a rung higher on the social ladder. My parents own an organic restaurant in town, and I work there a few afternoons a week. There's a cemetery down the street from the restaurant, which is where I took the cover photo. I like walking through the cemetery. It's so peaceful. It makes me think about what really matters in life. I know it sounds pretentious, but what if we never think about it? About the purpose of this whole time of being alive? Most of us are going to end up in a cemetery with hardly anyone thinking about us. We act like our lives are so huge and important, but we're really just tiny specks in space. In the grand scheme of the universe, what do our little lives matter? I've been thinking about these things a lot lately, so I decided to write some of them down. I don't have all the answers, but maybe other people think about the things that I think about? I like how zines connect us with people we might not otherwise meet, and how we can use them to share ideas that mainstream magazines ignore. Let me know what you think about what I've written. I'd love for this zine to spark conversations and I'm definitely open to differing viewpoints. I'd like to do a second issue with more ideas, so if anything you read makes you want to write, please send it to me, and I'll publish it in Tiny Specks in Space #2. Thanks for reading!

Opposite the intro is a table of contents, lines of typed text cut out and copied on top of a photo of a huge waterfall.

I turn to the first article.

What Matters?

Do you ever think about how many things we've made up? So many things that seem essential to us are no more than human inventions. Immediately after birth, we're classified - pink or blue, boy or girl. We're assigned a race, a nationality, a religion. Rich or poor, gay or straight, man or woman. Grow up, go to school, read what they tell you to read, learn what they say you need to learn, get a job, and make money.

But how many of these things are real? How many of them do we need? Our ancestors only cared about finding food and staying alive, but we're stressing about grades, SAT scores, getting into the right college so we can trade our time for money. We don't need sports cars, diamond rings, or the perfect lawn, but we're convinced that we do. We're really just animals, but we act like we're so much more important, so much more intelligent. At least animals focus on the essentials, not all this extra bullshit. Find food, stay warm, stay alive. We take those things for granted. I guess that's why we have so much free time to want other things. Get a degree, get a job, get a car. Get get get. Spend spend spend, and work yourself to the bone to be able to afford more more more.

What if I don't want to do it anymore? What if I don't want to follow the rules someone made about what a girl should be like? What if I don't want what I'm "supposed to" want? What if I want to decide for myself?

So what is the meaning of life? I think it's to stay alive. And to do it in a way that feels right, a way that matters. Because when you're gone, the cars and the degrees don't matter. What matters is how you treated people and how you lived your life. How true you were to yourself.

I turn the page.

What's Next?

Work all your life, and then you die. Then where do we go? It seems to me that the choices are pretty much:

1. Become a ghost, haunt the living, resolve your unresolved issues and then?
2. Afterlife (good, awful, or Purgatory)

3. Reincarnation

4. Nothing

I don't really understand the logistics of any of the options, other than option D. I've only been to church a few times in my life, but I feel about religion like Fox Mulder does about aliens: *I want to believe.* It would be such a relief to be able to put all my faith in some all-knowing being and believe that they have a plan for me, but I haven't been able to believe so far. Option D might as well stand for "depressing." If nothing really happens, then what IS the point of all of this? What's the point of being a good person if, in the end, we all just disappear?

If I could choose, I would pick reincarnation. Heaven sounds boring, and I've always hated the heat, so Hell is not for me. But I could take another shot at life. I'm sure I could do better. I would be nicer to my neighbors, swear less, and I would lock my bedroom door the first time I bring a girl home, in case my new mom is anything like my current mom and would walk in without knocking and completely lose her shit.

Oh, who am I kidding? I wouldn't be any nicer to the judgmental bitches who live across the street, and I'm actually glad my mom found out about me and Tracie. I've never been any good at lying. I guess I'm trying to live as honest of a life as I can. Sometimes I'm too honest, as evidenced by my complete lack of friends at school. I'm still working on finding the right balance between being honest and being nice. But if we're all just going to rot in boxes, does being nice really matter that much? How much is the right amount to change yourself to make other people comfortable?

Well, that certainly went off on a tangent! What do *you* think happens after we die? Write me a letter and let me know. Maybe we can figure this all out together. Or maybe there's no point in even thinking about it, since we won't actually know until it's our time. Maybe that's the point of life, that we're all in this

mystery together, and then once you know what happens,
it's too late to use it.

   The zine is full of lists and collages, pictures of stars and space, mountainous landscapes and tombstones. Near the end, there's a list titled "Bands that Give Life Meaning." I've heard of some of them, like Bikini Kill, but there are plenty that I haven't heard of. Team Dresch, Heavens to Betsy, Slant 6, Bis. I make a mental note to look for their albums next time Liz and I go to Island. I turn the zine over again, feeling glad that things like this exist, that people make their own places to share big ideas and have conversations about things that matter, instead of relying on glossy magazines and their diet tips and ads.

15

I force myself to start *Great Expectations* on Sunday morning, deciding to save my math homework for last because I know it will be the easiest. I'm only a few pages in when I hear the phone ring downstairs, then my mom calls my name.

"It's Liz!"

I meet her on the stairs and take the phone.

"Hey," I say as I walk back to my room. I'm pretty proud of myself for not calling her yesterday and demanding an explanation for her never showing up at Paula's.

"How's it going?" Her voice is casual, like everything is normal.

"Fine."

"Want to go get lunch at Shari's?"

Shari's is one of the few restaurants in town that's open all night, so we started going there after parties or shows or football games. But Liz loves the diner food and cheesy, cheery atmosphere so much that now we go there during the day as well. Especially after she goes on a big date. Sometimes I think she enjoys recounting her dates to me as much as she enjoys going on them. But the thought of listening to her rave about Joel seems particularly unappealing this morning. I don't say anything for a moment.

"Come on, Han . . . I'm sorry I never showed at Paula's on Friday. Things just got really intense with Joel after the show."

"Yeah, I thought you were going to come over after your date."

She giggles a little. "Yeah, the date ended up going a lot longer than expected. I'll tell you all about it."

I give her another second of silence, then she sighs.

"My treat? I know you can't say no to the strawberry waffle breakfast."

I do have a weakness for strawberries and whipped cream.

"Okay," I say finally.

"Cool! Can you be ready in like ten?"

Since that means twenty, minimum, I agree. I take a fast shower and don't wash my hair, just pull it into a messy bun, and I'm waiting on the porch when she pulls up, *Great Expectations* in hand.

She gushes about Joel from the moment she pulls out of the driveway.

"It was so intense," she says over and over. They talked about music and musicians and had so many favorites in common. They took his pickup to the old, abandoned drive-in movie theater on the edge of town. They spent the night laying in the truck bed and looking at the stars. He brought his guitar, and they took turns playing.

"So, what, you had such a good time together that you forgot to come over?" I ask when we're in the booth, waiting for our breakfasts to arrive. I choose an omelette and toast, just to be contrary, and she gets her usual, hash browns stuffed with sour cream and cheese with scrambled eggs and sausage on the side.

"Well, you know," she stirs her coffee thoughtfully, "you can't really talk at a show, so we had a lot to talk about after. He'd never seen us or Huckle Cat play, and he had a lot of good feedback. And since I already told my parents that I was spending the night at Paula's, I didn't really *have* to go home."

"So we were your cover story?" I'm irritated and not bothering to hide it. "What, so you could drive out to a field and have sex in the back of a truck?"

Her face flushes. "We didn't *just* have sex," she whispers harshly. "I'm trying to tell you it was an amazing night. I haven't felt like this with a guy in a long time." She pauses and takes a breath. "I'm sorry I didn't show up. I didn't know it was such a big deal. I figured Brian would come over anyway and he and Paula would sneak off to screw around and ditch us. They do that all the time at practice."

"No, he wasn't there," I say. "It was actually really fun. Those friends of Kathy's from beauty school came, and they brought alcohol."

She raises an eyebrow. "Drunk Hannah?"

I shrug. "Not out of control or anything. It was fun. I always thought Paula was so tough, but she was really sweet."

"Yeah, Paula's all bark no bite."

"I mean, I still wouldn't want to cross her," I say, and Liz rolls her eyes and chuckles.

"Like you would ever want to cross anyone." She stretches her hands across the table and looks at me seriously for a second. "Come on, don't be mad. I had an amazing weekend and I want everything to be cool. I'm sorry I flaked and used you as my cover story." She gazes at me with her deep brown puppy-dog eyes until I can't resist reaching my hands out to her.

The waitress interrupts with our food, and we pull our hands apart. Liz cuts off a chunk of sausage and pops it into her mouth.

"So did I tell you what Joel said about our cover of 'Come As You Are?'" she asks as she chews. I shake my head, and she launches into it.

16

I make myself finish all of my homework before I write back to Corey that night. After my last math problem, I turn to a fresh page in my notebook and start writing.

Dear Corey,

Thank you for sending me your zine, Tiny Specks in Space. It gave me a lot to think about. I don't know what happens after we die, but lean toward believing that nothing happens. Math and science are my favorite subjects in school, and I haven't found anything to prove that Christianity is real, so why should Heaven and Hell be real too? And why should I believe that one religion has all the answers when there are so many different ones that think they do? I like The X-Files a lot (although I'd take Scully over Mulder any day), but I think aliens are more likely to exist than all the stuff religion says. But I don't think that means there's no point to being a good person. I think it means there's <u>more</u> of a point. If now is all we have, then why not spend it being as nice to each other as possible? It seems kind of sad to be nice only if you get a reward. Just my opinion.

I've been thinking about stuff like this a little lately, because my grandma is dying. Sorry to be so dramatic. She's not sick, at least not physically. She has Alzheimer's. My mom calls it "the long goodbye" because the grieving goes on for a really long time. It seems wrong to even talk about grieving right now, since she's not dead. But she's different. If she goes to Heaven, would she be the person that she is now, or the one that I remember from when I was younger?

My genetics teacher says that the point of life is reproduction. That all species want to reproduce, and some only live long enough to pass their genes on, then they die. Obviously, she's pretty focused on genes, since she talks about them for a living. I don't know what the purpose of life is. I like what you said about being true to yourself. I know I should be truer to myself. Most people don't even know that I like girls.

Well, I guess that's all. Thanks again for sending me your zine. I liked it a lot. I love reading, but this was actually the first zine I've ever read. I hope you do make another one, because it would be interesting to see everyone's responses to your questions. Have you been making zines for a long time?

You don't have to write back or anything if you're busy.

     Thanks,

     Hannah

I write Gran's address under my name, then fold the letter up and put it in an envelope before I can reread it and think about how stupid it sounds. It has a lot of personal information, but she did say she liked honesty. I wonder if I should include some other things in the envelope, like she had in her package. I have some old stickers at home, but I don't really have anything here. I glance around the room and then remember my paper dolls under the bed. I pull the shoebox out, then pause. Is this weird? Sometimes, I do or say things that make sense to me, but then people look at me like I'm crazy, so I always second-guess myself. It's like I don't know how to be normal sometimes.

Well, I rationalize, she cut up a lot of pieces of paper for the zine, so maybe she won't think it's weird. And she doesn't have to write back if she doesn't want to. I pick two of my old favorites, the same model in two different outfits. In one, she wears a high-necked white blouse with a huge bow at the collar, a too-long skirt, and her hair pulled back in a loose bun. The other is from the underwear section, and her hair is down. She's wearing a lace-trimmed camisole, pulling up the bottom hem to show the waistband of her high-leg briefs. When I played with these paper dolls, they were twin sisters, one stuffy and one a wild girl, lounging at home after a long night of partying. I can't help but giggle thinking of young Hannah, playing with a paper doll of an underwear model, completely oblivious to how gay it would seem in retrospect. I smile to myself and fold the twins in half, adding them to the envelope and sealing it closed.

17

On Monday, in genetics class, Mrs. Halliday rolls out a metal supply cart piled with dishes and vials. She's holding a clear plastic container with little black dots inside. Paula's in my class -- our school lets juniors choose between chemistry, genetics, or both. She chose genetics, and I'm taking both. I have them back-to-back, fifth and sixth period. Our seats are assigned alphabetically in genetics, so we don't sit together. I share a table with Philip Lawson. Of course. Paula sits a few rows ahead of us, with an even worse seatmate, Josh Cramer.

Mrs. Halliday tells us that the little dots in her container are fruit flies, and we're going to breed them to see genetics in action. Next to me, Philip perks up.

"What do we do?" he asks eagerly.

I look over at Paula, to roll my eyes at her over Philip's excitement, but she's not looking at me. She's sitting up straight, paying rapt attention to Mrs. Halliday as she explains that the flies in her container are asleep from an anesthesia called FlyNap, so we can sort them into male and female, then breed them based on different traits. Any flies we don't use, she says, will go into the "fly morgue." She holds up a jar with a funnel in the top, half-full of a murky brownish liquid.

Paula's hand shoots into the air, but Mrs. Halliday is already turning to her supply cart and doesn't notice.

"Philip," Mrs. Halliday continues, "will you please distribute the materials on the cart to each table?" She follows him as he moves around the room, and shakes a few flies into each petri dish.

"Mrs. Halliday," Paula calls. Mrs. Halliday snaps the lid onto her container and looks up.

"Yes, Paula?"

"I can't do this assignment. I'm against animal experimentation."

Mrs. Halliday nods and moves to the next desk, shaking out more flies. "I'll come over after I finish giving these out."

She and Philip give out the supplies, which include a paintbrush and a vial with a white substance in the bottom. Philip returns to sit next to me, and I watch Mrs. Halliday walk over to Paula. She's probably in her sixties, and she wears jeans and running shoes and works out in the gym on her lunch break. She's a decent teacher. She didn't take any crap from the Christians in class when she taught evolution last year in bio, just said she was there to teach science.

"Paula," she's saying, "you don't have to participate in any class assignment, but you'll get a zero for today if you choose to sit out. We're going to check on our next generation of flies next week, so you'll get a zero that day as well."

"I know." Paula nods. She leans back in her chair, arms crossed in front of her. "I think it's wrong to breed animals just to experiment on them and to make them live in little vials."

Philip shakes his head. "What a waste of time," he says under his breath. "They're just fruit flies."

Without really thinking, I stand up.

"I feel the same as Paula," I say, and hear a scraping sound as Philip moves his chair away from me.

Mrs. Halliday turns to me, surprised. "Hannah? You don't mind missing today's points?" She glances down at Philip. She's well aware of our history.

"How many points is it?" I ask, starting to second-guess my impulse decision.

"Participation in daily class. Ten points today and ten points next week."

Twenty points is nothing. We take a quiz every Friday that's worth fifty, and I almost always get 100%.

"I think Paula makes an excellent point," I say.

Mrs. Halliday grants me a small smile. "Okay. The two of you can start reading chapter seven in the textbook. Josh, trade seats with Hannah and work with Philip, please."

She turns to go, and Josh starts gathering his stuff.

"Wait a second," Paula says when he reaches for the dish of fruit flies. "You can use Philip's. I want those."

Mrs. Halliday turns back in surprise.

"You just said you're against animal experimentation," she says.

"I am," Paula says. "I want to set them free."

At this, Josh Cramer lets out a hoot of laughter.

"It's forty degrees outside," Mrs. Halliday says. "They'll die."

"That's not *that* cold," Paula says. "They might not."

"You should let them loose by the dumpsters behind the Commons," Josh says with a grin. "At least they'll go happy."

He leaves the petri dish, and Mrs. Halliday sighs, then hands her container to Paula.

"This has holes in the lid so they can last until the end of class. Liberate away, Miss Connor. Just don't let them out *in* the Commons, please."

"So Paula," Josh says as Mrs. Halliday walks across the room to help Laura Salazar adjust her microscope, "you're against all animal experimentation?" I've come over to take his seat, but he hasn't gotten very far.

Paula nods.

"Does that mean you'd rather people die than animals?"

She narrows her eyes. "What are you getting at, Cramer?"

"Well don't you think it's better to test things on animals than on people?"

"Vaccines, for example. There would never have been a polio vaccine without animal testing," Philip chimes in like anyone asked him.

Paula rolls her eyes. "Give me a break, no one is asking us to cure polio in fifth period. There's a big difference between breeding animals just so to see what happens, and curing fucking polio."

"Mr. Cramer," Mrs. Halliday calls. "Is there a reason you haven't moved like I asked you to? You shouldn't need to consult with Miss Connor, since she's not even participating in this assignment."

After class, Paula and I go out the nearest door and down the stairs to the parking lot. She carries her plastic container like a precious treasure. The fruit flies have woken up from their anesthesia and are flitting around inside.

"Where should we go?" I ask. "Do you want to take them to the dumpsters like Josh said, or to the woods behind school?"

"You know, considering the source, I thought the dumpster thing was a surprisingly good idea."

We follow the building around to the back and the scent of rancid fry oil hits us. It feels like it's coating the back of my tongue.

"Yechh," I say.

Paula nods, then runs over to lift the lid of the nearest dumpster, peel the top off the container, and tap the flies in. I see more flies swarming around the opening. That's nice, our flies can make friends. Paula looks at the empty container for a second, then drops it in and runs back across the parking lot. She's grinning when she runs back to me, and I high-five her.

"Nice work!" I say.

"It might not make a difference," she says, "but I'm glad we did something. Thanks for standing with me, Hannah, it really meant a lot."

She links her arm through mine and I feel pleasantly warm inside. Maybe it was silly to lose the points over some fruit flies, and I'm sure I'll have to deal with this again if I keep studying science, but I do think Paula made good points. The chapter we read in the textbook explained the experiment and some different possible outcomes, so it wasn't really necessary for us to do it again with new flies. And it feels wrong to just kill any flies that don't work for the experiment. What makes us so much more important than them?

Paula and I walk back into the school, disconnecting our arms to fit through the doorway. She gives me a quick hug before disappearing into the flow of students in the hallway, and I walk to chem, carrying some of her confidence with me.

18

I look forward to checking the mailbox every day after school. Finally, on Friday, I find an envelope addressed to me. I tear it open as I run up the stairs. It's blue and red Sailor Moon stationery this time, with the same messy print writing.

Hi Hannah,

I'm so glad you liked my zine! And I'm never too busy to write back. I don't exactly have much of a life outside of zines and pen pals. I have about fifteen now, and I want more! Do you have other pen pals?

I'm really sorry about your grandma. That sounds like such a hard thing to go through. I only know one set of grandparents, and they live in San Diego. My grandma recently discovered Jazzercize. My dad's parents died before I was born. He's a lot older than my mom, because we're his second family. I have two half-brothers, both in their thirties. Do you have brothers or sisters?

I don't exactly think that you should be a good person because you get something out of it. But don't you think it's shitty that people who are assholes could end up in the same place (nowhere?) that nice people do? That's more what I was thinking about. It almost makes me feel like nothing we do matters in the long run, you know? Then it opens up all these other questions like Why are we here? Is it all just biology, like your science teacher thinks, or is there a greater purpose, like religious people think? It can be really overwhelming, and writing my zine just touched on the tip of the iceberg.

Thank you for sending those 80's catalog pictures! I love how they show two sides of the same person. It reminds me of the virgin/whore dynamic, where women can only fit into a few little boxes. They gave me a great idea for a collage for my next issue. Where did you get them?

I've done one other zine, but this one is the first one I'm really proud of, which is why I decided to splurge on the ad in MRR. I'm including a couple of ads for my friends' zines, which I recommend. I mostly read gay and feminist zines, so I hope you like that! What are some of your favorite books? Are you in high school or college? My high school doesn't have classes like genetics, but it's a small town. Is Salem close to Portland? My favorite band, Team Dresch, is from Portland. Do you like them? Have you ever seen them play live? I would love to. What's the best band you've seen live?

That's probably enough questions for now, so write back if you want!

Take care,

Corey

I feel a stupid grin on my face as I read. She doesn't think I'm a complete idiot. She also seems like she wants to keep writing to me. I get up to push play on my stereo, and listen to the guitars grind to life on my new Team Dresch CD. Liz is happy to hang out at Island after school now, at least on days when Joel is working, so it was no problem to get her to drive me the other day. Joel brought out a stool and let her sit behind the counter with him, and I bought a few CDs by bands that Corey mentioned in her zine. After I paid, I walked to the used bookstore down the street so I didn't have to watch them make out. I pick up the white paper bag with the Island logo on the side, and pull out the flyer that I found on the bulletin board at the back of the bookstore.

"Rainbow Youth" it reads in big bright letters, then smaller underneath: "A group for people age 23 and under who are lesbian, gay, bisexual, transgender, or questioning. Every Thursday, 3-5 pm, in the basement rec room of the United Church of Christ, 505 State Street NE, Salem, Oregon." When the rainbow-colored letters caught my eye, I tore the flyer down and ducked behind a bookshelf to read it before anyone could see.

I take out a notebook, turn to a blank page, and start writing.

Dear Corey,

Thanks for writing back. I don't have any other pen pals. I had one from Germany when I was younger, but one of us stopped writing after a few months. Okay, okay, it was her that stopped. Where are your pen pals from?

I don't have any brothers or sisters. Right now, my mom and I are living in my grandma's house while we clean it up because my mom wants to sell it, and my aunt and two cousins recently moved in too. I guess my cousins are kind of like little brothers. I keep wondering if Mom is going to tell me it's time to move back to our house, but she hasn't yet. We've gone back a couple times to get more clothes, and that's it. Maybe she wants to hang on like I do.

The best show I've been to lately was Huckle Cat, have you heard of them? They're from Salem, so you might not have, but I like them a lot. They're all girls, and my friend Paula says that the drummer is gay. Paula and my best friend Liz are in a band together, and they also played that show, but I didn't see them because I was working at the merch table. They're called Susan B. Dangerous. They're very talented. I wish I was creative like them. Sometimes I get so full of feelings that I wish I could get out. I wish I could smear them on a page and not carry them inside anymore. I like your collages, and I'm glad that you can use those magazine ladies in one. They were actually my paper dolls when I was little. I remember reading about people in the old days making paper dolls that way. My grandma always got a ton of catalogs, so there was plenty of material.

I have a lot of favorite books. Some of my favorites are Weetzie Bat, Bastard out of Carolina, Annie on my Mind. Have you read any of those? I like science fiction and fantasy a lot too, even though I know they're dorky. But they also remind me of how incredibly unspecial my life is. Reality seems so boring after space travel and dragons and stuff. I recently read a magazine article about people's favorite books, and everyone said the Catcher in the Rye. We had to read that for school last year, and maybe that's why I didn't like it, but it just seemed like another stupid guy whining about his stupid life and we're all supposed to be so impressed with how clever and deep he is. I hope it's not your favorite!

I'm in high school. I'm a junior. I'm not sure where I'm going to college, just anywhere that's not Salem. It's so boring here. Nothing ever happens. Sometimes I feel like my life is a movie and I'm waiting for it to get good. But if it were a movie, I would probably have walked out of the theater by now, because it's so freaking boring. What colleges are you thinking about?

Sorry, back to your questions! Salem is about an hour from Portland. I don't drive, so I only go to Portland for shows when Liz wants to go see one. We saw the Foo Fighters a few months ago, because Liz is obsessed with Nirvana and never got to see them live. The Foo Fighters were ok, but no Nirvana. I like Team Dresch a lot but I've never seen them play. What's the best band you've seen?

Okay, I better get to my homework, so I'll get this ready to mail now.

    Talk to you later!

    Hannah

19

When Liz is single, we'll hang out on Valentine's Day. We watch one of our favorite 80s movies like *Dirty Dancing* or *Desperately Seeking Susan* and split one of those big cardboard hearts of chocolates. It's really fun. But when Liz has a boyfriend, she gets into all that romantic Hallmark crap. It takes me a second to figure out where my feeling of dread is coming from when I wake up on Valentine's Day morning, until I remember the date.

Mom meets me in the kitchen when I stumble down the stairs, pulling on my hoodie. She's wearing a red sweater and beaming like it's a real holiday. I half-expect her to hand me a stack of heart-shaped pancakes, but her holiday spirit hasn't extended that far. I drop two slices of bread into the toaster.

"Why aren't you getting ready for work?" I ask.

"I took today off," she answers. "I have a meeting with Gran's lawyer, and then I thought we could go to this together." She waves a piece of pink paper under my nose.

I take the flyer and read, "You're invited to celebrate Valentine's Day with Silver Wells! Cookie decorating, games, and fun! Wednesday, February 14th from 3-5 pm."

"Leticia puts together something like this for every holiday. Something different for the residents."

"When did you and Leticia become best friends?"

"She's a nice lady," Mom replies. "She has a hard job, trying to keep the residents engaged."

I roll my eyes. "It doesn't seem that hard. Can't she just do the same thing every day? I mean, the old people don't notice, do they?"

She sucks in a slow breath. "Did you wake up on the wrong side of the bed today or what?" My mom loves phrases like that.

Like all you have to do is get up on the right side and everything is perfect.

"Sorry," I mutter. She sighs and sits down at the table, taking a serious tone.

"I know it's hard to watch what's happening with Gran, but please don't avoid her. You'll regret it later. You need to spend time with her while you can. I know I wish I'd spent more time with your grandpa when I could."

I drop my gaze. I shouldn't be such a jerk. I pick the flyer up from the table.

"What time do you want to go to this thing?"

Her smile returns. "My meeting is at two, so I'll meet you here after school and we'll go."

Mom offers to drops me and my bike off at school, so I'm early enough to wander into the Commons for once. The cheerleaders have a table set up to sell Val-O-Grams. They do this every year, and they get to skip class to deliver the cards to classrooms. Maisie Palmer, Liz's little sister, is standing behind the table in her orange cheer uniform, the winter version with the sweater and white leggings. She sees me and calls my name.

"Hannah, come send some Val-O-Grams!" She's grinning like a maniac. Maisie usually pretends not to know Liz or her friends, not wanting to get tainted by Liz's reputation for getting high in the locker room and dating a different guy every few months. But she'll acknowledge us if we can help her. I walk over obediently and listen to Maisie's spiel.

"They're just a dollar each, and you can pick your design from all of these. The money goes to buy new uniforms for the football team! Tell us the person's name, and we'll find out what classroom to deliver the Val-O-Gram to." She smiles and spreads her hands over the designs like a model on *The Price is Right*. I look them over. Black outlines and cheesy messages are copied onto pink, purple, and red paper.

"Isn't it kind of gross," I say, "that the girls have to sell crap so the guys get new uniforms? What do they ever do for you?"

Maisie rolls her eyes. "Spare me the feminism lecture, it's called school spirit. You can just send them to your friends." She holds up one with a heart-shaped box of chocolates on it. "Here, send this one to my sister to remind her of all the calories you two like to ingest together."

I take the card from her and have to admit it's kind of perfect, but not for the reason she's thinking. I see another card, pink with a picture of a cat, and remember how fast Paula befriended Olive the one time they met. I think briefly about getting one for Brian or Colin, but they probably won't care. Plus, two dollars seems like plenty to give to the football team.

I hand a five-dollar bill to Maisie and she gives me three crumpled ones.

"Put them here when you're done," she says, pointing to a box that's covered with pink paper as she moves on to catch another customer. "Janie, come send some Val-O-Grams!" she calls, motioning a small dark-haired girl over.

There's an empty plastic ice cream tub on a nearby table full of colored pencils, markers, and broken crayons. People lean or sit and write their messages, draw hearts and flowers, sign their names or leave them anonymous. I push close enough to dig through the tub. The first bell rings before I get to write anything, but Maisie jumps onto a chair to announce, "Someone will be here between classes all morning and at lunch. Turn your Val-O-Grams in by lunchtime today to be sure they get delivered!"

I stuff everything into my backpack and began my morning jog to calc. Coach Roberts would be so proud.

I drop my notes off with Maisie at lunch before heading over to our table. I haven't received any Val-O-Grams, not that I was expecting any, but each of my morning classes was interrupted by a cheerleader passing out pink and purple envelopes.

Maisie wrinkles up her nose when she sees how I've decorated my cards, but she takes them and picks up matching envelopes. I drop my borrowed markers into the bin and head to the hot lunch line. On Paula's card, I drew a star around the cat's right eye, and colored red lips to make a decent replica of Paul Stanley from KISS, if he were a cat. I colored the rest of the cat's fur black and gray like Olive's, and wrote "A big KISS from Hannah." I hope she likes it.

For Liz, I colored the chocolates to look like eyeballs, because actually referencing our candy sessions felt too sentimental. I added blue irises, black pupils, and colored the whites with crayon. I added red veins and blood vessels hanging off each one. I went back and forth on what to write, and finally settled on a simple "Eye hope you have a good Valentine's Day."

At the table, I sit next to Colin, instead of my usual spot between Paula and Liz. I'd definitely rather be next to him than between the two couples today. Brian and Paula act normal, talking about a new song they're working on. Paula has a rose sitting in front of her crumpled lunch bag, but I know she has Mr. Harvey for algebra, and he always brings a big bucket of roses to school on Valentine's Day. He gives them to all the girls, announcing, "Every woman should get a rose today." I had him freshman year. Liz and Joel, meanwhile, are sitting so close they might as well only have one chair. Gross.

Maisie comes over after we've all finished eating, drops two colored envelopes on the table, and spins away.

"Hey," I protest, "I thought you were supposed to deliver those in class!"

She calls over her shoulder, "And *I* thought it was Valentine's Day, not Halloween!"

"Then why are you wearing that butt-ugly mask?" Liz shouts after her. Our table erupts into laughter and Liz looks over at me, eyes round. "What was that even about? I was just going on pure instinct."

I laugh and reach out to pick up the envelopes, which are each labeled with Maisie's bubble handwriting. I pass them to Liz and Paula. They open them and both grin.

"This is awesome," Paula says, making devil horns with her pinkie and index finger and waving them around. She shows the card to Brian, who laughs.

The bell rings, and we all stand and gather our garbage. Liz steps around Joel and Colin to hug me.

"You know me so well!" She holds the eyeball picture out to show everyone.

After school, I see my card taped up inside our locker door, right next to one I haven't seen before. It's a store-bought card with a red guitar on the front. Joel didn't write anything inside, just scribbled his name. I make a face, then reposition the cards so mine is in front.

20

It's pouring rain by the time school gets out. I'm glad I brought my raincoat, even though it's ugly, and that I convinced Mom to get the nice fenders for my bike. Despite my rain gear, I'm still soaked by the time I get home. I leave my wet jeans and sweaty hoodie in a pile on the floor and flip through the clothes in my closet. I'm about to go with a fresh pair of jeans and hoodie for the Silver Wells party when I see the red dress in the back of the closet. I threw it in when I was packing to move to Gran's because it's my only dress that fits. I remember Gran telling me how nice I looked when I first tried it on, so I know she likes it. I slide the dress over my head, then wrestle my way into a pair of brown tights, and finish the outfit with the chunky Mary Janes that are the dressiest shoes I own.

When my mom gets home, I'm lying on the living room couch, flipping through one of Gran's catalogs. We haven't stopped any of the subscriptions. Mom doesn't see me, just sticks her head up the stairs and yells, "Hannah, are you ready?"

"Yeah," I call without lifting my head. I hear her give a squeak of surprise, then she comes into the living room.

"There you are!" she says like she looked all over. "Are you rea-"

She stops when I stand and she sees my outfit. Her hand goes to her mouth.

"Oh, you look so pretty," she says. I roll my eyes and her excitement evaporates. I feel a stab of guilt, but I just grab my raincoat and clomp over to the door.

Paper hearts and streamers are taped up all over the Silver Wells activity room. Gran is waiting for us, sitting at a table, talking to another lady. She seems animated and cheerful. I'm immediately glad I came, glad I dressed up.

"Mom!" Gran turns at this, and her eyes lock with Mom's. I see a moment of confusion before she smiles tentatively. I nod to encourage her. I hug her after Mom does, and her body feels so light. She always used to seem really solid to me, lifting me with no problem when I was little, hauling around bags of groceries, huge turkeys in roasting pans, both twins at once. I'm not sure when she got so frail.

"It's Hannah," I say awkwardly. I leave my arm loose around her shoulders.

Gran's companion has become engrossed in conversation with a man next to her wearing big white velcro shoes. Gran is wearing her Keds with a dark pink sweatsuit. The top has a white sewn-in collar peeking out. I wonder if someone picked it out for her, or if she did it herself. I always thought those fake collars were so silly and trying-to-be-fancy, but seeing hers today makes me glad that she can still have her fanciness even now that she can't wear her old clothes, with all their zippers and buttons.

Leticia is holding court in the kitchen area wearing an apron printed with cartoon hearts. She has a silver tray in front of her stacked with heart-shaped sugar cookies, and bowls of red, pink, and white frosting with plastic knives sticking out.

"Georgia!" she calls like my mom is her long-lost best friend. "And Hannah! So great to see you here today!" I smile tightly. So great.

The three of us move to sit near Leticia, across from a lady in a fluffy sweater and a man who I guess is her son. Mom reaches over for a paper plate and three cookies. She positions bowls of frosting so we can reach them, and hands a knife to Gran.

As we work, I notice Gran's nails, filed perfectly and painted a pearly shade of pink.

I clear my throat and say, "Your nails look nice, Gran."

She looks down at her hands, spreading white frosting on the cookie, and smiles.

"Thank you," she answers. "A nice lady came in and did them for me this morning."

I look at my mom, who smiles tightly and says, "I did them for you last night, Mom."

Gran looks dismayed to have gotten it wrong, and I feel a flash of anger toward Mom. Who cares whether it was this morning or last night? Gran did say she was nice.

"Well, they look great," I say, and smile at her. I stick a knife into the pink frosting and spread it on my cookie, looking for a way to change the subject. "We get to eat these, right?"

We only stay about a half an hour, frosting cookies and eating them while Mom recounts some story Uncle Richard told her about my cousin David's super-exciting job selling cars, which sounds like a total nightmare to me. All I can think about are sleazy used car salesmen on TV. After a while, Gran seems to have a harder time following the conversation, and Mom says, "Are you getting tired? Want us to walk you to your room?" She talks to her like she's a little kid, but I caught myself doing the same thing earlier.

Gran nods, and Mom helps her to her feet while I crumple our paper plates and napkins and drop them in the garbage can. I follow Mom and Gran out the door of the activity room, then we each walk on either side of Gran, holding one of her hands. In her room, I kneel and untie Gran's Keds while Mom folds back the blankets on her bed. We settle her in for a nap, and Gran sighs contentedly, reaches out and pats us each on one hand.

"You're such sweet girls," she says, her eyes already closed. Mom leans over and kisses her head, where I can see her scalp through her thinning white curls. She seems so delicate. I wish I could keep her safe, and keep her with us.

"I can't believe how much worse she's gotten since she moved,"

Mom says as she pulls the car into the street.

"She doesn't seem that bad," I say. "So she doesn't remember exactly everything right. She's still nice. This was fun."

I see Mom's arms stiffen as she grips the steering wheel. "If it was so fun, why is this the first time you've been for a real visit?"

"I went!" I protest. "Right after she moved in."

"That was weeks ago! It's a lot, Hannah, going there every night to see my mom when she doesn't have any idea who I am." Her voice sort of breaks in the middle, and I cross my arms in front of me, the risk of her starting to cry getting way too close for comfort.

"Well you don't have to make her feel bad when she forgets things," I say, and she sighs.

We're quiet for a few minutes, then Mom says, "You're right. I shouldn't. And I'm glad you came. Marion still hasn't been to visit once. And Richard's been telling me to move Mom somewhere since Christmas, and he hardly even asks how she is. I'm sorry to take it out on you."

I sigh too. "I'm sorry too. I'll try to visit more. I've just been really busy lately. Did I tell you that Mr. Keller asked if I want to take math at the community college next year?"

Sometimes I wonder if my mom and I would even have anything to talk about if it weren't for school.

21

I decide to go to the youth group the next day after school. Liz hardly ever has time to hang out these days, between Joel and track practice and the band, and Mom is pretty focused on the new person she's training at work, so I don't even have to make up any stories to tell anyone. After the last bell, I wait with the mob of kids who take the city bus that goes downtown. I have to take the second bus that comes, since there's only room for two bikes on the front of each one. I planned my outfit out the night before -- a yellow t-shirt with blue sleeves and collar, jeans, and my green zip-up hoodie. I recently sewed a Huckle Cat patch onto the front of the hoodie, which Brian described as looking "very punk rock." Translation: not the neatest sewing job, but I think it passes.

The bus lets me off a few blocks from the church, and I unload my bike and ride slowly to the parking lot. I'm glad that the meeting isn't close to school. Most of the people who got on the bus at school got off much earlier than me. Although I've read the flyer so many times that I've basically memorized it, I pull it out of my pocket and double-check the address, time, and date. Yes, I am in the right place at the right time. I climb the steps and enter the church. The lobby is dark, but I hear voices coming from downstairs, and I can tell that the lights are on down there. I take the stairs down and follow the sound.

I go through the open door, and see a pool table, one of those TVs that's strapped to a rolling cart, a little kitchen area, and a few people sitting in a circle of battered couches and armchairs. Really, I only see one of the people, a face I recognize from every advanced class I've ever taken. Philip Lawson. He's sitting in an armchair, laughing at something someone has said. I step back, my first thought that I need to get out of there as quickly as possible, but a blonde woman stands up and waves me in.

"Hi!" she says. Her voice is all cotton candy and cheer. "Welcome to Rainbow Youth! Please come in!"

Philip's eyes meet mine and widen, then quickly drop to his lap. He's wearing the same khakis and sweater vest he was wearing in school today, and he looks so small in his tall chair. I turn and focus on the blonde woman. Her hair is pulled into a high ponytail, and she's wearing a Willamette University Soccer sweatshirt and shorts, even though it's February. Two other boys sit cuddling on a loveseat to her left, and that's the whole group. There is a very real possibility that I'm the only teenage girl in Salem who is gay, lesbian, bisexual, transgender, or questioning.

"I'm Olivia," the blonde says. She reaches her hand toward me.

I smile involuntarily at the familiarity of the name, then shake her hand and say, "I'm Hannah. I have a cat named Olive."

One of the cuddling boys starts giggling, and I can feel my face heat up. Really? That's what comes out of my mouth when I'm meeting a group of actual gay people for the first time ever?

Olivia smiles warmly. "Aw, that's a sweet name for a cat!"

I smile, glad she doesn't already seem to think I'm an idiot, and sit on the couch where she gestures.

"I'm in the law school at Willamette," Olivia continues. "Usually I co-lead this group with one of our counselors, but she's at a conference this week, so you just get me for now." She gives a little self-deprecating smile, and I immediately like her.

"It's been a while since we've had a new member," she says, "so let me see if I remember what we do. How about we each introduce ourselves, and then we'll do our usual weekly check-in. Tell us anything you want about your week, what's been going on, any concerns, anything you want to talk about." She looks at me to make sure I understand. When I nod, she turns to her right.

"Would you like to start?"

All eyes turn to Philip, who squirms in his seat. "My name is

Philip," he says to the floor. "Nothing has been going on this week. Everything is normal."

"That's it?" Olivia sounds surprised. Philip nods resolutely, and I feel suddenly guilty, like I'm intruding into his private world. "Okaaaay," Olivia says, then turns to the boys on her left. "Spencer? Joey? How are you?"

The dark-haired boy, the preppier of the two, untangles himself and holds out a hand to me, knuckles up like I'm supposed to kiss it or something. I reach out and grasp his fingers briefly.

"I'm Spencer, and this week has been *out* of control."

"It has," Joey agrees. He is rail-thin, has curly blonde hair sticking up everywhere, and is wearing an Ani DiFranco t-shirt. Spencer and Joey launch into the story of their week. I gather that they go to South Salem High, and they're trying to set up a Gay-Straight Alliance.

"We've gotten eleven students signed up to join," Spencer says, and Joey interrupts, "All straight," with a roll of his eyes. Spencer pats him on the arm and says, "But that's *fine*," before continuing that their current struggle is getting approval from the principal to start the new group.

"Do you have a teacher advisor?" Olivia asks, and Joey nods proudly.

"Yes, Ms. Jamieson, the art teacher. She even said we could use her classroom. But Mr. Putnam is giving us all this crap about hanging up posters. He doesn't want us to be an official club."

"And we want to be official," Spencer says, "so more people can find us."

They nod in unison.

"I think it's great that straight people have expressed interest," Olivia says. "Allies never hurt, plus you never know who might not be out yet."

Joey nods. "I know," he says with a slight whine. "It would just be nice to know some other gay kids at South. As much as I *love* being the poster child for teenage homosexuality, it does get a little exhausting."

"Yeah, heavy hangs the head that wears the crown and all that," Spencer says, patting Joey's shoulder.

Olivia nods sympathetically. "Well, let me know if you need any help. I mentioned your group to one of my professors -- without specifics of course -- and they think you might have a discrimination case if the principal continues to try to block your efforts."

"Thanks," Spencer says.

"That reminds me," Olivia says, turning to me. "I'm sorry I didn't say this right away, Hannah, but everything said here is confidential. Nothing leaves this room without permission from the person who said it."

I nod and glance involuntarily at Philip, but he's not looking at me.

"How about you?" Olivia asks me. "Do you want to tell us a little about yourself?"

"Well, my name is Hannah, and I go to East." I'm not really sure what to say next.

"Oh, do you already know Philip?" Olivia says. We look over at him, and he nods at the floor.

"Yeah, Philip is like, the main reason I get as good of grades as I do," I say with a smirk. He keeps his eyes on the floor, but I think I see the edges of his mouth turn up, so I continue. "He's always right there, ready to do better than me on every test."

"You definitely don't make it easy," he says.

"What would be the fun in that? When it bothers you so much?" I hope he can tell that I'm joking.

"You *are* cute when you get angry," Joey says with a smile that could only be described as charming, and I watch Philip's cheeks flush a few shades darker.

"Well, welcome Hannah," Olivia says, jumping to Philip's

rescue. "We're very glad to have you."

She reaches down and pulls a couple of books out of the backpack that's sitting on the ground next to her. They have "Willamette University Library" stamped across the tops of the pages.

"These are the books I was telling you all about last week," she says. "This one is about the Stonewall riots, and this one is a biography of Billy Tipton."

I lean back into the couch and we all listen while Olivia talks. She passes the books around and I feel back on steady ground with facts and books. Talk of Stonewall turns to talk of Pride, and Spencer and Joey tell a long story about their disastrous road trip to Portland Pride last summer. Philip even laughs at one point. I'm glad I didn't run when I had the chance.

22

I wonder if Philip is going to act differently toward me the next day at school. Nothing happens in calc, which isn't a surprise since we sit far apart. At lunch, I glance over to his table, where he sits with a bunch of other nerds, mostly seniors. Do any of them know? Maybe one of them is his boyfriend. Even dorky old Philip is probably more experienced than me.

When I sit next to him in genetics, he doesn't even look up. His textbook is open in front of him, and he's staring at it intently.

"Hey," I say, but he still doesn't look at me. "So . . . have you gone to that group for a long time?"

He glances around to see if anyone is listening, then meets my gaze and hisses, "We are not talking about this."

I furrow my eyebrows and lean back in my chair, but I'm not ready to let it drop. I'm dying to know more. Mrs. Halliday comes in and starts writing on the chalkboard. I pull out my notebook and write, "Do more people usually come, or just the ones that were there yesterday?" I slide it over to his side of the table and he looks down at it, then picks up his pen and writes, "S&J always, sometimes others. A few from McNary." The high school across town.

"No one else from East?"

"No."

"Olivia seems nice. Is the other leader nice too?"

"She's fine."

I'm about to write another question when he pulls the notebook in front of him and scribbles something, then pushes it back to my side of the table.

"This doesn't make us friends, you know."

I stare at it for a second, his blue letters small and deliberate, then I sigh and nod. I turn my notebook to a new page and start taking notes. When I leave class, I can't remember a thing Mrs. Halliday said.

23

Corey and I start writing regularly, not even always waiting to get a reply before we send a new letter to the other. I order some other zines, too, and I write back to each of the authors after I finish reading, telling them what I liked about their zines. Most of them are written by teenage girls, mostly gay and feminist, like Corey said her recommendations would be. But they're still pretty different. Some of the zines are handwritten, some typed. One is written entirely with a typewriter that's missing the letter "e," with handwritten replacements scattered throughout. Some are personal, some are political, and some are a combination of both. Most arrive with little ads falling out like Corey's did. I order any that sound good to me, but Corey's is my favorite, and she's the only zine maker that I want to keep writing to. I feel different in the letters I write to her than I am with people in real life. I'm more clever, less neurotic. But I'm also more open, writing to her about my dad and about how scared I am to go see my grandma. She writes about her family too, and how her parents got together while her dad was still married to his ex-wife. She says that's why she tries to be as honest as she can, because her dad wasn't honest and now her brothers resent her and make snide comments about her mom under their breath.

When I open one of her letters, a wallet-size photo falls out along with the usual stickers and zine ads. It has the mottled blue background of a photo studio, and a teenage girl stares out at me defiantly. She has choppy dark brown hair, wire-frame glasses, and is almost smirking, her chin raised and eyes focused on the camera. She wears a short ball-chain necklace and plain black t-shirt. I turn it over, and she's written "Senior picture, 1996, huge disappointment." I look at the picture again. Her nose is kind of big, lips narrowed from being pressed together, but she doesn't look like she cares what I think. She looks smart and confident. And, if I'm being honest, she's kind of cute. I unfold the letter.

Hey Hannah,

We got my senior pictures back, and Mom and Dad are pissed! I didn't even want to get senior pictures. None of the assholes at my school need to remember what I look like. But my parents kept saying it's not for me, it's for them, and they were paying anyway. They made me go to this cheesy-ass photo studio, but they couldn't make me smile. And now we have a million copies of this stupid picture. So, here you go. Something to remember me by.

This girl in my math class brought her senior pictures in today to hand out, and she even wanted to trade with me. Senior year must really be getting to everyone if they're starting to think they might miss me, of all people. I've gone to school with most of them since we were little, but I doubt if half of them even know my last name. It's not like I try to be friends with them, though. Everything here just seems so fake. We're all playing this game and the prize is college. I wish colleges didn't care so much about grades and test scores, and more about interest in learning or capacity to think creatively or something. Of course, I'm a total hypocrite and my grades are okay and I'm applying to colleges like I'm supposed to. So far, I think my top choice is Reed, assuming I get in. Have you been to the campus? I visited last fall, and it seemed like a lot of the students were into brooding and complaining, like I would fit right in. For once in my life!

Remember when you wrote about creativity, and about wanting to reach in and smear your feelings across the page? I've been thinking about that a lot lately. I wish creativity were that easy! I like the image a lot, though. I've always liked cutting paper up, so I mostly make collages, but maybe I should try painting again. Or maybe you should, since you're the one wanting to spread your insides across some paper, you know? I don't think that art is some great achievement. I think it's necessary, but I don't think it's something that only certain people can do. Does that make sense? People act like only those precious few can make art, but I think anyone can. Just get some paint or some markers or crayons or whatever, and try it.

The other day at the restaurant, these assholes from the college were getting drunk and acting like they were so much better than us because we're "townies." If I ever act like that, you have my personal permission to slap me. It makes me so mad to serve jerks like that, because my parents work hard at the restaurant and my mom is a great cook. Case in point, as I write this, I'm eating my favorite garbanzo bean and parsley salad that she makes. It's from last night, and it's always better after it sits in the fridge for a day or so. Aw, shit, now I'm thinking about what a brat I was about the pictures. Should I have been nicer? I love my parents, but why can't they let me be myself?

I keep forgetting to ask, how's the rainbow group you started going to? Have you made any new gay friends?

Well, I guess that's all for now, so write back when you get a chance!

> Love,
>
> Corey

Dear Corey,

Wow, thank you for the senior picture! I'll cherish it always. I can't wait to get dragged to a cheesy photo studio next year to get my picture taken!

I don't have any school photos left, so I'll have to find a picture of me to send you sometime soon. And unfortunately, I'm a terrible person to ask if you were too bratty about your pictures. I say things all the time to my mom that I regret. I know she works really hard and is taking care of me and my grandma and kind of my aunt and her kids too, but it's like she knows exactly what to say to me to make me mad sometimes. And I also feel like you do, like why can't she see things more from my perspective? It's like she has this idea of how my life should be, but she never asked me what I want.

If you end up going to Reed, that would be so cool! I haven't been to the campus, but I know it's a really well-respected school. The salad that your mom made sounds really good. When I was little, I would come to my grandma's house every day after school, and she had this big garden in the backyard. It's mostly all dead now. But anyway, whenever I could, I would sneak out and sit in the garden and eat the parsley because I loved it so much. My grandma once said that if she couldn't find me, she always knew the first place to look was the garden. Now when I eat parsley, I always remember sneaking out and sitting in the dirt and sun.

I only went to the rainbow group once. I don't think I told you, but this guy from my school was there. We're not supposed to tell anyone about what happens in the meetings, so I'll call him P, even though it's not like you'll ever meet him. But he's my enemy. I know, it sounds stupid, it's not like we're nations at war or anything, but we're the top two in our class and we're always trying to knock each other out of first place. But then, seeing him there, it made me think maybe I've misjudged him this whole time. Maybe he's secretly cool? Not that being gay makes everyone automatically cool. But then I tried to talk to him about it at school the next day and he was a jerk and seemed mad and told me we're not friends. So I felt too nervous to go back. Maybe one day. There were a couple of other guys there who seemed nice, and the leader was nice too, so I should go back. I'll let you know how it goes.

Well, I'm almost to the bottom of the page, so I'll say goodbye now.

Talk to you soon!

Hannah

It's a complete lie that I'm out of school pictures. I actually know exactly where they are, in my mom's top desk drawer at our house. But I don't know if I'm ready to send one to Corey. She says that she doesn't care about regular beauty standards, but that doesn't mean she'll think I'm cute. And, I'm realizing, I really want her to. She's smart and interesting, and she acts like I am too. Will she still like me after she sees what I look like?

I fold the letter up, stick it in an envelope, and address it. I don't need to look at Corey's return address anymore; I've memorized it. I pick up her senior picture again, and can't help but smile. I like how insistent she is about being herself. I always feel weird, but I also feel like I try to hide it. I'm always trying to be normal, like everyone else. Kids used to make fun of my body when I was younger, and I can't handle it anymore. I just want to be nice and quiet and make it through the next year and a half and move far, far away from here. Or maybe I should apply to Reed. Maybe Portland would be far enough, especially if Corey was there. She's started signing her letters with "love," but I haven't. I'm sure it's just something she says. There's no way she could really care about me like that.

24

I tell Mom that I need new clothes and ride my bike to our house after school, partially to fulfill my promise of sending Corey a photo. We'd only lived in this house a few years when we moved in with Gran, so it never really felt like home, and certainly not as much as Gran's house does. We've come back a few times to get new clothes, and I know Mom has come back on her own more than she's come with me. I haven't been back alone. I'm almost expecting some Miss Havisham-style cobwebs, dead spiders in the corners, and mice scurrying around, but when I unlock the door and step inside, the house looks like I remember it. A little dusty, but we never exactly kept on top of the dusting. I use my finger to write my name in the dust on the TV in swirling cursive. I love how my name is a palindrome, each side a mirror image of the other, easy to break in half, into thirds. Neat and orderly.

Unlike my room, which I left a complete mess. I step out of my sneakers and prod at piles of laundry on the floor with my socks. There are the jeans I've been looking for, and my faded black Pearl Jam t-shirt. I gather the dirty clothes in my arm and carry them to the garage, dump them into the washing machine before I realize that this means I'm committing to at least an hour here, where the cable has been turned off and I don't have any of my favorite CDs. Good time to get started on some homework, I guess.

Back in my room, I open a desk drawer and dig through the yellow envelopes of photos. I always get doubles when I get pictures developed, so I can give copies to Liz or Paula, which also means that I end up with a ton of pictures of blurry backgrounds, people with their eyes closed, unflattering angles. Not that I have any flattering angles.

The top stack is from last summer, when we went swimming

at the river. Liz and Paula wore bikinis and I wore a one-piece with gym shorts. In one picture, Liz and I are looking at each other and laughing, our hair all messy from the wind and the water, our shoulders brown from the sun, and my nose spattered with freckles. It was a really fun trip. The five of us piled into the station wagon with air mattresses stacked in the back and a cooler full of sandwiches, pop, and beers that Colin's older brother bought for us. We swam and floated and stretched out on blankets on the rocks that lined the edge of the river. Paula knew a secret place that not too many other people used, so it wasn't too loud or splashy.

I take a couple of pictures to hang in our locker, ones where I'm smiling and don't have double chins or too much arm fat showing. At one point, Brian grabbed my camera and took a bunch of pictures when no one was ready. In one, I'm leaning back on my towel, my stomach all scrunched up and looking extra bulgy, and even worse, I'm clearly gazing at Liz, who's laughing with Colin and looking gorgeous as usual. I can't help but cringe, looking at the picture and seeing my body in comparison to theirs. I look so different. But I don't feel different when I'm with them, and they don't act like I am.

I put the river pictures back in their envelope and open the next one. This one has photos from school and some Susan B. practices, when I was taking pictures to put in the liner of their tape. In the end, they decided that Colin's line drawings copied better, but the pictures are cute. The band messing around in the empty bleachers in the football stadium, standing on different levels of the concrete steps, sticking their faces through the bars of the fences. There's a cute one of me and Liz, her arm thrown around my shoulders and our faces pressed together, smiling hugely. I set that aside, along with a couple of others that might be good to send to Corey. One my Grandma took of me on the couch in her house. It was a cold day and I was snuggled under a blanket, so my stomach is covered. After Gran took that picture, I snuck up and snapped one of her, stirring pots on the stove and smiling to herself. I set this one aside, touching her smile lightly, so I don't leave fingerprints.

Why do things have to change? I wish I could go back to when I was younger, when I went to Gran's house every day after elementary school, and spend more time with her. She was always offering to take me to the park, to the mall as I got older, but I wanted to be by myself. I've always felt out of place, even with Liz and Paula and this group that's supposed to be the outcasts. I'm too naive for them, but I'm too loud and messy for the brains and boring kids in the advanced classes with me. Gran never acted like I was weird, though. She seemed like she thought I was this sweet treasure that she was lucky to pick up from school and take care of. I wish I had spent more time with her, but I just wanted to read or watch TV. I wanted to check out, to take a break from struggling through the world.

I can't hear the washing machine anymore, so I quickly sort the pictures into two piles, combining the ones I don't want into one envelope, and the smaller pile of good ones into another. I go to the garage and stuff my clothes into the dryer, then settle at the kitchen table and solve math problems until I hear the dryer buzz.

25

The ride back to Gran's house is harder than the ride from school, mostly because I've stuffed my backpack full of clothes and have a full tote bag hanging from one handlebar. I keep hitting it with my knee, but it's the only way I can figure out to get everything back. I should have called my mom and asked her to pick me up on her way home, but by now she's already visiting Gran at Silver Wells, and I don't know the phone number.

I'm slowing to keep from hitting a lady with a stroller when I hear a yell from a passing car.

"Lose some weight, fatass!"

The car zooms off, laughter trailing back like exhaust. I brake and let one foot hit the ground, my face burning.

"People are so rude," the lady says. She has an apologetic look on her face. I shrug. She's small and thin, probably has never been called fat in her life. What does she know about rude?

"You're obviously working on your problem," she continues. "Good for you, getting out there and getting some exercise."

Her words are like another punch to my gut. She looks at my body and sees a problem. I know I should smile at her, thank her for congratulating me or whatever, but when I open my mouth, what comes out is, "Fuck off, lady."

Her face closes up immediately. She glances down at her baby, who's way too young to have registered what I said, then walks off with a huff. I sigh, readjust my bags, kick off from the ground and continue riding. When my tears come, the wind chills them into icy tracks across my cheeks.

When I get to Gran's house, I'm sweaty and out of breath, and the first thing I do when I get to my room is pull a fresh tank top and gym shorts from my backpack and change out of my damp school clothes. Then I sit at the desk and start the letter that I'll send to Corey with the picture. I don't intend to tell her about my ride home, but it's all that's there when I start writing.

Hey Corey,

Here's a picture of me and my friend Liz at the river last summer. I'm the one on the right. The fat one. Which people all over town are all too eager to keep reminding me. I was just riding my bike home, and first a car drove by and these assholes yelled at me to lose some weight, as if I were not in the process of riding a fucking bike at that exact moment. And the thing that pisses me off is that I'm not even riding to lose weight or get exercise, I just don't have a driver's license. My mom has made it clear that we can't afford a second car, plus driving seems like way too much responsibility to me. I don't feel ready to operate this giant machine that could kill people at any moment. But people see me, a fat girl huffing along on a bike, and of course they think, "Good for her, she's trying to lose weight." That's basically what this lady who heard the assholes said. I guess she was trying to be helpful or encouraging or whatever, but all I heard was that my body is wrong. Do they think I haven't considered that? Do people really think that I've been able to live sixteen years on this fucking planet without realizing that my body is not how it's supposed to be? Every magazine and TV show and movie and every person I meet is already sending me that message loud and clear. And the thing is, I don't even understand how people are thin. I've never been thin. I remember people saying it was baby fat and I would grow out of it, but I never did. I got taller, but I got fatter. I see thin people and I don't know what's different about them and me. I know I don't exercise much, and I hate gym class, but I bike and I don't think I eat that differently than my mom or Liz or other people. And so fucking what? What does it matter to anyone? What if I didn't exercise or ate Cheetos all day? Why is it anybody's business but mine? I know people are nosy and always want to tell each other what to do, I'm just sick of it.

Ugh, this letter is turning into a total downer, I'm sorry. Things are actually not so bad really. One or a couple of people can so easily wreck my day. I wish I was tough, but everything gets to me.

Thanks for listening,

Hannah

26

Hannah,

I'm so sorry that people are giving you shit about your body. You're right - it's completely no one's business but your own. Your body = your business, all the way. And I definitely understand being told that you're not right or your body isn't right. My parents are always ragging on me for not being a girl the way they think I should. The doctors told them I was a girl, and their heads immediately filled with all this bullshit about pink and princesses and long hair and dresses. I don't want any of it. I've never been a girl the way they want me to. It's not that I feel more like a boy than a girl, it's more that I feel fine with my body and my gender, but no one else does! Why does being female have to equal all these things? Who says????

This stuff is really surging over here right now, actually. One of my brothers asked his girlfriend to marry him last weekend, which means we have a wedding to plan. My mom isn't really involved in the planning, since my brothers view her as a bit of an Evil Stepmother, despite the fact that she's been married to my dad for almost twenty years. But the girlfriend asked if I would be a bridesmaid, and it's very important to my mom. I was really hoping I would be able to escape this whole thing without the dress argument, but it doesn't seem like it's going to happen. My mom hasn't started really pushing it yet, but I know it's going to get worse. It's sad to see how much she wants them to like her, and they refuse. It's like she thinks that me being a pretty little bridesmaid will show them that she raised such a sweet young lady. As if they'll care! There's no way I'm wearing a dress to this wedding.

You should give me a call sometime, especially if this shit

comes up again. I like letters a lot, but calls can be better in terms of actual communication, you know? My number is (707) 442-2811, and I'm pretty much never busy if I'm not at school or working at the restaurant.

Stay strong,

Corey

27

Sunday is Aunt Marion's birthday, so Mom orders her favorite, Chinese food from Kwan's. When she tells the boys where she's going, they get excited because they love the giant wooden Buddha in the Kwan's lobby. Everyone but me ends up piling into the car to get the food, so I offer to unload the dishwasher. I'm about to start setting the table when the phone rings.

"Hello?"

"Is Marion there?" It's Uncle Richard.

"No, she went to pick up dinner."

"Well, I called to tell her happy birthday, so can you tell her when she gets there?"

"Sure," I say. "Do you want her to call you?"

"No need. Just tell her when she gets there."

"Yeah, sure."

He's quiet for a second, then says, "Has she gone to see Mom yet?"

"I don't think so."

He sighs. "It's been what, a month?"

"About a month."

"I don't know why you let her get away with this, Georgia. It's her *mother*. Marion needs to visit her. Quit babying her. You can't protect her from everything her whole life."

"Um, this is Hannah."

What follows is the definition of the phrase "awkward pause."

"Wow, you sound just like your mom!" He switches to the fake jovial voice he reserves for me and the twins.

"Yeah, we get that a lot."

"Well . . . tell Marion I called to say happy birthday, okay hon?"

"Sure." Then before I can lose my nerve, I say, "And Uncle

Richard?"

"Hmmm?" He sounds distracted.

"She's your mother too."

I hang up the phone before he can reply.

I wait a second to see if the phone rings again, but luckily, it doesn't.

The last time I saw Uncle Richard was last Christmas, and he had plenty to say about me then. Mom and I had just moved here, and I stayed by Gran's side most of the day, reminding her of names and running interference when Uncle Richard tossed out questions she had no idea how to answer. As the afternoon wound down, I went into the kitchen to grab a garbage bag to gather up the wrapping paper and ribbons. I could hear Uncle Richard talking to Mom in the dining room.

"So, you let her eat whatever she wants?" he said. They were in the corner of the room, where hidden wall panels slide back to reveal a full bar with glass shelves and a tiny sink. It was Grandpa's bar, and Gran had kept it stocked out of habit, even though it only saw any serious action on holidays.

"Hannah's diet is none of your concern," Mom whispered back. I flattened myself against the kitchen wall, right outside the doorway to the dining room.

"And you let her dress like that? She looks practically homeless."

"That's what kids are doing now. Her friends all dress like that."

"You don't see *my* kids looking like that." None of his kids were even there. The older two went home with their spouses for Christmas, and the younger one was studying abroad in Spain and having too much fun to come home. And, Uncle Richard had been sure to point out, they could afford it.

"Richard, we have different parenting styles. I thought we were over this."

They fought about it before? About me?

I heard ice clink as someone sloshed liquor into a glass. "She should play sports. Does she get *any* exercise? Don't kids at school make fun of her? I worry about her."

"You don't need to worry. Hannah is doing great in school, she has friends, she's happy. And she's been a huge help with Mom."

I immediately vowed to do more to help.

"And speaking of Mom," Uncle Richard began, and I heard Mom groan. Plates clinked as someone started stacking the dinner dishes. I slid farther away from the doorway so they wouldn't see me. "It's not safe for her to be alone here all day."

"She's been okay so far," Mom snapped, and I could almost hear Uncle Richard rolling his eyes.

"Well if it's worked *so far*," he mocked. "I know you love playing the martyr, taking care of her like you took care of Dad, but she needs professional care. I had no idea she'd gotten so bad." I knew that my mom understood what he meant, like I did -- he meant that she'd *let* Gran get so bad.

Then there was only the sound of the dishes, and I exhaled and pushed myself away from the wall. It would be reasonable that I just happened to walk in now, right? I couldn't even remember why I'd come into the room in the first place.

Luckily, Taylor saved me, crashing in from the living room with a gray plastic shield strapped to his chest. He held a battery-operated gun, which he fired over his shoulder at Jeremy, who trailed a moment behind.

Aunt Marion's birthday dinner is uneventful, the takeout delicious as always. I tell her that Uncle Richard called to say happy birthday, but nothing else about the conversation. She and Mom shake their heads at each other and go on about how it's so like Richard to call before dinner even starts. On my other side, Jeremy and Taylor are engrossed in a conversation about something from TV, and I notice, not for the first time, how alone I am between the two pairs. I cut off a chunk of egg foo young and chew it slowly.

Liz is always going to abandon me for a guy. And Paula is cool and way nicer than I thought, but she has Brian. Am I always going to be the one left by myself?

28

Liz surprises me on Monday by asking if I want to hang out after school. I know I should say yes, but I don't feel like being available whenever she makes time for me. I tell her I'm planning on visiting Gran, which is a partial truth. Since Uncle Richard's call, I have been thinking I should go visit more.

"I've actually been wanting to come with you sometime," she says. "Maybe we could go together?"

We're at our locker at the end of the day, and she's waiting while I stuff books into my backpack. I turn to look at her. She looks hesitant, like she doesn't know how I'll react.

"You want to go to Silver Wells?"

"Yeah," she says. "I love Gran, and I haven't seen her in forever."

"Sure, of course you can come with me."

She rewards me with one of her gorgeous grins.

I call Mom from the pay phone in the Commons and tell her that Liz and I are going to visit Gran, so she can take the night off. She sounds surprised and relieved, and I feel like a hero.

I give Liz directions and tell her about the door code while she drives. Someone, probably Leticia, has made a collage of photos of residents on a piece of bright pink poster board in the lobby. We stop to look for Gran in the photos, and I only find her in one. She's sitting at a table, watching the person across from her work on a puzzle. When I point the photo out, it takes Liz a moment to recognize her.

Once we're past the lobby, I watch Liz look around, taking in the linoleum and whiteness. I reach out and link my arm through hers, and she pulls me close. I feel bad for her, seeing this for the first time.

Gran is in the activity room, sitting at a table with one of the other women I've seen her talking to before. She's smiling, although her smile seems a little bit nervous.

"Hey Gran." I sit next to her. Liz sits across the table from us. I look for recognition in Gran's eyes like I always do, but I can't find it.

"It's Hannah," I say, and point to Liz. "And you remember my friend Liz?"

Gran nods. "It's good to see you." She smiles warmly at Liz, and I take one of Gran's hands. Liz isn't looking at us. She's staring at her hands and picking at her cuticles.

"How are you doing?" I ask Gran, since it seems like Liz isn't going to say anything.

"I'm fine," she answers politely. "How are you girls?"

I tell her about school, about Liz's band and the Huckle Cat show. I don't get why Liz doesn't say much, especially after it was her idea to come. After we've been there fifteen, maybe twenty minutes, I say, "Well, I guess we should be going. . ."

Liz jumps to her feet and zips up her hoodie, ready to leave. I feel a flash of annoyance at her.

"Okay," Gran says, looking around. "Just let me find my purse."

"Oh, no," I say. "I'm sorry. Liz and I are going. You have to stay here."

Her brows furrow. "Here?" She glances around the room, confused.

"Yeah." I nod, biting my lips together to keep from crying all over the place. How can anyone deal with this? "You live here now."

"Oh." The resignation in her voice is too much.

"But I'll come visit again soon," I say in a rush. "And Mom will be here tomorrow. And your friends are here. . ." I gesture to the old people sitting around the room. Gran nods. I lean over and hug her gently. She returns the hug, and I meet Liz at the doorway, where she's waiting, jangling her keys.

"That was pretty fucking awful." Liz doesn't look at me as she starts the car.

"Yeah," I murmur.

"It's like she's already totally gone. Like none of the old Gran is in there."

I look out the window and nod even though she probably can't see.

"How can you stand it?" she asks.

"What else are we supposed to do?" I'm suddenly angry. She wanted to come, and now she's acting like it was the world's biggest pain. "Just leave her alone in there?"

"Well, maybe that would be better. It seems like going there confuses her."

"She has good days. I don't want her to think we all forgot about her."

Liz shakes her head. "How is that so bad? She's obviously forgotten about you."

"Don't say that," I snap. "You don't know. Since when are you an Alzheimer's expert?"

She's quiet for a moment, then says, "I'm sorry, Han. I know it must be way worse for you. I just wasn't really expecting her to be so far gone."

"I told you she doesn't remember me. How else could I have warned you?"

"I don't know. I guess I thought you were exaggerating."

I shrug. "It was your idea to go. Now you know how she is."

"Yeah."

We drive in silence for a few minutes, then Liz reaches over and turns on the stereo. The car fills with guitar and a man's voice. His voice is twangy, the song long and wandery. It's nothing like the fast rock songs Liz usually likes.

"What are we listening to?" I say when I notice her lips moving along with the words.

"It's Joel. Isn't he good?"

I wrinkle up my nose. Maybe it's objectively good guitar playing or singing, but it's definitely not my style.

"I guess," I say finally. "Are you into this?"

"Well, yeah. He's really talented."

"It kind of reminds me of Dave Matthews." One thing Liz and I have always agreed on is hating Dave Matthews. He's way too close to all those jam bands with their boring, never-ending songs and fans who haven't heard of deodorant. This is something we've talked about on multiple occasions, but apparently Liz has forgotten.

"Kind of," she says. "He'd love to hear that."

I smirk at my reflection in the window.

"So, what, you're into this kind of stuff now?" I can feel the edge in my voice.

"It doesn't make sense to only listen to one type of music." I can see her knuckles turning white as she grips the steering wheel harder. "If I want to get better at guitar, I have to expand my listening repertoire."

"Oh, what is that, a quote from the Book of Joel?"

She narrows her eyes. "God, Hannah, why do you have to turn into such a royal bitch anytime I get a boyfriend?"

I recoil like I've been slapped, but manage to come back with, "I just hate it when girls change for a guy. I *thought* we were on the same page about that."

"There's nothing wrong with trying new things. It's not like I'm the only one changing, he's interested in what I like too."

We sit in silence as one song ends and another begins.

I'm about to apologize when she says, "Maybe if you'd ever been in a relationship, you would understand."

29

After Liz drops me off, I run upstairs and take a shower. I want to wash the whole afternoon off. Marion and the boys are out, so I have the upstairs to myself and don't have to rush back to my room from the bathroom, wrapped in a towel that doesn't quite reach to cover everything. I dry off and flop back on the bed, still feeling crappy. I know I was awful to Liz. I should be more compassionate if she's my best friend. Is she really my best friend, though, if I'm always in second place to her boyfriends? I want to feel like I'm someone's first choice. I've never felt like I was.

I roll onto my side and wipe tears away with my damp towel. I should be tougher. I shouldn't let things get to me like this. I just want someone to care enough to see the tenderness that's inside of me, hidden under all the sarcasm and jokes. I don't want to feel like a disappointment like I sometimes do with Mom, or like I'm a backup like I do lately with Liz.

I push myself off the bed and pull on pajama pants and my balloon hoodie. The first thing I see when I shove my head through the neck hole is the photo of Corey. I tacked it to the bulletin board above my desk. She said to call her anytime, especially if I was upset. Maybe she only meant upset about body stuff, but it might help to talk. Before I can convince myself not to, I go into Aunt Marion's room and grab the cordless phone off her nightstand. I dial the number that I've memorized from reading Corey's last letter over and over.

"Hello?" a husky voice answers. I realize with a panic that I should have planned what I would say.

"Hi, um, is Corey there?"

"This is."

"Hey. This is Hannah. From the mail? From Oregon."

The voice changes from hesitant to happy.

"Hey, Hannah! I was wondering if you'd call."

"I wasn't sure if you wanted me to wait until I was in a crisis," I say, and immediately start blushing. I'm glad she can't see me. But she chuckles gently.

"No, anytime is great. But are you in a crisis?"

"No!" I say without thinking, then I remember why I called. "Well, maybe."

"Shit, what's going on?"

I tell her about my argument with Liz, leaving off her comment about how I've never been in a relationship. No need to reveal everything right now.

"She always does this," I finish. "Forgets about her friends when she gets a boyfriend. I should be used to it."

"Or you should get better friends," Corey replies, and I'm quiet for a second. "I'm sorry," she says. "Was that too mean?"

"No, it's okay," I say. "It's actually kind of nice for someone to stick up for me."

"Well, it's a lot easier to do from the outside. You two have been friends forever, right?"

"Yeah. Since elementary school."

"So if she's always done it, do you think she might always do it? Put her boyfriends before her other friends?"

I hadn't thought about it that way. In my fantasies about going away to college with Liz, it was always just the two of us. But what if I end up spending every night staring at an empty bed across the dorm room, wondering if she's going to come home? God, I'm pathetic.

"I guess so," I say.

"My therapist is always saying that you can't change anyone else's behavior, you can only change how you react to it. Or if it's someone you don't have to be around, you can leave."

I'm surprised that she mentions having a therapist so casually. My mom wanted me to go to counseling when I was younger, around the time I started my period. Sometimes I would get really sad for no reason, and cry and cry. I never went, though. I was so afraid that someone would find out where I was going and tell everyone. I was sure I'd be labeled crazy.

"I just don't get what she sees in this guy," I say, sidestepping the therapist thing. "He seems like such a tool."

"I'm sure you're right."

I smile. "Thank you."

"But even if you don't get what she sees in him, is that okay?"

"What do you mean?"

"Well, you don't really have to like him, right? As long as he treats her well, she could like him and you could be supportive because you want her to be happy."

I have honestly never thought about it that way. Do I want Liz to be happy, even if that means she ends up with some dipshit guy? Even if it means she doesn't end up with me?

I'm quiet for a moment, then finally say, "Why do you have to be so *rational* about it?"

I think I can hear her smiling when she answers. "I'm sorry, would you prefer I just agree?"

"Obviously."

"Yeah, he sucks," she says. "And she sucks for liking him."

"Hey!" I laugh. "That's my best friend you're talking about."

I feel a lot better when we hang up, and decide to go down and see if there's any Chinese food left. I scoop leftover chow mein and fried rice onto a plate and put it in the microwave. While it's heating up, a movement out the back window catches my eye. I duck behind the curtain, then peek out. I see the glowing end of a cigarette, and surprisingly enough, my mom. She's staring into space and smoking. She told me once that quitting smoking, which she did after my grandfather was diagnosed with lung cancer, was the hardest thing she'd ever done.

The microwave beeps, and I pull the plate out, stirring it all together the way I like it. I hesitate a second, then slide my feet into my untied sneakers and open the back door slowly. Mom sits in a folding chair by the giant rhododendron that rules the corner of the yard. It will burst with big pink flowers soon, but for now it's just a huge green bush.

"Hey," I say. She jumps and looks up at me with the distinct look of someone who's been caught doing something they're not supposed to. Another folding chair lays on its side near the house, and I drag it over to her. We haven't done a great job of maintaining the yard since we moved in. Gran's garden is a disaster, full of overgrown plants turned brown and mushy from the rainy winter.

"Are you okay?" I ask. The grass is also overgrown and soaks the cuffs of my pajama pants, making them cling to my ankles.

She lifts her cigarette and stares at the glowing tip, then shifts her gaze to me.

"These things are horrible for you," she says.

"I know."

"I smoked every day until your grandfather was diagnosed with lung cancer."

"Quitting was the hardest thing you ever did," I finish for her. "You told me."

She sighs, inhales off the cigarette, and blows the smoke away from me.

"You say you know, but I can smell smoke on your clothes after you go out with your friends." She waves her cigarette at me to make a point.

I feel my face go warm. It's not like I've never smoked a cigarette, but it me feel dizzy and sort of nauseous. I don't get the appeal. But everyone smokes when we go to shows. It's not my fault they let people smoke inside.

"I don't smoke."

"I know you're smart," she says. "I just don't want you to get swept up and start thinking it's cool."

I roll my eyes. "If it's so uncool, why are you doing it now?"

"Because I got two calls this afternoon at work. The first was Marion, in a panic because the boys need new baseball uniforms and cleats. She expects me to buy them!"

"Gran took them shopping a lot." I almost whisper it. I don't want her to get mad at Gran. Aunt Marion works as a waitress, but she always seems to be short on money.

"I know." She does? "But I'm not her. I can't start supporting Marion's family too. On top of being the person that Silver Wells calls whenever there's a problem. And working all day and spending every evening visiting my mother and wondering if she'll recognize me." Her voice breaks a little at the end. She sucks on her cigarette like it will keep her from crying.

"What was the other call?" I'm not sure if I want to know.

"The other one was your Uncle Richard."

I groan and she nods. "He called to tell me that my daughter was 'extremely disrespectful' on the phone last night, and I should know that, when you speak to people like that, it shows that I didn't raise you very well."

I exhale sharply. "*Asshole.*"

She doesn't even reprimand me. "He has always enjoyed cramming as many insults as possible into one sentence."

I take a bite of my leftovers. They're already cold.

"I'm sorry I was rude to him," I say through a mouthful of bean sprouts. I chew and swallow. "But he was being such a jerk, talking all this crap about Aunt Marion for not visiting Gran, when it's not like he's helping at all."

"He's paying for Silver Wells."

"He is?" I didn't know that. I assumed there was money somewhere. Grandpa was a successful dentist, and left enough money for Gran to keep living in the house without working after he died. And Gran never seemed short on money. She never bought generic groceries like we always do, had never hesitated to buy me anything I asked for.

Mom nods. "It's not cheap to have her there with around-the-clock nurses, meals, everything."

She looks smaller than I've seen her look before. She drops the end of her cigarette into the grass and steps on it.

"Let's go in." She reaches out and touches my head. "You shouldn't be out here with wet hair. You'll catch your death."

I nod and follow her inside.

30

I decide to go back to Rainbow Youth that Thursday. Philip and I have hardly spoken since he told me that we aren't friends, aside from the occasional "thank you" or "excuse me." Luckily, we haven't had any partner projects in genetics.

When I enter the church basement on Thursday afternoon, I'm surprised to see that Philip isn't there. A lady with short black hair shot through with gray, probably a little older than my mom, sits next to Olivia. She's deep in conversation with Spencer and Joey, who are curled up together on the loveseat again.

"Hannah!" Olivia says with a huge grin as I walk in. She stands and gestures for me to come in and sit. "I was hoping we would see you again! How are you?"

"Fine," I murmur, sitting in the same spot as last time.

"We've been a pretty small group for the last few weeks," Olivia continues. "Have you seen Philip at school? I've been worried about him."

"He hasn't come?" I ask. She shakes her head and I feel a stab of guilt. Probably because of me. "Well," I begin, "school has been crazy lately and midterms are coming up, so he's probably busy."

Olivia nods thoughtfully. "Well, if you see him, tell him we're thinking about him."

I tell her that I will. The other lady comes to a break in her conversation and turns to me.

"I'm Joanne Zeiner," she says, offering her hand. I wipe my sweaty palm on my jeans before I shake. "I'm a counselor at Willamette, and Olivia and I lead this group together."

"Hannah."

Olivia beams at both of us, so happy that we've finally met.

Joanne asks Spencer and Joey to give me and Olivia an update on the GSA they're trying to start. The two boys glance at each other, and seem to decide that Spencer will be the one to explain.

"So, remind me what was happening when you were here last?"

"You had people who wanted to join but the principal said you couldn't be an official club," I say.

He nods and purses his lips.

"Okay. It's gotten a little more . . . *contentious* since then. Olivia told us about the Equal Access Act, which is a law that says if a school has one club, it has to allow every club."

"Non-curriculum clubs," Joey interjects, and Spencer nods.

"Right. Spanish club and stuff are fine. But South has a Christian club, an Anime club, and all these other clubs, so legally, they *have* to let us have a GSA."

"Which we told Mr. Putnam, the principal," Joey adds.

"And now he's threatening to cancel all clubs," Spencer finishes.

My eyebrows shoot up. "Whoa."

The boys nod in unison. I glance over to Olivia, expecting her to look defeated, but she's fired up.

"This is exactly why I'm studying law," she says. "To fight this kind of oppression."

"But is not letting you have a club really oppression?" I ask. The boys and Olivia look at me like I'm crazy, and I feel my face heat up.

"They're treating us like second-class citizens!" Joey insists.

"Right," Spencer chimes in. "It's okay for Young Republicans to meet, when their agenda is explicitly anti-gay, but we can't meet to support each other?"

"GLBT teens have higher rates of suicide, smoking, running away from home," Olivia lists. "I would argue that a GSA is the most important club on campus."

"Okay," I say, raising my hands in surrender. Joanne winks at me.

"Aren't we lucky, Hannah, to see such passion in action?" She turns to the boys. "So the question is: what, if anything, is your next step?"

"If anything?" Olivia echoes in disbelief, but Joanne silences her with a touch on the knee. Olivia sighs and leans back in her chair, arms crossed.

Joey and Spencer glance at each other.

"I was thinking," Joey says, and Spencer looks at him encouragingly. "What if we do a walkout?"

Olivia nods enthusiastically.

"How many people would walk out?" Joanne asks. The boys don't look sure.

"Our club roster is at twenty," Spencer says like he doesn't think it's enough.

"Other clubs would probably join in," I suggest. "I mean, they're getting shut down too. So maybe talk to the other presidents or something and see if they support a GSA?"

"Great idea," Olivia says, and I can't help feeling proud. I wonder if anyone has ever tried to start a GSA at East. Definitely no one I've heard about, and I feel like I would have heard. For a second, I imagine trying to start a GSA with Philip, but I just shake my head and hope no one notices my little smile.

We continue discussing the walkout, and Spencer and Joey agree to approach all the club leaders they know and see if they would also participate.

"There is one thing to consider," Joanne says after the decision has been made. We all turn to her. She looks at Spencer, then Joey. "Is this something you're able to invest yourselves in?"

They both nod and look confused.

"I mean," she continues, "a walkout is a big deal. It might even get media attention. How would you feel being the face of this movement?"

Joey scoffs. "No problem. Story of my life already!"

But I'm surprised to see that Spencer stays quiet. I thought they were both out and proud.

"Spencer?" Joanne says gently. He inhales deeply, then speaks.

"My mom knows. And everyone at school knows, duh. But I haven't told my dad. I know, it's like how could he *not* know?" He pauses, and we give him the chuckles and smiles he's looking for. "It's just . . . I haven't *told* him. It's different in Mexican families. He's Catholic and thinks being gay is a sin. And he and my mom don't talk since she married my stepdad, so I know she hasn't told him for me." He shakes his head, looking less than totally confident for the first time.

"It's so stupid," I say. "I mean, straight people don't have to tell their parents about their sex lives or like, their *desires* or whatever."

Joanne nods. "It's certainly not fair. Is it a conversation you've had with your parents, Hannah?"

I shake my head and roll my eyes.

"My mom doesn't really like to talk about things. Like, we talk about school and grades, but we don't talk about feelings. I guess I figured I would tell her if it comes up, like if I ever get a girlfriend. And I don't talk to my dad."

I wait for the usual questions -- What happened? Why not? But the group sits quietly for a moment, then Joanne turns back to Spencer.

"So, there's a lot to think about."

He nods, and Joey reaches an arm around his shoulder and squeezes him close. Spencer's frown dissolves into a smile, and I look away so they can have their moment to themselves.

31

I get to school early the next morning and find Philip in his front-row seat in calc.

"Can I talk to you?" I ask, sliding into the empty chair next to him. He glances around nervously, eyes lingering on Katie Tran, the only other person already in the room.

"At lunch," he answers. I sigh.

"Okay, where can I meet you?"

"I'll meet you in the language hall. You have Spanish before lunch, right?"

I nod, surprised that he knows that. I have no idea what language he's taking. Maybe Russian or German. Brainy boys love those harsh consonants for some reason.

I only have to wait a second outside the Spanish classroom before Philip appears at the end of the hallway. He gestures with his head for me to follow him, and leads me to a dead-end hallway that's empty aside from lockers and one of those hoses with the glass to break in case of fire. I feel like a secret agent. When I catch up with him, he's all business.

"What's up?" He's speaking quietly, even though we're alone.

"You don't have to stop going to Rainbow Youth."

"I haven't."

"I went yesterday and Olivia said you haven't been there since I went, and she's worried about you."

He smiles a little. "Olivia worries too much."

"Well, okay, but still, you don't have to stop going."

"I told you that I haven't. I've just been . . . busy."

I roll my eyes. "Oh yeah, I definitely believe that."

"Well, can you blame me for not wanting to spend more time with someone who obviously hates me?"

"I don't hate you." Yeah, he drives me nuts, but I wouldn't say that I hate him. And what I said at the last meeting was true -- if he wasn't around, I probably wouldn't work nearly as hard at school.

He stands and stares at me, arms crossed.

"Do you think I can't hear you groaning when I talk, or see you rolling your eyes and giggling with your friends?"

"I don't -" I start to say, but he gives me a look that shuts me up. "It's not like you've ever tried to be friends," I say finally.

"Remember the regional math tournament in sixth grade? Neither of us knew anyone, and I tried to talk to you between sessions, but you said you'd rather be alone."

I remember the tournament, but have no memory of that conversation. I had just started crushing really hard on Liz, and it felt heavy in my stomach all the time. I remember thinking that everyone could tell how different I was from them, how alone and confused. I'm sure I didn't want to hang out with Philip, but maybe he would have understood.

"I'm sorry."

He raises one shoulder in a shrug.

"Well you can have it," I tell him. "If you don't want to hang out with me at Rainbow Youth, I'll stop going. Or we can switch weeks or something. Joint custody."

He shakes his head. "No, you should keep going. You seem like you need it more."

"God, Philip, you wonder why people roll their eyes at you! What's *that* supposed to mean?"

"I didn't say that *people* roll their eyes at me, I said that you do."

It takes every ounce of self-control that I have to keep my eyes on his. He can tell, and his eyes crinkle as he smirks. I can't help smiling too, and we both start to laugh.

"No, I mean it," he says. "It's a good group. Keep going if you want to." We're both quiet for a moment, then he says, "Was that it? Just that Olivia misses me?"

"Well, I'm sure they all miss you."

"I'm sure. I bet Spencer misses me most of all."

"Spencer? Why him?"

He shrugs.

Wait a second. "Did you guys go out or something?"

He shakes his head, and I feel a second of relief. I'm not the least experienced person in the world after all. But then he says, "Joey."

Well, there goes that.

"When?" I ask.

"Freshman year. Right after I started going to meetings."

"Did Olivia and Joanne know?"

He smiles. "Yeah, it's not forbidden."

"Why did you break up?"

He shrugs, waves his hand in the air. "I wasn't out, and he wanted to run around holding hands and kissing on street corners."

I smile at the image, Joey's curls bouncing as he skips along, dragging a reluctant Philip behind him.

"Spencer's not out," I say a second before I realize that this is exactly the kind of information that wasn't supposed to leave the room. At least Philip is part of the group, so it could be worse.

"I'm sorry, have you met him?" Philip asks.

"No, I'm sorry," I say. "Forget I said that. Nevermind."

But that just makes him more interested, and I sigh.

"He's out to his mom, but not his dad," I say in a rush.

"Oh. Okay." He's quiet for a second, then asks, "Are you? To your parents?"

I shake my head. "There's just my mom. But I haven't . . ." I shudder. "It seems gross. She's already in my business way too much."

He chuckles, but stops when I ask, "You?"

"No," he says, his back straightening. "Maybe after I graduate from Stanford. I need them to pay for it, and they wouldn't if they knew."

"Are you sure?"

"My father volunteers for the OCA on the weekends."

"Shit." The Oregon Citizens Alliance sponsored a ballot measure when I was in middle school to make it illegal to even mention homosexuality in schools. It lost, but it didn't exactly create a welcoming coming-out environment for Young Hannah. I can't even imagine how it would feel if my mom worked for them. He nods.

Just then, Mrs. Halliday appears at the end of the hallway. "Oh, I'm sorry," she says when she sees us, like she realizes that she's interrupting a private conversation. Her face reddens, and she turns around and retreats.

"Great," I moan, "now she definitely thinks we're doing it."

Philip laughs. "There goes your reputation."

I cover my face with my hand, but can't help telling him, "You're welcome for the boost to *yours.*"

He shakes his head, but he's still smiling. "Let's go. I'm hungry."

I nod, and we split off in different directions to go to our lockers.

32

After school, I find two pieces of mail addressed to me. Mixed in with the usual bills and catalogs are both a letter from Corey and a new zine, one that I ordered after seeing it reviewed in a zine that one of Corey's pen pals made. The twins have taken over the living room and are beating the crap out of each other in their video game, so I head upstairs and flop down on my bed. A minute later, I hear a chirpy little meow and look down to see Olive pushing through the almost-closed door. I pat the bed next to me, and she jumps up. I open the letter first.

Hey Hannah,

How are you doing? Have things gotten better with your friend? I'm glad you called. You seem really cool, and I'm glad we've become friends. You definitely deserve to have people around you who care about you, so I hope your buddy shapes up! I hope I wasn't too advice-y. You don't have to do anything that I say. I really believe that each person is their own expert and you're the only one who really knows your own life and what you should do. People are going to be assholes no matter what, so you should at least be true to yourself.

Today was sunny and perfect, and I went on a long drive up the coast. It's not sunny that often here, and even when it is, it's not usually hot, which is great. You mentioned not having a driver's license, right? I don't know if I could handle that. I get along okay with my parents most of the time, but things have definitely improved since I gained the ability to take off when I want to. They're pretty cool about it, too. My mom is so busy, either working at the restaurant or trying out new recipes at home, that she doesn't have time, and sometimes I think my dad spent all his parenting on my brothers, so he mostly lets my mom take charge. Same with the restaurant. Technically, they co-own it, but she's definitely the boss. I think that's why we clash, because we both want to be in charge. But mostly, I just want to be in charge of myself, you know?

The ocean looked so pretty while I was driving today. I didn't go that far, a half an hour or so, and I took some pictures. I'm hoping they'll turn out well enough to use in my next zine. The ocean is kind of like space, something that's so huge that it makes me really aware of how small I am in the grand scheme of things. I kind of like thinking about that, do you? It makes me feel like my mistakes aren't as big of a deal. The ocean is one of those things that's hard to take a picture of, though. No photo can do justice to the real thing. Maybe I can collage some other stuff onto the photo to make it seem grander.

I really hope things are going better for you, and thanks again for calling. You should call again sometime! Or send your number and I can call you, so we can split the long distance charges.

Talk to you soon!

    Love,

    Corey

I smooth the creases out of the letter on the comforter, and trace the word "love" where she's written it, then re-read the beginning of the letter, where she called me cool. It's easy to seem cool through the mail. She doesn't have to know about all the stupid shit I say all the time, all the embarrassing things I've done in my life. How Liz isn't talking to me, and hasn't even been sitting with us at lunch anymore because I was such a jerk. Corey only knows what I choose to write, which isn't very much. But even so, could it be that she likes me? Even after seeing the fat picture that I sent her? Even after talking to me and hearing my pathetic voice? I know it's not likely, but it's hard not to hope, just a little.

I pick up the envelope that holds the zine and tear it open. The title announces in block letters, "Riots, Not Diets!" The cover has a drawing of a screaming little girl. The first article talks about how loving your body is political, how being fat when everyone wants you to shrink is revolutionary. I poke my stomach and watch it jiggle. Revolutionary?

The rest of the zine is political too, and not all about bodies. Toward the end is a piece titled "What History Class Lied About." It's a list of events that happened differently in reality than the stories that the author learned in school. The introduction explains that history is presented as a black-and-white thing, as if there's only one true story, but really, everything has multiple sides, and history changes depending on who you ask. I shake my head as I read, thinking about how different these stories are from what I've heard. The last item on the list reads, "Suffragists like Susan B. Anthony and Elizabeth Cady Stanton fought against slavery, but they also didn't want black men to be allowed to vote before them. Anthony said she would rather cut off her arm than let black men vote while white women couldn't. And did they care about black women getting to vote? Nope, not if they thought it would keep white women from getting the right."

I have to read the paragraph twice. She would rather cut her arm off? God, what a drama queen. I don't remember seeing anything about that when I was doing my report for US History, but I've learned that my US History teacher doesn't expect very deep research. After I finish reading the zine, I tuck it into my bag to make a copy of the article to send to Corey. Is it wrong to name a band after someone who sad things like that? I wonder what she'll think.

33

The next day, I go to the school library after my last class and dig a dime from the bottom of my backpack to make the photocopy. I'm about to sit down and write a reply to Corey's letter when I change my mind and head to the 300s shelf. I remember this area from my research paper, and recognize some of the books that I checked out when I was studying Susan B. Anthony. I scan the shelves and notice one book that I didn't see before. I take it over to a table and flip through until I find the quote that the zine referenced. It's not that I didn't trust the zine, but the quote somehow feels more real when I see it printed in a library book. She definitely said it. I check the book out and ride my bike home, thinking about what I read.

By the time I get to Gran's house, I've decided to call Corey instead of writing. She said to call anytime, after all. She seems happy to hear from me, which makes me feel all full of cartoon hearts, and I start explaining the zine and what I found in the book.

"Shit," she says as I finish.

"I know," I say. "And I suggested that my friends name their band after her. Do you think that was wrong?"

"You didn't know that when you suggested it, though."

"That's true."

"Would your friends change the name if you asked them?"

"I'm not sure. A lot of people tell them how cool it is."

"It is really clever."

"Thanks."

"And if you think about it, this country was pretty much founded on racism, right? So it's not like she was some extremist for thinking that way."

"I never really thought about it," I say. "But if it was normal to think that way back then, does that make it okay?"

"Well, is the band about her?"

"No. Not at all. I think they just liked how it was like a prim lady name mixed with the word dangerous."

"What if they made it clearer that the band isn't about Susan B. Anthony? Tried to differentiate themselves, you know?"

"I don't think anyone thinks it's really about her," I say, and I almost laugh. "I mean, people don't think they're coming to see a band that sings about American history or anything."

She laughs too. "Hey, it could happen. I'm sure it does, in fact."

"Do you think I'm a bad person? For not knowing about Susan B. Anthony?"

"I don't think you're a bad person. I think it's hard to put anyone up on a pedestal, or think that anyone is all great, you know? People always disappoint you somehow."

I can't help but think of Liz when she says this. I guess being a feminist doesn't automatically make someone not wrong in other ways, just like seeming so perfect for me doesn't mean that Liz will want me.

"How are things with you?" I haven't even asked yet. Rude Hannah, I chide myself.

"Well," she begins, and I settle back on my pillows to listen, "my invitation came in the mail today for Stephanie's bridal shower. That's my brother's fiancée. It's in a few weeks."

"Are you going?"

"I don't know," she says, an edge of whine creeping into her voice. "I've never been to a bridal shower. What happens at them?"

"I've never been to one either, but I did help my mom plan my aunt's baby shower when I was younger."

"What did you do, smash candy bars into diapers and make people guess what kind they were?"

"No," I laugh. "But they did have to taste baby food and guess the flavor."

"So gross."

"And people had to guess how big around my aunt was and she was so embarrassed."

"Why?"

"No one wants their measurements announced to a room. Especially when they're pregnant." Doesn't she know that?

"I guess, but why does it matter? You're supposed to gain weight when you're pregnant!"

"Well, yeah, but people act like gaining weight is the worst thing that could happen to them. Don't you read fashion magazines? There are people who would rather be dead than fat."

"It sounds like you read too many fashion magazines."

"That's true," I say. "My grandma gets every magazine and catalog in the world, I swear. Every day, there's at least one in the mailbox."

"I avoid that shit. They tell you that you're not good enough as you are, so they can sell you a bunch of crap that's supposed to make you feel better. But you're never going to be good enough, so you're always going to have to keep buying."

"A perfect system," I joke, but she doesn't laugh.

"Yeah, for the ones making the money."

I'm quiet for a second, then I say, "I never felt like those magazines were for me. Like, they aren't talking to me. They're talking to a different kind of girl."

"I hear that."

"Speaking of other kinds of girls, how's your bridesmaid dress battle going?"

She blows a raspberry into the phone and I laugh.

"That well?"

"Even better! We're going dress shopping next weekend. Fucking nightmare."

"Oh, man. What are you going to do?"

"I'm considering getting sick. I know my mom won't believe

me if I fake it, so I think I have to go all the way and poison myself."

"Get some ipecac," I suggest. "It makes you throw up. This family I used to babysit for had some in their medicine cabinet in case the kid ate something he shouldn't."

"You know, that might work. She can't make me go dress shopping if I'm blowing chunks all over the place. Thanks for the tip!"

"Yeah, anytime." I chuckle. We're both quiet for a second, and I hear music playing in the background. "What are you listening to?"

"Excuse 17. Do you know them?"

"I've heard of them."

"We should trade mix tapes. Do you want to?"

"Sure!" I immediately start thinking about what songs I'll put on her tape.

"Do you ever do a theme to your mix tapes?" she asks.

"I never really thought about it. I mostly just make them for myself or for Liz to play in the car. What kind of themes?"

"I have one pen pal who's really into themed mixes. We've done songs by local bands, songs from movies, covers. Once we did an autobiography mix, which was pretty fun. Your favorite song from childhood, current favorite song, the song that was playing during your first kiss, stuff like that." She pauses for a second, then laughs. "Mine was 'Hold on to the Nights' by Richard Marx. How about you?"

I feel heat creep up my neck. How did I lose control of this conversation so quickly?

"Uhhh," I say. Brilliant.

"Oh shit, I'm sorry," she says, seeming to realize that I've never kissed anyone. I feel like we were equals a second ago, and now I'm back to being dumpy old Hannah, who no one will ever want to kiss.

"It's okay," I say. "We can do a theme if you want."

"Nah," she says. "For the first one, let's just do whatever songs we want. When we get bored of trading mixes like that, we can start thinking of themes."

"Okay."

I hear a click, and then Aunt Marion's voice comes over the phone. "Hannah?"

"Yes?"

"Sorry hon, but I need the phone."

"Okay." I wait for another click before I say, "Corey?"

"You have to go?"

"Yeah, sorry. I don't have my own phone line." She does, which means I never run the risk of her parents answering when I call.

"No problem. We can talk later. I'm going to start working on your tape."

"That sounds great! I'll talk to you later."

"Bye, Hannah."

"Bye."

34

Corey and I start talking on the phone more often than we write. One of us calls the other every few days. We talk about the books we're reading and shows we're watching, what we're doing in school, and she tells me about her art projects. We exchange more pictures, too. I even send her one that shows my full body, and she still wants to talk to me after she gets it.

I want to talk to Paula about Corey, but there never seems to be a good time. Part of me wishes I could talk to Liz, but we're just being polite to each other at the locker and haven't really talked in weeks. She and Joel have lunch with his friends sometimes, or with us sometimes, but they're always together. And how could I tell Liz without her thinking about all those nights we cuddled together, wondering whether me being into this girl means I'm into her too?

Finally, Mrs. Halliday is out sick and we have a substitute teacher in genetics, so everyone goes wild and we all sit wherever we want. Paula and I take a table in the back. The sub sets us loose filling out a packet of worksheets that Mrs. Halliday left, telling us we're allowed to work with our partners, so I get my chance.

"I have a question," I mutter to Paula, and she looks up from her packet.

"Is it about sex-linked traits? Because those are my favorite kinds." She gives me a cheesy grin.

I smile, but say, "No, it's not about school, it's about real life."

"Oooh, like about this big fight that you and Liz are having? Because she doesn't even remember why she's mad at you. She's just mad because you're mad."

I roll my eyes. "I'm not mad, I'm just sick of it."

"Of what?"

"Of always coming in second to her rotating cast of boy toys."

She laughs. "Well don't hold back!"

"It's not even about Liz," I continue, and she lets me talk. "I just . . . I was wondering how you can tell if someone like . . . likes you."

"If someone likes *me*?"

"If someone likes . . . someone else."

"Someone like you?"

"For example."

She raises one eyebrow. "Hannah Lewis, do you have a new crush?"

I glance around quickly to see if anyone is listening, but Paula is the only one who can see the lovely crimson shade that I know my face has turned.

"I have this pen pal," I begin.

"From another country?"

"No, she lives in California."

"Handy."

"Right. And we talk on the phone sometimes. Like, all the time, actually."

She's grinning like a maniac.

"Oh my God, Paula, don't make a whole thing out of it."

Her face falls.

"Of course," she says. "We'll keep it cool Hannah style."

"What do you mean?"

She shrugs. "You're always so into things being *cool*, but cool can get cold sometimes."

"You think I'm cold?"

"I think you're hard to get close to. You really intimidated me when we first started the band."

This is news to me.

"I always thought *you* were intimidating," I say. "You're so cool." There's that word again. I shake my head. "I'm sorry."

"No need to be. . . So, you think this girl might be into you?"

"I don't know."

"But you're into her?"

I nod slowly and she grins.

"You should ask her to come visit," she says.

"God, Paula! Don't you think that's too forward?"

"What's forward about that? You're being friendly! And who wouldn't want to come visit beautiful Salem, Oregon?"

"Don't you think it's sketchy to come to a different state to visit a stranger? I mean, I could be anyone."

"So could she."

"Yeah, I know, but we talk on the phone. . ." I trail off.

"Have you exchanged photos?" She's getting excited again. I nod. "Do you have one with you?"

"No, jeez, I don't carry her picture around in my wallet or something."

She looks disappointed. "Well, bring one tomorrow."

I tell her that I will, and the sub interrupts us with an announcement that she'll be collecting our packets at the end of class and that's how Mrs. Halliday will grade our participation for the day. I look down at the first page and start filling it in, then slide it over so Paula can see my answers. As she's copying them, I say again, "So . . . how do I know if she's into me?"

She smiles and starts singing "How Will I Know" by Whitney Houston. One of the girls sitting in front of us turns around and gives her a look. Instead of making her shut up, that just makes Paula start dancing in her chair too. The girl rolls her eyes and turns back around, hair whipping behind her. I can't help giggling.

"What do you two talk about?" she whispers after a moment.

I shrug. "Just whatever. What we're doing that day, or what we're doing in school. Her brother is getting married and her mom wants her to wear a dress but she doesn't want to."

"Is she into girls?"

"Yeah, she's had a bunch of girlfriends."

"Nice, I told you that you needed someone more experienced. To show you the ways of love." She gives an exaggerated wink.

"But don't you think her being so experienced makes her less likely to be into me?"

"How so?"

"I mean, if she knows she can get a girlfriend, why would she be interested in me?"

Paula gives me a stern look. "Hannah. We went over this. You're awesome. You're interesting and smart and cute. Do I need to write this all down for you?"

I smile weakly, but don't say anything, so she continues.

"Have I told you about my first guitar teacher?"

I shake my head.

"He always made us address ourselves as 'wonderful musician.' Like if we were stuck on something, we were supposed to be all, 'wonderful musician, what should I do next?' He said we had to be nice to our brains to make them help us."

"But your brain is your brain," I say. "Don't you think it knows if you're lying to it?"

She shrugs. "He said you can convince yourself of things. If you keep telling yourself you suck, you're going to start believing it. But if you tell yourself that you're great, you'll believe that too."

I look at her, skeptical. "Did he have a psychology degree or something?"

She rolls her eyes. "You don't always have to have a *degree* to know things. I think he knew how to help people make music. Isn't that enough?"

"I guess so. I mean, I guess it wouldn't hurt."

"Exactly," she says. "What's the worst that will happen, you delude yourself into thinking that you don't suck? Which everyone else already thinks anyway? Ask her if she wants to come visit. If she turns you down, at least you don't have to wonder."

"Spring break is coming up," I say slowly. Her face lights up.

"Does she have the same spring break?"

"I don't know."

"Is she in high school?"

I nod, then answer the rest of the questions that Paula fires at me. What does she look like? What bands does she listen to? What is her zine about? I tell her everything I know, and my mind is busy forming a plan.

35

I know Corey is working after school, so I take the cordless phone to my room and work on homework while I wait for her to call. She usually calls when she gets home from the dinner rush. Mom and Aunt Marion assume it's Liz that I'm talking to every night, and I haven't corrected them. I figure I'll deal with the phone bill when it comes.

The phone rings around nine o'clock, and I answer it on the first ring.

"Hey!" Corey says when I pick up.

"Hey," I say. "How was work?"

She groans. "So busy. There was a birthday party at one end of the dining room and a retirement party at the other, and they both had a *lot* of needs."

"I'm sorry."

"Aw, it's okay. It went fast, at least."

"That's good," I say.

"What are you up to?"

"Just finishing up my homework."

"Which class?"

"Calc."

"Ugh, I'm so bad at math."

"It's my favorite."

"I know, but I can't say I understand. I just get stuck and start spinning in my head, thinking about how I'm never going to use it in real life. Really, do you think you're ever going to use calculus?"

"If I become a math teacher."

"Is that a possibility?"

I shrug even though she can't see it. I don't think it would be the worst job. "I mean, isn't anything a possibility at this point?"

"Very true."

"And anyway," I continue, "when am I ever going to need to know how to diagram a sentence? They're not exactly teaching life skills."

I hear her warm chuckle, and I'm glad no one is around to see the dopey grin that takes over my face. I decide to jump in.

"Hey, speaking of school, when is your spring break?"

"In two weeks," she says.

"Mine too!"

"Nice. Do you have anything planned?"

"No," I say, "but I had an idea."

"Yeah?"

"Yeah. Do you want to come visit?"

She's quiet for a second, and I'm sure she's trying to figure out how to say no, or maybe even *hell* no. But when she speaks, she just says, "Yeah."

"Yeah?" I say, not really believing it.

"Yeah! The first weekend of spring break is that bridal shower I've been dreading, so I could come then. That would be the perfect excuse!"

My heart sinks a little. She just wants to get out of the party.

"Totally," I say weakly.

"Not only because of that," she says like she can read my mind. "That's just a bonus."

I laugh. "Sure."

She laughs too, and I feel my tension melt.

"I'd like to see all the places you talk about."

"I can see if there's a good show scheduled at the Loyola," I say, getting excited. It would be fun to show her around town. "It's not too far of a drive, is it?"

"I think it's around seven hours," she says. "The longest I've driven before was to San Francisco, which is four and a half, so it'll be a good challenge. I kind of love driving, you know?"

"Oh yeah, I remember."

"This will be fun!" she says, and she sounds like she's getting excited. I grin, proud of myself for suggesting it, for putting myself out there. I can't wait to tell Paula tomorrow.

36

Liz is alone at the lunch table when I get there on the Friday before spring break. I'm surprised to see her without Joel attached to her side.

"Hey." I swing my backpack onto the table. She looks up and I notice that her eyes are red.

"Are you okay?" I sit next to her. She bites her lip and shakes her head, then starts crying. I reach out and pull her to me, and she buries her face in my hoodie. I feel her thin shoulders shake.

"What happened?" I ask. "Didn't Mr. Walters like your song?" I know that she and Paula have been working on a new song for class, and they were supposed to present it today.

"It's not that." She talks into my shirt, then pushes herself upright and lets loose a fresh batch of sobs.

"Do you want to like, go to the bathroom or something?" It's not like Liz to lose her composure in public. People at nearby tables are staring at us openly.

But then Paula appears, and she's pissed.

"Where the hell *were* you?" she hisses at Liz, who just cries harder.

"God, Paula, give her a break!" I put a protective arm around Liz's shoulders. "She's obviously upset."

Paula stands back, hands on her hips. "Oh yeah? Are you upset about being ditched for our midterm? When we were supposed to play our new song for the class? Are you upset because you had to explain to Mr. Walters why your partner didn't bother to show up?" She snaps her fingers in the air. "Oh, no, wait! That's me!"

Liz doesn't say anything. I rub her arm, trying to be reassuring. Brian and Colin walk up, talking to each other, but then Colin looks at us, taking in the scene. Paula standing over Liz, who's curled into me, crying. He elbows Brian and they stop walking like they don't know if they should come any closer.

I look at Liz, not sure what to say. She seems completely and utterly defeated.

"Hey guys," Brian says carefully, coming to stand next to Paula. He puts his hand on her arm. "Everything okay?"

No one speaks for a moment, then Liz says, "Joel dumped me."

I drop my arm and straighten my spine, pulling myself away from her. Liz's words have the opposite effect on Paula, whose face softens.

"Okay," Paula says. "Let's go. We'll see you later, boys." She grabs Liz's arm and pulls her up, and Liz takes my hand, pulling me with them.

Paula shoves chairs out of our way and leads us to the bathroom in the back of the art wing. It doesn't get a lot of use because it's a small one; just two stalls, two sinks, and a freshman washing her hands. Liz stands behind Paula and me while we wait for the girl to leave, then Paula says, "Okay, what happened?"

Liz sniffles. I get a wad of toilet paper from the nearest stall and hand it to her.

"Thanks." Her voice is quiet. I've never seen her so upset by a breakup. But, I think quickly, I can't actually remember a breakup that she didn't initiate.

"He met some other girl," Liz says finally. She leans against the wall, tipping her head back and closing her eyes. "I was asking him about *prom*. God, I'm so stupid. He was like, 'Oh I didn't think you'd be into that kind of thing,' and I was like, 'What does that mean?' and he was like, 'I didn't think you would want to wear a dress and get all fancy and whatever,' and I told him that I did. I thought it could be fun, and we could go with you guys," she gestures to Paula. "And we can find a guy for you, or you could go with Colin or something." She looks at me and I nod like sure, of course we could have done that. She swipes at her eyes. "And then he started talking about how everything is all about me, and how I don't support his music enough, which I *totally* do, but he said all I do is talk about my music and my band. That was last night, and then before composition he said he met some other girl at his coffeehouse show last week. The one I had to leave early from because my mom made me go to Maisie's dance thing, remember?" She looks at Paula, who nods.

"What a dick," Paula says. She stands with her feet wide and her hands on her hips. "He was in class too, that smug asshole."

Liz blows her nose loudly into the wad of tissue. "He has the worst timing on earth. Right before the midterm, spring break, and my birthday?" She sticks out her lower lip. "My birthday better make up for this."

Her birthday is Sunday. Even though we haven't been talking, I haven't forgotten.

"It will," Paula promises, looking pointedly at me.

"It will," I agree.

Liz exhales heavily. "This is such bullshit. I want to go home." She looks at us, eyes red and hopeful. "Do you want to come with me?" Paula and I look at each other. We have genetics next, then I have chemistry, and I can get all those notes from Philip at Rainbow Youth during break. My last class is US History, which is based on a textbook that I can read at home, and our teacher's rambling memories of the 1960s, which are almost never on the tests. I shrug and nod, and Paula nods definitively.

Paula goes to update the boys while Liz and I go to our locker, and we all meet at Liz's car. We stop at the 7-Eleven for snacks, then Liz drives us to her house. We sit on her bed with a bag of chips and a tub of ice cream with spoons sticking straight up. Liz lies with her head in my lap, and I run my fingers through her hair. It could stand to be washed.

"Okay, babe," Paula says, licking potato chip salt off her fingers, "what are you thinking for your birthday? It's Sunday, right?"

I feel Liz nod against my leg. She twists her head so she can look up at me. "So Hannah, I had this idea."

"What idea?" I feel instantly suspicious. She pushes herself up to sitting and glances over at Paula. Great, an idea they've been working on without me.

"What if we have a party at your house?" Liz asks.

"But my mom and everyone will be there." I'm confused.

"No," she says with a sly smile, "your *other* house. It's just sitting there, right? Not to be insensitive or whatever, but it's kind of begging for a party."

"But it's a Sunday."

"So what? It's spring break!"

I think for a second, trying to see if I can think of a reason not to do it, but all I have is my fear of getting caught.

"How many people?" I ask slowly. At least they won't be at school to invite anyone. And it's such short notice, maybe no one will be able to come.

Liz and Paula exchange a look like they know they got me.

"Not too many," Liz says. "The five of us, of course. And a few people from school. And maybe. . ." She looks over at Paula. "Do you think your sister would get us alcohol? She could come. And those friends of hers. Do you think they know any guys they can invite?"

Paula snickers. "What, they can only come if they bring a buffet of guys?"

Liz shrugs. "Well, why not?" She breaks into a grin, and the two of them laugh.

"Wait," I say, remembering the plans I've been making. "My pen pal is going to be in town."

"Oh yeah, I forgot!" Paula says with a huge grin.

"Your *pen pal?*" Liz says at the same time.

"Yeah," I say, feeling guilty that I haven't told Liz anything about her. "I have a pen pal in Northern California. She's coming to visit tomorrow."

"Bring her," Paula insists. "I wanted to meet her anyway!"

Liz looks back and forth between the two of us.

"You knew about this?" she asks Paula. She just shrugs like she doesn't have any information.

"We talked about it in class," I say. Liz and I don't have any classes together this semester.

"Did you find her through school? Like some class project?"

"No," I say, "I saw an ad for her zine in *Maximumrocknroll* and we started writing."

"And having long phone calls," Paula sing-songs.

Liz looks suspicious.

"And you're just friends? Just . . . pen pals?" She looks at Paula, who's the one making all these stupid faces.

"There's nothing going on," I say. "We're just friends."

"Okaaaaay," Paula says, wiggling her eyebrows.

Liz turns to me. "Why are you keeping secrets?"

"It's not a secret," I say. Liz hates being left out of anything. "It's just nice to have someone to talk to, someone who listens and doesn't only talk about herself."

"Is that a dig at me?"

"No," I say, harsher than I mean to, "not everything is about you."

"Well, you don't exactly open up and talk about yourself, Hannah," she snaps. "You guys are acting like there's something going on. Are you like, *into* her or something?"

I shrug. "Yeah, I guess." This isn't exactly how I planned my coming out to Liz, but here we are.

She leans against the wall. "Wow, I've been waiting for this moment for years. The moment when Hannah the nun finally likes someone."

"I'm not a *nun*," I protest.

"You're always so secretive about everything," she says. "I'm over here spilling my guts all over the place, and you're just like, 'oh that's interesting.'"

"Don't be mean," I say.

"Like keeping secrets isn't mean?" she says. "So what, are you like, a lesbian now?"

"I don't know, Liz. God, back off."

She turns to Paula. "You knew all of this?"

Paula nods. "Yeah, it came up. Not this girl specifically, but like, girls in general. At that slumber party after the Huckle Cat show."

Liz pushes her hair back roughly. "Oh my God, I'm so sick of hearing about that fucking slumber party!"

"Well, jeez, Liz," I say, moving to the edge of the bed. "It's not like you've been *available* lately for me to talk about my feelings with. You've been off with Joel or -" I stop talking suddenly, remembering the reason we're in Liz's room in the middle of the day.

"Right," she says when she sees my face. "Thanks for bringing him up."

"Babes," Paula says, holding out her hands like a crossing guard telling us to stop. "Can we please chill? Liz, can't you smoke a bowl or something and be nice?"

"*Me?*" Liz's eyes are round. I bite my lips to conceal a smile.

"I mean, okay, it's kind of a long time not to say anything." Paula shoots me a pointed stare, and my smile falls. "But she obviously had her reasons."

We all sit in silence for a moment, then Liz pushes herself off the bed and moves to her desk chair. She opens her bottom drawer and pulls out the Batman lunchbox. She rolls a joint, shoves the window open, lights her joint, and inhales hard. She takes a second hit before offering it to Paula, who sucks briefly and hands it to me. I accept it and inhale, imagining the smoke coating my insides and filling in the cracks.

By the time Maisie gets home from school, the three of us have moved to the couches in the basement, watching bad TV and munching on bowls of popcorn. Liz and I lay on different couches. Paula sits by my feet, her own socked feet stretched out onto the coffee table. Maisie slams the door and is able to make her sneakers surprisingly loud as they stomp down the carpeted stairs. She comes to rest in front of the TV, hands on her hips.

Liz groans and waves at Maisie to get out of her view of Jerry Springer.

"Um, what happened at school today?" Maisie says, not moving. "I heard you had a total meltdown at lunch."

Liz groans again and covers her face with her hand.

"Who did you hear that from?" Paula asks. She tosses some popcorn into her mouth.

Maisie's eyes roll to the ceiling while she thinks. "Janie, Lauren, Stacy, everyone. Stacy said she saw you and Joel having some huge fight in the hallway before fourth period, and then a *bunch* of people saw you totally crying in the Commons."

I feel a stab of anger toward Maisie, who seems less concerned about her sister's well-being than about catching up on gossip.

"And what?" I say. "You just had to rush home and see if it was true?"

Maisie shrugs. "Everyone was asking me what was happening, and I had *no* idea."

"Tell them it's none of their beeswax."

She looks at me like I've completely lost it.

"Joel dumped me, okay?" Liz says. "It fucking sucked and I don't need your stupid friends sticking their noses in it."

Maisie takes a small step back. "Okay, jeez, I just thought I'd see if you were *okay*."

"Thanks very much for your concern, sister *dear*," Liz says. She shoves herself up to sitting and grabs a handful of popcorn for herself. She raises it to her mouth, then changes her mind and throws the kernels at her sister. "Now fuck off."

37

I wake up Saturday morning with my stomach full of butterflies. I know that Corey is leaving this morning, so she won't be here until the afternoon at least, but I want everything to be perfect. I spend the morning cleaning my room. I stack my new Team Dresch and Bikini Kill CDs on top of the Pearl Jam and Soundgarden ones and arrange my growing zine collection on a prime shelf. I called her Friday night after I got home from Liz's and told her that my mom thinks that Corey used to go to school with me and has moved away. I could hear her hesitation, but I explained that there's no way my mom would let a stranger stay with me, no matter how well we know each other.

Like we planned, Corey calls me from a pay phone in Eugene, which is about an hour from Salem, so I know she'll be here soon. I have so much extra energy that I can't sit still, and I keep pacing back and forth, checking my hair and outfit in the mirror every five minutes. I change my shirt probably ten times, rearrange the photos on my bulletin board, and smooth out invisible wrinkles in my bedspread. Around five in the evening, I hear a car pull into the driveway. I run down the stairs and past Mom, who's unloading the dishwasher. She smiles as I breeze past her, and I try to ignore the twinge of guilt about all of the lies I've been telling lately. What if Corey is a creepy serial killer who preys on young girls who read *Maximumrocknroll?* I'm suddenly glad I'm not home alone.

A faded tan Mercedes with California plates is parked in the driveway, and behind the wheel, the girl from the photos on my bulletin board is smoothing down her hair in the rearview mirror. I want to play it cool, but I can't help grinning as I walk down the front steps. She sees me, grins back, and steps out of the car.

"Hey," I say.

"Hey." It's the same voice from the phone, and I feel my stomach tighten in a way that I usually only feel when Liz is around.

She steps toward me.

"Are you a hugger?" She looks kind of unsure, which makes my heart thump. Could she be as nervous as me?

"Sure," I say, and she closes the distance between us and wraps her arms around me. I hug her back, inhaling her unfamiliar scent. She's a little sweaty from the drive, but she feels strong and solid and I don't really want to let go.

When we step apart, we smile shyly at each other, and I try to break the awkwardness by waving my arm toward her car.

"Can I help you with your bags?" God, I sound like a bellhop or something.

She smiles. "Yeah."

From the passenger seat, she produces a duffel bag, which I pull onto my shoulder, and a beat-up backpack that's splattered with paint.

"Do you paint?" I ask when she grabs it. I thought she only did photography and made collages.

"Ehh, not much. I'm not that good at it."

"I doubt that," I say, and she smiles.

"Well, thanks."

"You must be Corey," my mom says with a huge smile when we walk through the front door, and I cringe at her excitement. "I'm Georgia, Hannah's mom. How long has it been since you've been back in Salem?"

Corey glances at me, then says, "It feels like forever."

Mom nods knowingly.

"We're going to take Corey's stuff upstairs," I say. I lead Corey through the kitchen and up the stairs, pointing out the bathroom, the boys' room, and Aunt Marion's room.

"This room used to be my mom's," I tell her as I push my door open. "Then my grandma used it as a guest room, but it was always my playroom when I was little."

I set her duffel bag down on the desk and sit on the bed, watching her take in the room.

"I love the bookcase," she says, looking at the shelves that cover the wall behind the bed.

"Me too."

"Have you read all these books?" She steps toward the wall to read a few titles.

"Oh, no," I say. "A lot of them are old books that have been left here."

Olive steps through the door, then stops when she sees Corey, her green cat eyes wide.

"It's okay," I tell her, sliding off the bed and crouching on the floor, wiggling my fingers at her.

"Is that Olive?" Corey asks.

"Yeah," I say. "You're not allergic to cats or anything, are you? I should have asked."

"Nah, I knew she'd be here. It's fine." She smiles, and I smile back, then quickly look back at the cat. Olive steps toward me and I stroke her head reassuringly.

"Are you hungry?" I ask, looking up. "We can go get dinner."

"Yeah, that would be great. But would it actually be okay if I shower really quick? All that time in the car, you know?"

I nod. "Totally. Let me get you a towel. I'll wait downstairs. Come down when you're ready, okay?"

She grins and nods, and I feel another little flutter in my stomach.

"I'm so glad you came to visit," I say before I even think about it.

She looks at me for a second, the smile returning to her lips, then says decisively, "Me too."

38

An hour later, we're seated in a booth at Shari's, orders taken and glasses of water in front of us. The waitress offers us coffee, which Corey accepts and I decline.

"You don't drink coffee?" she asks like it's a normal thing to drink with dinner. I shake my head.

"I never got to like it. My mom doesn't like it either, so it's not like I grew up with it or anything."

"Mmmm, I love it," she says, taking a sip from her cup. "This isn't the best, but even bad coffee is good to me."

"The smell used to make me gag," I say. "When I was little, I couldn't even walk down the coffee aisle at the grocery store."

"Shit. Is this grossing you out?"

I shake my head, feeling stupid for telling that story. "No, I'm better now."

"I'm glad."

"My aunt drinks coffee. So you can have some of hers in the morning or whenever."

"I was just thinking I should have packed my French press," she says with a laugh. I grin, even though I don't know what that is. But I can't resist smiling when she does. She's not what people would call pretty, but her grin is infectious and I love knowing that I'm the one that made her smile. Besides, pretty is way overrated.

I'm nervous that we won't have anything to talk about, or that we'll feel like strangers, but we talk easily. I realize that we already know each other from our letters and calls. She feels like an old friend. I fill her in on Spencer and Joey's GSA woes. I learned at Rainbow Youth last week that the principal is canceling all clubs despite the walkout, so they're talking now about protesting outside of the district office after spring break.

"That is so cool," Corey says. She drags a French fry through ketchup and pops it into her mouth. "Are you going to go?"

"I hadn't thought about it. I don't go to their school."

"But it's the same district, right? What if someone wants to start a GSA at your school and the same thing happens?"

"That's true."

"Are you scared? You're not out, right?"

"Right." I wonder if she'll judge me as she chews thoughtfully.

"Since it's a gay-straight alliance, you could just be a straight ally."

"Sure," I say. "A straight ally who's very passionate about something that's happening at another school?"

She grins. "You're a really good ally!"

I laugh.

"Oh, hey," she says, motioning to her plate, where a garnish of an orange slice and a sprig of parsley sits. "Do you want this? I remember you saying you liked parsley."

I smile, pleased that she remembers.

"Yeah, I used to sneak into my grandma's garden and eat the parsley. The smell always puts me back there in my mind."

"They say that smell is the strongest memory sense."

"I've heard that."

She holds the sprig out and I take it, our fingers brushing briefly. I pop it into my mouth.

"What does it taste like?" she asks.

I close my eyes as I crush the leaf with my teeth, and I remember sitting in the sun, feet sunk in the soft dirt, hidden away where no one could find me.

"Like freedom."

I pay for dinner, since she came all the way to visit, but she insists on leaving the tip. We walk to the car in air that's cooling rapidly, feeling like cold water against my skin. There aren't many cars in the parking lot. It's late for dinner and too early for the middle-of-the-night crowds.

"Where to now?" she asks as we slide into the car.

"There's not a lot to do in Salem." I wish I'd thought of things to do. "Especially at night. There's a 24-hour grocery store, and sometimes Liz and Paula and I go and wander up and down the aisles."

She laughs. "Wild times."

"Totally."

She starts the car and we drive, then I get an idea. "Hey, how about you turn left up here?"

She follows my directions and I lead her to the parking lot behind my elementary school.

"Did you go here?" she asks, and I nod. We get out and walk toward the playground. She breaks into a run and starts climbing the jungle gym. By the time I catch up with her, she's at the very top.

"When I was little," she says, "I always raced all the boys to the top of the jungle gym."

"I bet you always won."

She nods like it's obvious, and I grin. I grab a bar and pull myself up, climbing carefully. She makes room and I balance myself next to her on top of the metal bars.

"Everything was always a competition," I say. "Whoever was on top of the jungle gym was like the coolest kid in school."

"Everything is still a competition at school."

"What do you mean?"

"No one supports each other. Everyone's always trying to knock each other down, prove how cool or smart they are. Who cares about cool? I'd rather be interesting and real, you know?"

I feel my face heat up, thinking of Philip and our constant battle to be first in our class. Thinking about how Paula said I focus too much on what's cool.

I change the subject. "Was your mom mad about you missing

the bridal shower?"

"A little bit. She's still going, but now she doesn't have a little buddy to go with her. But I would probably hold her back. She can bond with all the ladies over their frilly wedding shit, and not have to worry about her grubby, ugly daughter complaining."

"You're not ugly!" I'm surprised. She's far from it.

"Well, thanks."

"Does your mom say that you are?"

"No, but I can tell she thinks it."

I frown. What a horrible thing for your mom to think about you. Although my mom occasionally leaves magazines around the house with the pages open to new diet ideas, she's actually pretty supportive. I remember crying at night after kids at school made fun of me, at the very school we're outside of now, and my mom wiping my tears away, telling me that I was pretty and so much smarter than all those kids anyway.

I work up my nerve for a second, then blurt, "I think you're cute."

She smiles and looks down. "Thanks. I think you're cute too."

I bite my lip, my heart pounding. Is this a moment? Should I kiss her? But I take too long, and she swings to the outside of the jungle gym, climbing down. I shake my head, disappointed in myself, and climb down after her. I lead her the long way back to the car because I want it to take longer, along the trees that line the edge of the field. We're almost to the car when she stops and grabs my arm.

"Look!" she says, pointing. I stop walking and look, and see a shrub move. A rabbit hops out, eyes catching on the street lights. We both stand frozen. It turns and sees us, then runs back into the bushes.

"That was so cool!" I breathe when it's gone.

"Have you ever seen rabbits here before?" she asks as we start walking again.

"Never! I remember other kids talking about the wild bunnies around school, but I wasn't sure if it was just a myth. I always wanted to see one. Rabbits are one of my top five animals."

She laughs. "I can honestly say that I've never thought about my top five animals."

My face heats up again. That was definitely something a little kid would say. Then I decide to tell her something I haven't told anyone.

"Sometimes I think about becoming a vet."

"That's cool. And I bet you'd be really good at it. You're good at science, right?"

I nod, then worry that I'm coming off like a jerk. "I'm okay," I amend.

She chuckles. "You can say you're good at something if you are."

"I know," I say, but I get a flash of a memory from middle school, a science lab with big black tables. Before class started, Levi Hilton, who sat in front of me, dumped his books on his desk and announced, "Last night's homework was so confusing. Does anyone get this stuff?"

"I do," I said, reaching for his notebook to see where he went wrong.

"You're so arrogant, Hannah," Karen Barrett said. She sat a few seats away, and everyone knew that she had a crush on Levi. "You used to be cool, but now you're just full of yourself."

I sat, the words washing over me like ice water. Levi looked at me expectantly, holding out his notebook, but I waved him away, saying, "Ask Philip, he can help you."

When we get back to Gran's house, Corey opens the trunk of her car and pulls out a sleeping bag, which solves one problem I'd been worrying about. Was she going to expect to share my bed? It's queen-sized, unlike my little twin at the other house, so there would have been enough room. But maybe this is easier. Besides, we have plenty of time.

Corey takes her pajamas into the bathroom with her. I pull mine on while she's gone, then slip under the covers. Olive usually sleeps with me, but she's keeping clear of the room tonight. Probably too many new smells.

Corey comes back and settles into her sleeping bag, then I click the lamp off and ask, "So, what do you think of Salem so far?"

I hear her chuckle.

"Seems like there's not much to do at night."

Oh great, she's bored already.

"Sorry it's boring," I say in a rush. "Tomorrow we can check out Island and the book store. There's a craft supply store too, if you want to go there."

"Sure," she says, "but it's fun just hanging out, too. You don't have to keep me constantly entertained."

"I don't want you to think your trip wasn't worth it or whatever."

"I'm not worried about that."

"Okay, cool. Sorry I'm so neurotic."

"No need to apologize," she says, and I can hear a smile in her voice. Lying here, talking in the dark, reminds me of talking on the phone.

"Sor - I mean, okay."

She chuckles, and I can't help laughing too. I roll over so I can see her outline amongst the other shadows.

"Do you visit a lot of your pen pals?" I ask.

"Most of them live too far away. I had one in San Francisco, and I went down and visited and went to Pride. That was wild."

"Whoa, that sounds so cool. I've never even been to Portland Pride."

"I imagine it would be difficult, not having a car."

"Yeah." Then I realize something. "You said you *had* one in San Francisco. Not anymore?"

"Things kind of went south after I visited. Some people are different in person, you know?"

"Isn't everyone?"

"Yeah, but sometimes it's a *good* different."

I wonder what kind I am.

"Plus it didn't help that I had a big crush on her and she was *not* interested," she continues.

"That sucks."

"Yeah. But I get crushes on everyone, so it was to be expected, I guess."

"I've only had a few in my life," I say, wondering if she can hear my heart pounding as the conversation turns to crushes.

"Only girls?" she asks.

I shrug even though she can't see me.

"When I was little," I say, "I liked a few boys, but looking back I'm not sure if I really liked them, or if I was just going along with what my friends were saying."

"How can you not be sure?"

"I don't know, I don't feel like I can say with certainty that I'm never going to fall for a guy."

"Bisexual, then?" she asks.

"I guess," I say. "That word just sounds so clinical, like you don't say 'homosexual' or 'heterosexual.' They're too formal. What word do you use for yourself?"

"I just say I'm gay, usually. 'Lesbian' feels so seventies to me."

I laugh.

"I like calling myself a dyke, too," she continues.

"Oh, right. You did in your ad."

"And look how well it worked!"

We both laugh this time.

"Most people are so sure about everything, but I can almost always see both sides of arguments," I say after we're quiet for a moment. "Most things don't really seem black-and-white to me."

"A lot of things aren't."

"That's why I like the word 'agnostic' instead of atheist, even though I'm not interested in religion. Like, who am I to know what's out there?"

"Sounds like a great start to an article for the next issue of my zine," she says. "I started working on the next issue earlier this week. I've got a couple of pieces so far that people have sent me."

"Cool, I look forward to reading it."

"You should write something. Will you?"

"Yeah," I say without thinking. "I don't know what I would say, though."

"Write about things not being black-and-white, or what you think matters in life."

"Okay." I'm quiet for a second, then I say, "That's why I like math, because it *is* black-and-white. It's reassuring. There's a right answer."

"Math is another big mystery to me. The rules never make sense."

"Sometimes I feel like they're the only thing that makes sense."

"Write about that," she says through a yawn. "I like hearing your perspective."

We're both quiet for a moment, and it feels good, a comfortable silence.

"Tomorrow is that party, right?" she asks. Her voice is a little softer, like she's drifting away.

"Yeah. Are you up for it?"

"Yeah, I'm looking forward to meeting your friends."

"Totally," I say, but I wonder how it will go. Will Paula be a huge dork about my crush? Will Liz be nice? I hope she didn't invite too many jerks. I'm about to say something else when I notice that Corey's breathing has changed. I hear a quiet snore, and smile to myself, snuggling deeper under the covers and closing my eyes.

39

Corey's sleeping bag is empty when I wake up, and I find her in the kitchen, already dressed, drinking coffee with Aunt Marion.

"You didn't tell me that your friend is an artist," Marion says when I walk in. There are a bunch of photos spread across the table. At first I think Corey brought them with her, but when I get closer, I see people that I recognize. A much younger Mom making a goofy smile at the camera, Taylor and Jeremy sharing an armchair while they examine a picture book, and Gran holding a baby with dark brown hair sticking up in all directions like mine always did. I reach for that one and Aunt Marion smiles.

"That's one of my favorites," she says. I examine the photo. I've never seen this picture before, but Gran is looking at me with such love that it makes my throat get tight.

"Did you take these?" I ask.

Aunt Marion nods. "I thought about going to school for photography, but Dad didn't think it was serious enough."

"That's rude," I say. "I never knew you were such a good photographer."

"We were talking about the schools she was thinking about going to," Corey says.

"Didn't you already do all your college applications?" I pull out a chair and sit, still holding the photo.

Corey shrugs. "Yeah, but there's always time to switch it up if it's not right. Sometimes I think about taking a year off or doing a year or two at community college and then transferring."

"I didn't think you needed to save money," I say. I've gotten the impression that her family has money, and her car hasn't done anything to dispel that idea.

"Not so much to save money. But what if I end up surrounded by rich jerks? Plus, I get nervous about moving into a dorm and being around so many people at once. You know how I don't have a ton of friends other than pen pals."

"Oh yeah." I didn't realize that she had doubts about her plans for next year. I thought she was always so sure of herself.

"You should keep that picture, Hannah Banana," Aunt Marion says, standing from the table and ruffling my hair. She starts gathering the other photos, stacking them and sliding them into a manilla envelope.

"What do you two have planned today?" she asks as she carries her coffee cup to the sink. Corey looks at me expectantly.

"I was thinking we could go downtown?" I say it like a question, looking at Corey. She nods. "We can check out the record store and see if there's anything good, and any other stores or whatever."

"Works for me."

"Then we're spending the night for Liz's birthday tonight," I say, carefully wording it so it's not exactly a lie. Liz, Paula, Brian, Colin, and I all decided to spend the night at the house after the party so we don't have to worry about driving drunk.

"I haven't heard about Liz in ages. I wasn't sure if the two of you were still hanging out," Aunt Marion says.

"Yeah, she's just been really busy."

"Well, I'm glad you can spend her birthday with her. You two were always such good friends. What time is the party?"

"She wanted us to meet up around six."

"Then you should get going, sleepyhead. Daylight's wasting."

I duck my head so she can't mess my hair up again. It really doesn't need any help.

"Where's my mom?" I ask her, and she looks down at the envelope in her hands.

"She's visiting your grandma."

"Oh, cool," I say quickly. I don't want to make her feel bad about not visiting, even though I do think she should. But it's not like I visit all the time, so I'm not exactly in a position to judge. I turn back to Corey. "I'm going to go up and get dressed, then I'll be ready in a few, okay?"

"Sure," she says, lifting her coffee cup. "I just need to finish this and I'm ready."

"There's more coffee if you want it," Aunt Marion offers. "And I think there's a travel mug somewhere in here." She opens a cabinet and starts moving dishes around.

"That is not something I'm ever going to turn down." Corey takes a long drink and stands. I leave them to it and run up the stairs.

Corey drives us downtown, and I point out the church where Rainbow Youth meets, the Loyola, the mall. All the big sights of Salem. She acts interested in all the boring stuff I point out, and I'm struck by how comfortable I feel with her. I rarely make friends on my own. Usually, I meet people through Liz. She's an excellent shield. Everyone gets so distracted by her perfect golden glow that they don't notice that I do not belong, that I have no idea what I'm doing. Today, there's no shield, just Hannah. And Corey makes me feel like I'm worth hanging out with. She laughs and acts interested in me, and I feel like I'm actually funny and interesting.

We start at Island, and I show her Monica the mannequin, who today is wearing a tutu and cowboy hat, and holding a sign listing the new releases. They must have a whole room of costumes somewhere.

"This is where I got the *Maximumrocknroll* and saw your zine ad," I say as I pull the door open for her.

She grins. "Where it all began, eh?"

I giggle and nod.

Luckily, Joel isn't working today. Larry is stationed behind the cash register, and a jazz album is playing over the speakers. He smiles and nods at me when we come in, then goes back to typing on an adding machine that whirrs and prints numbers onto a little roll of paper.

We spend a while at Island, pointing out our favorite albums and laughing when we both reach for the same Team Dresch CD. I confess that I hadn't heard of them before I read her zine, and Corey smiles like she's proud. She tells me that she's glad I like them.

We leave her car parked outside of Island and walk to the book store, then the few blocks to the craft supply store and the mall. The day goes quickly, and I'm kind of sad for our time alone to end when I check my watch and realize that we should get dinner and go back to Gran's to change for the party. We buy limp slices of pizza at the Sbarro in the mall and eat at a little table, our shopping bags tucked between our feet.

"Your aunt seems cool," she says between bites.

"Yeah, she's a lot younger than my mom, so she always seems a little more like a cousin or something."

"Your mom's the oldest?"

I shake my head. "She has an older brother, but he lives in Washington and doesn't visit much."

"Wow, so that means your mom is the only one who visits your grandma? You said that your aunt never does."

"I visit sometimes," I say defensively.

"Oh yeah, I'm sorry, I didn't mean to imply that you don't."

We eat in silence for a moment.

"That must be really hard," she says. "I hardly see my grandparents, so we're not close or anything. But you and your grandma were close, right?"

I nod.

"Sometimes I feel like everyone is just waiting for her to die," I say. "And sometimes I think I am too."

Corey's eyebrows go up.

"I don't mean I *want* her to die. But it's like part of her is already gone, but we're not allowed to act like she's gone."

"You can't grieve," she says.

"Yeah. Like I don't want to downplay the person that she is now, or her existence or whatever. But the woman who helped raise me, and taught me to write in cursive and all that, she's already gone."

She nods thoughtfully, then wipes her greasy fingers on a napkin before reaching over and putting her hand on mine. I turn my hand over without thinking and we grasp hands. I can feel her heat radiating up my arm, and I start to feel guilty like I'm using my sadness over Gran to get sympathy and make her touch me. I pull my hand back and use it to shove the last of my pizza into my mouth.

"We should go," I say around the crust.

Corey is looking down at the spot where our hands were, but she just nods and pushes her chair back.

40

Aunt Marion is at work when we get back to Gran's house, and the boys and Mom are in the living room. Taylor and Jeremy are stationed in front of the TV as usual, and Mom is leaning back in the recliner, flipping through a copy of *Good Housekeeping*.

"How was your shopping trip?" she calls when we come to the doorway to wave hello. I hold up my bags.

"Productive," I say. She smiles. "We're going to go change and head over to Liz's party," I continue, and she nods, eyes back on the article she's reading. She's making this way too easy. One of the advantages of sixteen years of playing the good daughter.

Brian's Camry and Liz's Subaru are both parked in the driveway when Corey pulls up to the house, so I tell her to park on the curb, but she drives another block and then turns, parking a block away.

"You don't want it to look like you're having a party, right?" she asks. I didn't think of that, but make a mental note to ask Liz and Brian to move their cars. I carry Corey's sleeping bag to the house, and she hikes her duffel bag onto her shoulder.

Everyone piles out of the cars when we walk up, and all eyes are on Corey.

"Hey everyone," I say, feeling weirdly nervous. "This is my pen pal Corey. She's visiting from California. Corey, these are my friends -- Colin, Brian, Paula, and Liz."

Corey smiles and nods at each one in turn. Paula grins like a maniac, Brian and Colin seem marginally interested, and Liz surprises me by narrowing her eyes, making a whole point of looking Corey up and down. She's holding a Slurpee that she must have gotten at the 7-Eleven around the corner, and she chews on the straw as she takes Corey in.

"Happy birthday," Corey says when she gets to Liz, which

makes her expression soften a little.

"Thanks," she answers, then turns to me. "You're late. I was afraid you chickened out."

I glance at Corey. We can't be *that* late. She shrugs.

"Sorry," I say to Liz. "We had to go to Gran's house and get our stuff."

"It's just not like you," Liz answers. "You're always on time or early. But," she looks pointedly at Corey, "I guess you're doing all sorts of new things these days."

Even the boys notice that one. Tonight is going to be a disaster, I can already tell.

"Well," I say, turning to walk to the front door and pulling out my key, "we're here now. Let's go set up."

Brian and Liz open their cars and pull out their stuff, then everyone follows me into the house. One of the bags that Brian hauls out of his trunk makes noticeable clinking noises. He drops it on the kitchen floor, ignoring Liz's cry of "Careful!" and unzips it. It's full of bottles of liquor.

"Jesus, Liz, how much money did you give Paula's sister?" I ask. And exactly how many people are they expecting?

"My aunt's birthday check came early," Liz says with a sly smile. "And Paula threw a little in too." Liz has a rich aunt who sends her $100 checks every Christmas and birthday. I've always wished that Uncle Richard would take a page out of her book.

"You gave it *all* to Kathy?" I'm surprised, but Liz shrugs.

"I'm only going to turn seventeen once," she says, a little defensively.

"Sure." I count the bottles as Brian and Liz unload them onto the counter. Twelve bottles, plus a few two-liters of pop. There's the white-labeled Malibu from the slumber party, but the others -- vodka, whiskey, gin, rum -- have plain labels.

Paula opens the fridge and starts stacking the soda inside, pushing Tupperware containers of shriveled veggies to the back.

Liz, meanwhile, pops the plastic dome lid off her Slurpee, reaches for the bottle of rum, and pours some in. I turn to Corey.

"I guess the party is starting," I say. "Do you want a drink?"

"Sure," she says. I pull two glasses from the cabinet, part of the set of commemorative Portland Trail Blazers glasses that we got at Dairy Queen when I was young, and hand one to Corey. She pours a small amount of rum in, then fills it the rest of the way with Coke.

"So, this is the house you grew up in?" she asks, looking around.

"No, not really," I say. "We moved here like three years ago. We moved around a lot when I was younger."

I try to see the house how she might see it. I grab a washcloth from the drawer, wet it, and wipe the dust off the countertop.

Everyone else starts making drinks, and we go to sit in the living room. Liz pulls an Altoid tin from her pocket, removes a joint, and lights it. I notice that Corey just passes it, so I do the same.

"So, who did you invite?" I ask as the room starts to fill with blue-gray smoke.

Paula and Liz exchange glances, then Liz says, "Just a few people from school. And Kathy and her friends, like we were saying."

"And Miya's bringing her little brother," Paula says with a grin.

"How little?" I ask, imagining a kid running around. Liz and Paula seem to think is the funniest thing they've ever heard.

"He's our age," Brian says when it's clear that they're not able to answer. "He goes to North. His name is Jack."

"Yeah, he's old enough," Paula says through her giggles. "We told her to tell him to bring friends, but she said no promises."

"Oh yeah," I say, turning to Corey to explain. "Liz wanted a buffet of guys for her birthday." Corey raises her eyebrows, but just nods.

"And," I say, remembering the present I bought Liz this afternoon, "speaking of your birthday." I get up and grab my backpack, which I dropped by the front door, and pull out the paper Island bag. I hand it to Liz, and she removes the new Weird Al album. It's dorky, but we were both really into him when we were little. The first movie we saw in a theater without our parents was *UHF*. Her eyes soften, and she gives me the first sweet look she's given me all night.

"Ooooh," she says, tearing at the plastic with her stubby fingernails. "Should we put it on?"

"Uh, no offense to your memories or whatever," Paula says, "but I think we can do a little better for party music." She grabs her overnight bag and pulls out a few CDs, then turns on the stereo next to the TV and puts one in. I'm not the 80s hair band expert that she is, but I think it's REO Speedwagon.

A few minutes later, we hear a noise at the door, then the doorbell rings. Liz pops up to answer it, and Kathy steps in, followed by Miya and a teenage boy that I assume is her brother Jack. He's tall and thin, wearing baggy jeans held up with a studded leather belt. His black hair hangs in his face, and he's wearing a Black Flag t-shirt. I glance at Liz, and she winks at me. I feel instantly better. Maybe tonight will be fun after all.

Heather arrives next, trailed by a thin man in jeans and a polo shirt. He looks a little older than her, and I can't help but wonder if he's the same guy she told us about, the one who talked a big game but didn't have any idea what he was doing when it came down to it. I bite my lips to suppress a giggle.

I sit back and let Liz play hostess. It is her party, after all. She shows everyone the drink supplies and open bags of chips in the kitchen. I turn to Corey.

"You okay?" I ask her, and she nods and smiles. She's wearing a pair of forest green cords, worn almost smooth at the knees, and a blue t-shirt with "Bratmobile" written on it in glitter paint. She told me while we were getting ready that she made it herself. She's so cool and creative. I should make a move tonight. It would be a good time, with the party and the alcohol loosening everything up. Or maybe she'll make a move on me. I'm sure less likely things have happened.

"Hey, Hannah," Heather says, leading her date to sit with us in the living room. "This is Ed." He's drinking a bottle of beer from the six-pack that he brought, and Heather has a plastic cup of clear liquid. She's wearing cutoff overalls and a pink tank top, another outfit that I would never wear. The denim hugs her stomach, putting it all out on display. I self-consciously tug at the red ringer t-shirt I'm wearing, smoothing it out over my own stomach.

I introduce Corey and Heather explains, "Ed and I used to work together before I quit that job to go to school. We ran into each other at the grocery store the other day, and were trying to find a time to get together to catch up. Then I asked him if he wanted to come provide alcohol to an underage party, and how could he resist?" Her face breaks into a grin. I chuckle. Ed shrugs and leans back, making himself comfortable.

We chat for a while. Heather tells us what she's working on in school, and Corey seems really interested, more interested than I would expect her to be in beauty school. I finish my drink and get up to make another. I glance at Corey to see if she wants one, but she's hardly touched her first one and just smiles at me. Liz and Jack are standing by the sliding glass door to the backyard, Liz waving one hand around while she explains something. The other hand has a firm grasp on a bottle of beer that matches the one Ed was drinking. Jack laughs at something Liz says, and she leans toward him, touching his shoulder softly, smiling that smile of hers. He's toast.

"Hey, girl," Paula's sister Kathy says, opening the fridge behind me and pulling out a beer for herself.

"Hey."

"How're you doing?" she asks. She glances over at Liz. "How's *that* whole drama?"

I shrug. "I think it's over," I say. And I realize that it's true. I'm sick of waiting for Liz to realize that I'm the one for her, sick of being mad at her for not liking me the way I like her. I feel a sudden warmth toward my best friend, the girl who remembers listening to Weird Al together and still wants to hang out with me, even though she's become effortlessly cool while I stumble along behind.

"How are you?" I ask, but she's focused on a point above my ear.

"Do you ever think about cutting your hair short?"

"What?"

"You always just pull it back. What's the point in having long hair if you don't even do anything fun with it?" Her own orange curls have been twisted into little knots all over her head. It's very Gwen Stefani, and looks cute with the baggy jeans and tight crop top she's wearing.

I remember a Great Clips salon when I was little, my butt sliding on the vinyl salon chair. I said that I wanted my hair shorter once, twice, three times when the stylist turned me around to the mirror. Finally, she turned to my mom.

"I wouldn't want to go any shorter," she said.

"Why not?" Mom asked.

"When they're so . . . round like she is, longer hair is better. Distracts the eye."

I've worn it past my shoulders ever since. But really, it's pretty unlikely that the size of my hair has ever made anyone fail to notice the size of my ass.

"Yeah, maybe I should cut it all off," I say to Kathy, but she's already distracted, looking toward the living room, where Miya is trying to get her attention. I turn back to the counter and focus on making myself a new drink.

More people arrive as the night goes on, and I talk to some of

Liz's track friends, then a girl from my English class, and eventually find my way back to Corey. She's still on the couch, her glass now full of water. She's in a serious-looking conversation with Heather's friend Ed. As I get close, I hear the word "zine," and see her hold her hands out, measuring the dimensions in the air. He nods, interested.

"Hey," I say, sinking onto the couch next to her. She smiles at me, and I feel my insides heat up even more than they already have from the alcohol.

"Ed's a writer," she says. "We were just talking about self-publishing."

"Oh yeah?" He looks so normal, but I guess normal people have things to say too.

Heather comes up behind the couch and leans across the back, running her hands down Ed's chest. He turns his head up and their mouths meet, the back of his head pressed into her cleavage.

I gesture toward Corey's water.

"You don't really drink, huh?" I ask. I can't believe I didn't ask before. She shrugs.

"I don't like to lose control. Especially when I don't know a lot of people." She takes a sip.

"That makes sense," I say, wondering if she wishes I weren't drinking. I'm a little tipsy. "Hey, do you want to see my room? Since we're here and all." I grin. She nods, and I lead her down the hall to my closed door. I should have checked it before anyone arrived, but it's not too bad. Same pictures torn out of *Spin* and *Rolling Stone* hanging on the walls, same laundry on the floor that I didn't wash when I was here before. I quickly kick the dirty clothes under the bed and smooth the comforter out, then sit. She walks around the room, examining the books on my shelf and the CDs on my desk like she did at Gran's house.

"I could probably get rid of a lot of this stuff," I say, starting to feel embarrassed by my dorky things. "I mean, I've been living without it for like six months and haven't missed most of it. That's something one of my grandma's magazines would say -- if you don't use it in six months, get rid of it." I'm rambling. She just smiles, then sits on my bed. I sip from my drink. I suddenly feel very intentional about the fact that we're alone, on my bed. Even though we were alone at Gran's house, there's something about being in this house, with my friends out in the living room, music pumping from the stereo, and no parents in sight.

"I'm so glad you asked me to come visit," she says after a moment of silence. I look into her eyes. They're bluish green, more blue with specks of green radiating out from her pupils. My eyes can't help but flicker down to her mouth, and she licks her lips. My heart is pounding, and I feel like the room has gotten twenty degrees warmer since we came in.

"I'm glad you wanted to come," I answer. She smiles. One of her front teeth is a little crooked, leaning out in front of the one next to it.

My bedroom door bursts open, and I jump to my feet instinctively. It's Paula and Brian, his hand on her lower back, both grinning.

"Oh, shit! I'm sorry! I always forget which door is the bathroom!" Paula says, her words slightly slurred. With the door open, I can tell that more people have arrived. It actually sounds like a party out there.

"Are you okay?" I ask, stepping toward her.

"Yeah!" she says, brushing away the hand I reach toward her shoulder. "We're great babe, don't let us interrupt . . . *whatever* was going on here." She giggles and shoves Brian back out the way they came. They close the door and I turn back to Corey, but she's already standing, reading the text at the bottom of a picture of Kurt and Courtney that's hanging next to my closet.

"Well," I say, feeling awkward, "this is my room. Should we go back out?"

She nods, and we step into the hallway.

41

Corey and I stand to the side of the living room for a little while, and I point out people I know, then we join the small crowd that's started dancing along to the 80s mix that's playing on the stereo. We move to the songs, smiling and singing along, then Corey excuses herself to go to the bathroom. I head back to the kitchen and pour myself another drink, adding more liquor than I have previously. I grimace at the taste, but keep drinking. I need courage. Maybe I'll have another chance with Corey. We are both spending the night, after all.

I feel a breeze and glance toward it. Someone left the sliding glass door open, and the cool air feels delicious compared to the stuffy kitchen that stinks like beer and bodies. I push the door open wider and step out, shutting it behind me and flopping down on the bench on the tiny concrete square that Mom insists on calling a patio. I see movement on the edge of the lawn, and realize it's Liz.

"Hey," I call. She turns, and the light from the kitchen catches her smile. God, she's gorgeous.

"Hey, Han," she says, coming to sit next to me. She wraps an arm around my shoulders and I lean into her.

"We're good, right?" I ask, and I feel her nod.

"I want us to be."

"Me too."

"I'm sorry I freaked out when you came out or whatever."

"Or whatever," I giggle. Maybe I'm drunker than I realize. She continues talking.

"It's not like I'm some homophobe. You know that, right? It just hurt that you didn't want to talk to me about it. Especially since you'd talked about it to Paula."

I straighten up and turn to face her.

"I know. I'm sorry I didn't tell you. I just didn't want things to be weird between us."

She laughs. "Why would things be weird?"

I shake my head. "I didn't know how you'd react. Thanks for being cool."

She nods and looks out across the lawn. I feel unusually controlled by gravity, like I have to work hard to lift my arms. My feet are glued to the concrete.

"How's Jack?" I ask after a moment. She groans, and I laugh. "That bad?"

"He's okay," she says, "but after feeling like I did with Joel, I want more."

I nod. "Yeah, I know what you mean." She looks interested, so I continue. "I mean, I've had crushes before, but the way I feel when I'm with Corey, it's so much more *real*."

"Who did you ever have crushes on? You've been so secretive lately."

I shrug and look at my lap.

"Come on, Hannah! Tell me something so I don't feel like you've been pretending about everything the whole time we've been friends!"

"Don't be so dramatic! I just haven't talked about who I'm into. Everything else has been totally real." I look at her face.

"So who are you into?" She stares back, almost challenging me. Does she know? Is she trying to get me to say it?

"Erin Everett in sixth grade," I say. Erin wore overalls with the knees perpetually grass-stained or torn, hair always in a ponytail, and got picked first for sports. Her family moved away before we started middle school.

Liz squints and says, "I guess I remember her?" She leans toward me. "No one else since elementary school? Or not until you met this girl, or what?"

Our faces are close, and I look at the curve at the end of her nose, the chicken pox scar above her eyebrow, her eyes red but still endless brown fading into her pupils, eyes that I could stare at forever.

"You," I exhale. "Other than that, it was always just you."

I glance down at her lips, chapped and thin. One day when we were standing next to each other at the mirror in the school bathroom, she stuck out her lips and said, "God, Hannah, your lips are like, full. You should give at least 50% of them to me." I would have if I could.

And then I can't see her mouth anymore because it's coming toward mine, searching for mine. I kiss her back, and she opens her mouth. Her tongue presses through my lips and I open my mouth to her. She tastes like smoke and liquor. I reach for her shoulder and she leans into me, kissing me hard. Every cell in my body comes to attention, my heart thumping.

And then I hear the whoosh of the sliding glass door opening, and the voice of Josh fucking Cramer. He sounds positively gleeful as he calls back into the house.

"Holy shit you guys, Liz and Hannah are totally lezzing out back here!"

I pull back from Liz, who puts her hand to her mouth, her eyes wide. Her back is to the people that are squeezing to look out the door, so I see Corey first. She's watching us, her lips pressed together. She looks surprised and maybe a little sad. She turns and starts pushing her way out of the kitchen. I shove myself up and through the crowd to follow her. I hear Josh calling after me, "Hannah, don't go! It was just getting good!"

I'm so stupid. I imagine Corey standing there, watching me grasp onto Liz like I was drowning and she was a goddamn life preserver.

Corey is thinner than me, so she slides through the crowd easier. I don't know who invited all these people or why they won't get the hell out of my way. By the time I get out the front door, she's already at the corner. She turns and I follow, heading for the tan Mercedes parked halfway down the block.

And then, everything gets worse. Running makes the liquor slosh around angrily in my otherwise-empty stomach, and I feel a thickness under my tongue that means my body does not want this alcohol inside of it anymore. I manage to shove my ponytail behind one shoulder before I bend and vomit into the neighbor's lawn. The contents of my stomach come out easily, but that doesn't mean that I don't make a ton of gross gagging noises.

I straighten up and spit, then swipe at the tears that automatically start streaming any time I puke. I look first at the house in front of me, to assure myself that no lights have turned on, then toward Corey's car. She's standing about halfway between me and the car, in the middle of the street, arms crossed in front of her.

"Are you okay?" she asks. She sounds tired. I cover my face with my hands and begin to sob. She takes a step toward me, but I move toward her instead, to get farther from the scene of my most recent humiliation.

"I'm so sorry," I wheeze. She puts a hand on my shoulder.

"It's okay."

I want to fall into her arms, but I feel super gross and just lean a little into the hand she has on my shoulder instead.

"Do you feel better?" she asks, and I nod like a kid. She walks to her car, and I follow her and lean against the side. The coldness of the metal seeps through my clothes. I'm not even wearing a jacket, and I'm kind of sweaty from the alcohol and the run and puking in the street, and oh my God, kissing Liz. I look over at Corey. She's staring straight ahead, and I see a tear trickle out from under the frame of her glasses.

"How do *you* feel?" I ask.

She exhales and shakes her head.

"Pretty stupid."

"You didn't do anything wrong."

"I thought you were into me," she says.

"I was. I am."

"So you invited me to come visit to watch you make out with someone else?"

"That was stupid. I'm the stupid one, not you. I'm so sorry."

She shoves herself up off the car and takes a ragged breath. "I think I need to go and take some time to think about things."

"Go? Go where?" I say. I don't want her to leave. I need to convince her that I know I was wrong, that I can do better.

"Anywhere but here," she says, unlocking her door. "I'll talk to you tomorrow, okay?"

"You can't *leave*," I say. Where is she going to go in the middle of the night?

"Watch me."

She sounds pissed. I step away from the car and let her drive off. We could have spent the whole night alone in my room, whispering secrets to each other, cuddling and kissing under blankets. If only I weren't such a screw up.

My body heaves with sobs as I watch her car disappear around the corner. I cover my face with my hands and stand there, letting the horrible feelings wash over me. I can't bear the thought of facing Liz or any of the other people at my house right now, so I walk in the opposite direction. With every step, I berate myself more. Stupid. Careless. Bitch. I flash to what Paula told me in class, about how I should talk to myself nicely and try to convince my brain to help me. But surely, Paula's music teacher wasn't thinking about assholes like me. People like me deserve to feel bad.

I end up at the 7-Eleven. I wish I could buy a drink to rinse the taste of puke from my mouth, but I don't have any money with me. I stand on the edge of the parking lot, debating whether I want to try to shoplift and end my night with a trip to the police station. I decide to just keep walking. Finally, I realize that I have nowhere else to go but back to the house. By the time I turn onto my street,

I'm crying again and my nose is running from the cold. What am I going to say to Liz? Of all people to see us, why did it have to be stupid Josh Cramer? Who even invited his annoying ass? Maybe I can barricade myself in my mom's room, since it's the only one with a lock, until everyone leaves.

But something is off about the house when it comes into view. When I ran out the door, cars lined the street, but now I only see Liz's Subaru and Brian's Camry in the driveway. I forgot to tell them to move their cars. The street is empty and the house is quiet. I glance at the house number to reassure myself that this is, in fact, my house, and turn the front knob. It's locked. I dig my key out of my pocket and let myself in.

The living room is dark, but I hear the sliding glass door unlatch and open in the kitchen.

"Hey! Who's there?" I call, running toward the sound.

"Hannah?" I hear, and I round the corner to find Colin, already halfway across the concrete patio.

"What happened?" I ask. "Where is everyone?" I step out the back door after him. He looks like he still wants to take off. He glances through the door behind me, I guess to reassure himself that I'm alone.

"Your mom showed up."

The words hit me like a punch, and I collapse onto the bench. It doesn't escape me that I've come full circle, back to the place where Liz kissed me. I let the words repeat in my head for just a second. Liz *kissed* me. Colin sits carefully next to me, perched on the edge of the bench so he can run at a moment's notice.

"Where is she now?" I ask.

"Driving everyone home."

"Everyone?"

"Liz and Paula and Brian."

"Our everyone."

He nods, and I sigh.

"Why are you still here?"

"I uh, hid? In your bedroom closet."

I laugh in spite of myself.

"I was going to clean up a little and see if you came home, but then I heard the front door and just bolted again."

He shakes his head and laughs too, which makes me laugh harder. We crack up for a moment, but then my laughter turns into a kind of sobbing. Colin stops laughing and stretches his arm tentatively around my shoulders. When I turn against him and bury my face in his jacket, he tightens his grip.

"What a fucking mess," I groan into his shoulder. It smells like smoke and dirt and is weirdly comforting.

"Yeah, your mom was pretty mad," he agrees, like that's the worst of my problems.

"How did she know we were here?" I pull away from him. He shrugs.

"I don't know, she was just like, 'Who are you?' and everyone scattered. I was in the hall, so I ran into the closet, but your mom saw Liz and was demanding to know where you were, and Liz didn't know."

"I am so dead," I say. I honestly have no idea what my mom is going to do. I never break any rules, so I can't remember ever actually getting punished and don't have a point of reference.

We gather a few cups and bottles from the backyard, then I tell Colin to go home. He doesn't argue, just lets himself out the gate.

42

I'm wiping the sticky counters with a sponge when I hear a key in the front lock. Several of the bottles still had liquor in them, but I upended them all in the sink. The smell still lingers, threatening to make me puke again. When the door opens, I toss the sponge into the sink and turn to face the music.

"Hey," I say. Mom is wearing her flannel nightshirt half-tucked into a pair of jeans. Her hair is a mess. When her eyes meet mine, I take an involuntary step back. I've never seen her look so pissed, and certainly never seen a look like that turned toward me.

"Where the *hell* were you?"

"I'm so sorry," I begin, but she cuts me off.

"I get a call in the middle of the night from the neighbor, saying they're concerned because there are cars here and music and lights on, and they didn't think we'd moved back yet. I called and no one answered, so I drove over. And do you know what I found?"

I shake my head slowly. I don't really want to know.

"Your buddy Liz was drinking in the living room with a bunch of boys I'd never seen before. Music *blaring*. Paula and her boyfriend were in my bed. *My bed*, Hannah."

My mouth falls open.

"I'm sorry. I didn't know all of that was happening."

She doesn't seem impressed.

"And where were you? No one had any idea where you were. You opened up our home to these . . . these *hooligans*, and took off?"

I cover my face with my hand and the tears start again.

"Corey and I got in a fight. I was walking around."

"In the middle of the night?"

"Obviously," I mutter, and her eyes flash again. Okay, not the time.

"I thought you were more responsible than this."

"Well, we were all going to spend the night. So no one would drive drunk."

She just glares.

"I shouldn't have agreed to let them have the party here," I say.

"I thought we were a team, you know? I thought I could trust you."

"But that's the thing. I want to be a stupid kid sometimes. I don't want to have to be responsible all the time."

"Do you think I want to be responsible all the time?"

"No." I know she doesn't. We're silent for a moment, then I say, "Thank you for driving everyone home."

"I only drove a few of them home. Most of them ran. You're friends with a lot of chickens, do you know that?"

I laugh through a fresh sob. "Most of those people are not my friends."

"But driving around gave me some time," she says, "to think about the right punishment."

"Yeah?" I walk into the living room and drop to sit on the loveseat.

"Well, no phone is probably already clear. And no social life. No friends, no parties, no 'sleepovers.'" She uses finger-quotes as she paces in front of me.

"For how long?"

"At first, I was thinking a month."

"A month!"

She raises her hand. "Then I decided that was too harsh. And I realized that I don't have a way to monitor you while I'm at work, so you could just go wherever you want and do whatever you do when you're out with your friends and don't tell me any specifics. And then I had a better idea."

I swipe at my tears and look at her.

"You can visit your grandma. I'm going to call Leticia in the

194

morning. I'm sure they can use some volunteer help this week."

"That's not nice, to treat Gran like a punishment."

"Then don't think of it as a punishment, and you get off easy."

We stare at each other for a second, then I nod.

"How long?"

"The rest of spring break at least, then we'll see how I feel. I'll pick you up after work, and we can have dinner together."

I realize that she's punishing me not only by making me hang out with Gran, but by making me hang out with her too. I consider pointing that out, but decide not to push my luck.

"Okay," I say. I drop my eyes to the carpet. I screwed everything up. Classic stupid Hannah.

"And one more thing," Mom says, interrupting me from my self-loathing. I look back up at her. "We're moving back home. Tomorrow. Or, should I say, later today? After we get some sleep and you wash my sheets." She wrinkles up her nose, glancing back to her bedroom door.

"I can buy you new sheets. I have babysitting money."

"Don't waste your money. I just wish you could wash the image of those naked teenagers out of my mind."

I almost giggle, imagining poor Paula and Brian getting burst in on by my mom. I guess they didn't realize that the door locks.

"You're going to let Aunt Marion have Gran's house?" I ask to change the subject.

"Marion doesn't *have* anything. It's still in Gran's name. And we're still putting it on the market. I wanted to give you time there while we could, since I know how much you love that house. But I don't exactly feel like putting your needs first right now."

"I wondered why we were staying so long," I say. I didn't know that it was for me.

Mom rubs her face with her hands, then runs them back through her hair. Instead of smoothing it, this makes her bangs stick straight up. She looks around and seems to decide that the house is in an okay state to leave until we come back in the morning.

"Let's go," she says. She sounds more like herself, like most of the anger has drained out. Or been spewed out at me. But I deserve so much more, especially for the way I hurt Corey. Bread and water, solitary confinement. It's all too good for me.

Corey. I see her backpack and sleeping bag still sitting next to the fireplace, and I wonder where she is. Would she start driving home in the middle of the night? Without her bag?

"Corey's stuff is still here," I say, standing. Mom follows my gaze and sighs.

"Where did she go?"

I shrug. "She said she needed time to think about things and that she'd talk to me tomorrow."

"What did you fight about?"

I start to think of a cover story, but I don't really see any point any more. What's another disappointment now?

"I guess we kind of liked each other, but I screwed it up."

She raises her eyebrows. "What do you mean?"

I take a deep breath. "I'm . . . I'm not sure exactly what I am, Mom, but I like girls. I like her. And she liked me, but not after tonight."

"So this whole visit has been so you could have sex with this person?"

I cringe. "No, God, Mom, too much."

She laughs, for the first time tonight. "I'm sorry, *that's* too much?"

I can't manage a laugh. "Nothing happened. And nothing's going to happen, because I'm a stupid jerk."

She reaches out to smooth my hair back. "Oh Han, you're not stupid. You're just young."

My throat gets tight again, and I bury my face in my hands as a fresh wave of tears starts up. She pulls me into a hug, and rubs my back like she did when I was little.

"Are you mad?" I sob.

"I thought we established that."

"No, not because of the party. Because I like girls."

She steps back and holds me at arm's length. "It's a lot of information all at once, and in the middle of the night. We'll have to talk about it more. But first, we need to sleep. Come on, let's go."

43

I hear the doorbell through a thick cloud of sleep, and twist around to look at the alarm clock. Almost ten. My bladder is announcing its fullness as loudly as possible, so I shove myself out of bed and run down the hall to the bathroom. After I pee, I look in the mirror and groan. My face is puffy and red, and my eyelids feel like swollen sheets of sandpaper. As I stand there, the dream that I awoke from rushes back to me. I was in a big glass tank of water, like a mermaid on display at the circus or something. Corey was yelling at me through the side, pounding her fists against the glass, but I couldn't tell what she was saying. I tried to swim closer to her, but felt something grab my hand. I turned to see Liz, and she was pulling me down, deeper into the water, which wasn't a tank after all, but led down to dark purple water and jagged rocks. Unlike in real life, Liz was bigger than me, stronger, and I couldn't get my hand out of hers. She kept dragging me down into the deep. I shake my head and scoop water from the tap into my mouth to rinse the horrible taste out. I can still feel Liz's lips from the night before, the press of her tongue against mine.

I stumble back to my room and flop down on the bed, but the door swings open again after a minute. My mom doesn't knock. I guess I've lost the privilege of deciding who can come in and when.

When she steps inside, I see that she's not alone. Corey follows, eyes on the floor. She's wearing the same outfit as last night, and her hair is messy. I wonder if she slept in the car, or if she slept at all. She looks like she had a rough night.

"Hey," I say.

She gives a tight smile and meets my eyes briefly.

"I just need to get my stuff, then I'm heading home," she says. I look at my mom, not sure exactly what I'm allowed to do. I left

Corey's bags at the other house, since according to Mom, we'd be moving back today anyway. Then I realize that today is Monday.

"Why aren't you at work?" I ask Mom. She's wearing jeans and her gray Willamette University sweatshirt, not work clothes.

"I called in sick," she says. "I had a long night."

Corey and I nod in unison, and Mom smiles a sad little smile. "I guess we all did."

"Definitely," I say. "Can I go to the house with Corey to get her stuff?"

"I'll take her," she says, and Corey looks at her, surprised.

"I have my car," she says. "I can drive myself."

"Well, Hannah is not allowed out with friends right now. You and I can caravan over."

For someone who hasn't given many punishments in her life, she sure seems to have this down.

"I just thought," Mom continues, "I'd give you two the chance to say goodbye. You can start packing while we're gone, Hannah, then you and I will head back over there for the night."

I nod. The fact that she's letting me see Corey at all is probably more than I deserve, and I have to admit that I don't mind not getting stuck in a car with someone who can barely stand to look at me.

"I'll see you downstairs in five, okay?" Mom asks Corey, who nods, then she turns and walks out, leaving the door open.

"Do you want to sit?" I ask Corey. I pluck nervously at my tank top top.

Corey pulls out the desk chair and sits, facing me.

"I told you about that pen pal in San Francisco, right?" she says. "The one I was into who turned out to not be into me?"

"Yeah."

"I'm kind of sensitive about stuff like that, you know? It seemed like this trip was turning into a repeat of that one."

"That's really shitty," I say. "I don't want to make you go through that again."

"Actually," she says with a faint smile, "I still stayed at her house. So this was a little different. At least I could get away. Sometimes, things get overwhelming and I need to be alone to sort them out. Does that make sense?"

I nod. "But at least she didn't make you sleep on the street," I say.

"Yeah, that's true." She's quiet for a moment, then says, "Look, I know I overreacted. But I really thought you liked me. It was so surprising. Especially because you complain a lot about Liz. I wasn't sure if you would even be friends that much longer."

"I'm not sure either, half the time." She seems to expect more, so I go on. "Sometimes I think I get so mad at her partially because she's never liked me like that. Like, I'm always there for her, but she's never there for me the way I want her to be."

She smiles ruefully. "Well, congratulations, because it seems like she does like you."

"She was just drunk," I say, shaking my head. "And I wouldn't have kissed her back if I wasn't drinking. Especially with you there. I spent the whole weekend trying to get the nerve up to make a move on you."

"Me too. Too bad neither of us did."

"That's for sure." We're both quiet for a moment, then I say, "You don't have to leave."

"I kind of think I do. Your mom didn't really make it seem like I'm welcome to stay."

"Well, that doesn't have anything to do with *you*."

"When did she show up at the party?"

I roll my eyes. "While you and I were at your car."

"Really?"

"Maybe not exactly then. I walked around for a while after you drove off. When I got back everyone was gone."

"Shit," she says, and I nod. That is definitely one word for it.

She glances over at the clock, and I can tell she wants to leave.

"I'm sorry last night didn't turn out better," I say.

She nods. "Yeah, me too."

"At least you got out of the bridal shower, though, right?"

She lets out a little laugh. "Yeah, true."

I follow Corey down the stairs, where we find Mom digging through the kitchen cabinets, tossing things into a cardboard box. I look at her quizzically, and she says, "Your aunt is such a picky eater. I'm only taking the things I know she won't use."

I nod, and Mom turns to Corey. "Ready?" She wipes her hands on her jeans and gathers her purse and jacket from the table.

I follow them to the front door, and I'm not sure what Corey is going to do, but she turns and hugs me, hard. I let my body melt against hers, feeling her heat and inhaling her scent, incense and sweat, for possibly the last time ever.

"I'm really sorry," I whisper.

"I know," she says. She steps back, and gives me a small smile.

"Can I call you?" I ask, then look over at my mom, who's standing in the doorway, clearly trying to give us some space. She clears her throat, and I add quickly, "At whatever date my mother determines me to be rehabilitated?"

"How about you write?"

"Sure," I say, hoping that she can't tell how disappointed I am.

"I'll see you later, Hannah," she says. She follows my mom down the front steps. I stay in the doorway, watching them each get in the driver's seat of their own car. I wait until I can't see either car anymore, then step back in and close the door behind me.

44

That afternoon, as promised, Mom and I return home. It takes two trips to haul the stuff we want to take with us, which includes a few boxes of books for me, the box of food and kitchen stuff, and a box or two of mementos. Aunt Marion insisted on checking all the boxes before we carried them out. She almost didn't let me take Grandpa's marbles, but she finally just dug her hand into the bowl and came out with a large blue-and-red swirled marble that she stuck into her jeans pocket. She let me take the rest. I lift the wooden bowl from my box, surprised that it hasn't spilled, and set it on my desk. I run my mom's sheets and blankets through the washing machine twice, then make her bed when they're done. I find a condom wrapper, silver and slippery, under the bed, and shove it in my pocket without saying anything. I sincerely hope it belonged to Paula and Brian, and not to my mom.

"I called Leticia while you were packing," Mom says when I come out. "She said you can come in tomorrow and start volunteering. I'll drop you off on my way to work in the morning, so plan to be ready by seven-fifteen."

I groan, but she gives me a look like, "What do you expect?"

"She said you can wear your regular clothes," she continues, as if I were planning a special outfit for the day.

"Did you tell her why I'm going?"

"I told her you needed something to keep you busy during spring break, and that you want to spend more time with your grandma."

"Thanks." I'm glad I'm not starting my new volunteer job with Leticia thinking I'm a delinquent. "I think I'm going to go to bed early. Maybe I'll do some reading."

"Do you have homework over the break?" she asks. I'm

surprised she hasn't asked me already. I nod.

"Yeah, I'll do it. I don't want to do it too early and forget everything by the time I go back."

"Okay. Sleep well Hannah Banana. I love you."

"I love you too."

45

In the morning, I pack *The Clan of the Cave Bear*, the thickest novel I found at Gran's house, into my bag along with an apple and a peanut butter sandwich. Leticia is already grinning and bouncy when we emerge through the door with the sign that still says "Keypad broken, please use other door." The little frowny face seems like it's looking right at me today. I tell Mom that I can go in by myself, but she insists on walking with me. Maybe she's afraid I'll try to make a break for it. Only after I'm securely in the activity room with Leticia does she head back out to her car.

"Where is everyone?" I ask, looking around the room. I've never been here when it's empty.

"At breakfast. This is my special time to get things ready for the day. This morning is painting."

She leads me over to a wall of locked cabinet doors, pointing at a calendar taped to one. It's printed on bright yellow paper with flowers dancing around the border. Each square has multiple activities listed, and every Tuesday at 8:30 is painting.

"This is the easiest volunteer job you could have chosen, Hannah," she says as she unlocks a cabinet and pulls out bottles of paint and spattered cups with crusty brushes in them. "Many of our residents are used to doing chores at home, so they like to help out. You might even get bored."

"I'm sure I'll be fine."

"And you picked a good day to start," she continues, squeezing paint onto Styrofoam plates.

"Why's that?"

"My brother is coming in this afternoon to play music for the residents."

I glance at the calendar again and sure enough, "4:30 - Sing-along with Ernesto" is printed in today's square.

"What does he play?"

"He plays the guitar. He's a teacher, and he comes over once a week after class to help entertain everyone. He knows all the old-time songs, and the residents just love him."

"Is he a music teacher?"

She shakes her head. "Economics."

"Oh yeah? Where?" East doesn't offer economics classes, but I know it's math, so it sounds interesting.

"At the community college."

"Nice. I might take calculus there next year."

"Your mom told me that you're good at math. You and Ernesto can talk all about numbers when he comes in."

I smile, and take the wad of plastic tablecloth that she pulls out of the cabinet. I spread it out over the nearest table, smoothing out the wrinkles the best I can, then we distribute the plates of paint along the middle of the table.

Gran is one of the first people to come into the room, led by a woman in pale pink scrubs. I try to catch her eye, but she's drawn to the bright blue tablecloth and different colors of paint, just like everyone else. Leticia unlocks a different cabinet and pulls out a handful of fabric smocks and aprons that were hanging on a hook inside.

"The paint is washable," she says to me, "but most of the residents would still rather have an apron. Can you help your grandma get hers on?" I take one, a green smock with pink flowers that will probably be way too big for her tiny body, and walk over to Gran.

"Hi Gran," I say. She looks up as I approach and smiles her nervous smile.

"Hello."

"It's really nice to see you today," I say, stealing her phrase. She doesn't seem to notice.

"It's nice to see you, too."

"Do you want to do some painting?"

She looks over at the table again, thinking.

"Okay."

"Let me help you get this apron on, so you don't get paint on your outfit."

She nods and lets me tie the apron on her. She smooths it at her shoulders, and I notice that her nails are freshly painted. When did Mom have time to do that?

Leticia and I pass out sheets of paper, and I sit with Gran, watching her paint. She spreads blue across the top of the page, then sticks her paintbrush directly into the yellow, leaving a green spot in the puddle of paint.

"Oh, no," she says, looking over to see if I've noticed.

"It's fine," I tell her. "Don't worry about it. There's plenty of paint."

She nods, looking relieved, and paints green across the bottom of the page. I remember what Corey said about how I should try painting to get my feelings out, and stand to get a piece of paper for myself. I think about what I'm feeling, and mix together some blue and red on the edge of a plate. I smear the dark bluish-purple across the page, making a shallow u-shape to replicate the deflated way I've been feeling since Sunday night. I fill the concave with red for all the anger. For how I feel toward myself, how Corey feels toward me, and how I feel toward Liz. Both for kissing me and for the idea of having the party in the first place. I could have said no, but when do I ever say no to Liz? I shake my head.

Gran is watching me paint.

"That's pretty," she says. I smile weakly and say thanks. She reaches her brush tentatively toward the purple that I mixed, and I nod encouragingly and push the plate toward her. The paint is quick to dry, so the purple doesn't mix with the green she's already put down when she copies the shape I made onto her paper.

As promised, the residents all want to help with cleanup. They get distracted easily, though, and I find myself washing brushes and plates while Leticia gathers the aprons and rolls the tablecloth back into a ball that she shoves in the cabinet.

"We don't have anything planned for a while," she says. "Do you want to go on a walk with your grandma? Lunch is at 11:30, so bring her to the dining room around then."

"Sure."

Gran and I set off, and I take her hand like Mom always does. We pass a couch that's stationed in front of a TV playing golf, and Gran veers over to sit.

"Are you getting tired?" I ask, worried that I'm making her do too much.

"I'm fine," she says.

I sit next to her, and the cushion crinkles. All of the upholstered couches and chairs here have plastic coverings between the cushion and the cover, in case someone pees themself. I hope no one has peed where we're sitting, but I know it's likely that someone has.

A naked plastic baby doll lies on the coffee table in front of us. Once, when Mom and I were walking with Gran, we passed one of the women cradling a doll in her arms. Gran grabbed my arm and whispered into my ear, "She thinks that's real!" Now, she reaches out to pick the doll up, stroking its yellow plastic strands of hair and smiling faintly.

"You were born with so much hair," she says. I smile at her. We used to sit like this on the couch at her house when I was little, but I had to crane my neck up to look at her then. I'd lean against her, inhaling the perfume scent of the powder she fluffed on herself every morning. She doesn't smell like that anymore, and now she has to look up to meet my eye.

"What else was I like when I was little?" I ask. I don't really care if she's talking about Mom or Aunt Marion or me.

"You were a very good baby," she says. "I never had any trouble getting you to sleep." I know this was true of myself. My first word was "night," and I used it on repeat when I was ready for bed. "Night, night, night, night," I would chant sleepily.

She reaches up and smooths back my hair. "You've always been such a lovely girl."

When she says it, I almost believe it.

"I'm not so sure about that," I say. Scenes from Sunday night flash through my memory. Corey wiping away her tears in the street. Liz leaning in to kiss me. What is Liz thinking this week? My big, lifelong secret is out in the open now. "You," I'd said to her. "It was always just you." Does she even still want to be my friend?

Before I realize it, I'm crying. I remember Liz's face, surprised and confused when we pulled apart, Josh Cramer's gleeful yell when he found us, the look in Corey's eyes like I'd just stomped on her heart.

"Oh, honey," Gran says, noticing my tears. She reaches up to wrap her arm around me and the plastic doll clatters to the floor. The seat crinkles as I lean into her, trying to slide down to get smaller. I can feel her frail bones, but her ropy muscles are still there, squeezing me in.

"It'll be okay," she murmurs as she strokes my hair. "It's all going to be fine. Wait and you'll see."

46

I eat my lunch with Gran, then Leticia asks me to sit at the front desk for a while. I've never actually seen someone sitting there, and there's a doorbell that visitors can ring if they don't know the code to get in. But Leticia says they have several families on the schedule this afternoon to come by for tours, and since I'm here, it would be helpful for someone to greet them.

"Plus," she says, "we have another volunteer who comes in the afternoons."

"Yeah?" I imagine another screw up like me.

"Well, we *tell* her she's a volunteer. She's actually someone who's making a slow transition to living here. She was resistant to moving to a care facility, so her family told her that they found a volunteer job for her. She comes in and spends time with the other residents and does the activities with them."

"Oh." Is anyone here really doing what they say they are?

Leticia shows me the front desk and gives me a sticky note with the afternoon appointments and the phone extension of the person I'm supposed to call when they get here. I reach up to redo my ponytail and try to smooth it out a little. I hope no one judges Silver Wells based on me and my balloon hoodie and ratty jeans.

"You'll be fine." Leticia smiles warmly when she sees my nervousness. She pats me on the shoulder and lets herself back through the locked door.

The first two appointments are no-shows, but the last two show up. I dial the extension that Leticia gave me and a woman pops out of a door that must lead to the administrative offices, all smiles, to give the families their tours. Other than that, I spend the afternoon reading in peace. The book is about cave people, and it reminds me of Corey's zine and how we're all just animals but think we're so much better and smarter. If I were alive during caveman times, would I care about any of the things that seem so important to me now?

When the front door opens late in the afternoon, I look up, thinking there's another appointment that's not on my list. But instead, I see a short, muscular Latino man walk in holding a guitar case.

"You must be Hannah," he says with a grin. "I am Ernesto." He holds out his hand, and I shake it.

"You've heard about me?" I ask.

"Leticia told me that Sharon's granddaughter would be helping out this week. It must be so nice to get this extra time with your grandma."

"It is." I feel suddenly guilty for lying about the real reason I'm here. Leticia and Ernesto think I'm just a nice granddaughter and don't know it's a punishment.

We both look up at the sound of the door opening again, and I'm surprised to see my mom walk in. I didn't think she was off work yet.

"Hey," I say. "Is it time to go already?"

"No, I thought I'd come by and join the sing-along with you and Gran." She's answering me, but she's looking at Ernesto, who's gazing up at her. I feel suddenly invisible.

"The residents and I all appreciate your enthusiasm for the music, Georgia," Ernesto says to her. She positively beams.

"Okaaaay," I say, standing and dropping my book into my bag. The three of us go inside, and find Leticia turning the chairs in the activity room so they all face one end, which is where Ernesto heads with his guitar.

Leticia and my mom hug, and Mom greets a few of the residents by name. A woman wearing a handmade name tag that identifies her as Mrs. Boardman helps Leticia arrange the chairs. The fake volunteer.

"Do I get a name tag?" I ask, and Leticia turns to look at Mrs. Boardman.

"Oh! I didn't even think to make you one! I'm sorry, Hannah, I'll have one for you tomorrow."

She and my mom share a smile, and my mom leans over to whisper that Leticia only made that name tag for Mrs. Boardman to help sell the volunteer story. My face heats up and I feel silly for asking.

Mom goes to find Gran and steers her over to sit with us. Ernesto plays and sings for a half hour, old songs like Leticia promised, and some residents clap and sing along. Some just sway, and some don't seem to know where they are or what's going on. Mom sings along, and puts her arms around me and Gran at one point, pulling us to sway side to side with her. Ernesto ends with "Hound Dog," standing from his stool to swivel his hips back and forth like Elvis as he plays, and the crowd goes wild. If you can call a dozen or so Alzheimer's patients laughing and clapping out-of-time "going wild."

Mom grins over at me.

"This is fun, isn't it?" she asks, and I have to nod. I don't want to admit it to her, but I'm kind of glad she made me come. I look around her and see Gran, clapping and smiling at Ernesto with her teeth showing, and I feel a surge of love in my chest. I wish I could fold this moment up and take it with me when we leave.

47

Mom and I fall into an easy routine of riding together to Silver Wells each morning. I help Gran put together puzzles or fold socks or make craft projects until lunch, then I sit at the front desk and read until Mom comes to get me after work. She doesn't come as early as she did on Tuesday any other day, but she does always go inside to say hello to Leticia and Mrs. Boardman and sit with Gran for a little while. As promised, Leticia greets me on Wednesday morning with a name tag like Mrs. Boardman's, my name spelled out in round blue letters.

On Friday afternoon, I'm at the front desk settling into *The Valley of the Horses*, the next book in the cave people series, when I hear a tap at the front window. I look up, surprised to see Aunt Marion standing on the sidewalk. She motions for me to come outside, and I do, leaving my book face-down on the desk.

"I'm busting you out early!" she says when I step through the door.

I turn to look back through the glass, confused.

"But I'm supposed to stay until Mom comes to get me."

"She asked me to pick you up today. She has plans after work tonight."

"Plans?" My mom never has plans.

"Plans!"

"But won't Leticia tell her if I leave early? I don't want to get in more trouble than I already am."

Aunt Marion rolls her eyes. "You dress like you don't care about what people think, but you're such a good girl inside." She says it like it's an insult. "The trick is to look like everyone else, and then just do whatever the hell you want. Then, no one expects it."

"Okay, fine," I say, not really believing that my aunt is peer pressuring me. "But I have to get my stuff and say goodbye at least."

"Great, I'll go start the car."

"You should come in with me." She still hasn't visited Gran. Now that she's come this far, she can at least come in and say hello. But she shakes her head.

"No way. I can't go in there." She looks through the glass door, and I think I see fear in her face.

"It's not that scary," I say, then correct myself. "I mean, it's not scary at all."

She wraps her arms around herself and bites her lower lip.

"I don't want to see my mom like that."

"But don't you think she deserves to see you?"

"She won't know who I am." Her voice is getting thick, and I realize she's about to cry.

"Sometimes she knows. Or at least she knows that someone important is visiting. And even if she doesn't, she's still a nice lady. If you love her, you shouldn't want her to be alone."

"I told Georgia that I wouldn't pick you up if I had to go in, and she said you were at the front desk in the afternoons and I could just wave to you through the door."

It's my turn to roll my eyes at her. "Don't be such a baby, Aunt Marion. You're supposed to be the adult here."

That gets to her, and she gives me a defiant look.

"We don't have to stay long," I say. "But I need to tell Leticia I'm leaving, and it's stupid for you to stand out here when your mom is right inside."

"She's not my mom anymore."

I sigh and cross my arms. She looks away, swiping at her eyes.

"We can't stay long," she says finally. "We have plans."

"We have plans too?" Everyone has plans all of a sudden.

"It's a special surprise." Her voice is quiet.

"Well, great. That will be your reward for getting through this."

She takes a deep breath, then nods. I push the door open for her, and she steps inside. I grab my stuff from the desk, then lead her over to the locked door.

"The door code is 6041," I tell her, repeating the phrase I've heard Leticia say over and over. "Same as the street address."

I type in the numbers, then turn to her. She looks like a little kid, small and scared.

"The first time is the hardest." I'm not totally sure if that's true, but it sounds right.

We step through the door, and I feel her hand squirm its way into mine. I squeeze it and lead her into the activity room.

Friday afternoon is cookie time, so there are cookie sheets and tubes of dough on the counter, and Leticia is bending over one of the tables, helping a resident scoop out some dough. Gran is sitting at a different table, and we head that way.

"Hi Gran, look who came to see you today," I say. I pull my aunt forward, and Gran smiles her polite smile, teeth hidden away.

"Hello," she says. "It's nice to see you."

I gesture for Aunt Marion to sit, and she balances on the edge of the chair. She already has tears slipping down her cheeks, and I reach across the table for one of the boxes of tissues that are all over this place. I hand it to her, and she uses one to wipe her face. I hope she doesn't upset Gran.

"Hi, Mom," Marion says through her tears.

"Aunt Marion came to pick me up today," I tell Gran. "Wasn't that nice of her?"

She nods. "You're a very nice lady," she tells Marion. This just makes her cry harder, and Gran looks at me, alarmed.

"Marion's having a hard day," I tell her. "Remember when I had a hard day earlier this week?" I doubt that she does, but she nods.

"You girls always were so sensitive," she says.

"Totally," I agree, then I continue. "I remember once, you told me that it's good to be a little sensitive, and I shouldn't let the world take that out of me."

Aunt Marion gives a short laugh through her tears. "I remember that. It was that Christmas when Richard's kids were teasing you so bad."

I reach over and put a hand on Gran's, sitting on the table.

"You always gave the best advice."

"Oh, no." She waves me away, but I can tell that she's pleased. "I'm nothing special."

I shake my head, feeling tears coming into my own eyes.

"No, Gran, never say that. You're very special to us."

Aunt Marion pushes the tissue box back at me and nods.

"You're the most special person we know," she agrees.

Leticia comes over a few minutes later and I introduce Aunt Marion to her. She grins, thrilled as usual to meet another member of the family. She doesn't seem surprised when I tell her that Aunt Marion is here because Mom has plans tonight, and she doesn't have a problem with me leaving early. She takes my name tag to store in one of the cabinets, and rubs my shoulder as Aunt Marion and I stand to leave.

"You're such a good girl, Hannah," she says. "We'll see you next time."

I nod, and realize that Mom and I haven't talked about how much longer my punishment will last, or whether I'll come in on the weekend or once I go back to school. I look around. I'll kind of miss coming here every day.

"I'll see you again soon," I say.

48

Aunt Marion sits for a moment behind the steering wheel
before she starts the car. I pull out the handful of tissues that I
stuffed in my hoodie pocket before we left and hand them to her.
She separates one from the wad and blows her nose loudly.

"I really miss my mom," she says.

I nod. "I know. I miss her too."

She takes a deep breath, then gives her eyes a swipe and starts
the car. We pull out onto the street, and I finally think to ask, "So,
what's this big secret plan you have?"

She reaches into the purse that sits between our seats, digging
around with one hand while she steers with the other. I'm surprised
that I recognize the business card that she pulls out. It's a little more
crumpled, but the pink card with gold script is pretty distinctive.

"I found this in the living room, and I called and made us
appointments."

My hand goes to my hair.

"Are you trying to tell me something?" I ask, and she laughs.

"I figured we could both use a little updating." She reaches over
and pulls at a strand of my messy hair.

"Ow," I protest, even though it doesn't really hurt. She laughs
again.

"Talk about *sensitive*," she says, and I can't help but laugh with
her.

My appointment is with Heather, and Aunt Marion is with
another woman. I see Miya in the middle of giving a haircut near
the reception desk, and she pauses to wave at me. She has cute new
super-short bangs cut into her straight black hair, and for a second
I think I should do the same. But then I see Heather's short blonde
curls and go back to my original plan.

"Cut it all off," I tell her once I'm settled into the seat.

She meets my eye in the mirror and grins.

"You sure?"

I nod, and she grabs her scissors.

"So, Kathy said that party got busted?" she says as she sprays my hair with water and starts combing out the tangles.

I groan. I don't remember seeing Heather when I was running out the door after Corey, but I have no idea when she left.

"Yeah, it was a whole thing."

She nods encouragingly at me, and I tell her the story. Corey, Liz, my week at Silver Wells. While I talk, I watch in the mirror as long strands of hair fall to the floor.

"Well, your mom must not be too mad if she brought you to get all cute." She nods over to where Aunt Marion sits, getting chunks of her hair wrapped in foil.

I shake my head, which already feels lighter.

"Oh, no, that's my aunt. She thinks I'm a goody-goody, so she was proud of me for finally getting in trouble."

Heather laughs loud enough that Aunt Marion looks over at us, and I shrug at her in the mirror. She winks back.

Heather spins me to look at myself in the mirror. My hair is right below my chin.

"Keep going?" she asks, and I nod. "That's my girl!"

I try to explain a style I've seen in magazines, and she nods thoughtfully, then goes back to snipping away.

"Without all this length weighing your hair down," she says, "it's going to curl up a lot better. And I have some serum that will help with that."

"Okay."

"I really think you're going to like having short hair. It's so much easier."

"I always kind of thought fat girls shouldn't have short hair."

She rolls her eyes at me in the mirror.

"Fat girls aren't supposed to do anything fun. Can't wear stripes, can't have short hair, can't eat in public, can't live our lives in peace. When I was fourteen, my mom told me I shouldn't wear pink, because it would make people think of pigs."

"Whoa, that's so rude."

"So of course, the next day, I went out and bought a bunch of pink clothes."

I laugh. She's wearing a pair of skintight jeans today, with a black-and-white striped t-shirt. I'm wearing my usual baggy jeans and t-shirt, but I decide that next time I go shopping, I should look for some clothes that fit a little tighter. That fit a little *better*, I amend.

"Where do you get your clothes?" I ask her.

She tilts her head. "Oh, here and there. Sometimes Lane Bryant if I can afford it. I'm learning to sew and alter things, or like, sew two skirts together to make a skirt my size. How about you?"

"Mostly thrift stores, but I have to go to the mall for jeans."

"We should go shopping together sometime."

"Yeah!" I hope I don't sound too eager, but she smiles warmly at me in the mirror.

"I'll give you my number. Just let me know when you want to go," she says.

She cuts for a while longer, then trades the scissors for a hair dryer and blows my hair dry. She opens a drawer and pulls out electric clippers.

"You ready?"

I nod, and the clippers buzz to life. When she turns me back around to look at the mirror, the left side of my head is clipped close, and the rest of my hair is just long enough to tuck behind my ears. Heather flips the longer part over so it covers the stubble, then pushes it back to the right to expose it. She runs her fingers through my new, short waves.

"What do you think?"

I can't help grinning. It looks really cool, like I could be in *Spin* or something. Or on the cover of my own zine, even.

"Fun, huh?" she says, and I nod. She leaves me alone to find the curl serum, and I look around the room. Aunt Marion is in the back, getting her hair rinsed, but Miya has finished her haircut and I see her approaching.

"Wow, Hannah, you really went for it!" she says with a smile. I reach up to touch my hair, nervous about what that means, but she continues, "It looks great!"

"Thanks," I say. "I like your bangs a lot."

She reaches up to smooth them, then thanks me.

Heather returns, a small bottle in her hands. She squeezes a few drops out, rubs her hands together, then digs her fingers into my hair. She spreads the substance through, then scrunches up handfuls to make it curl. I smile at my reflection, and I'm actually pleased with the face that smiles back. Not bad.

49

Aunt Marion buys me the bottle of curl serum and drives us through the Taco Bell drive-thru on the way home. Mom isn't home when she pulls into the driveway, but she agrees to let me go in alone once I promise not to make any phone calls or do anything else I'm not supposed to do.

"Your mom is going to be mad enough at me already," she says, fluffing her newly-highlighted curls in the rearview mirror.

"Join the club."

"Oh, I've been in the club for years. I'm pretty sure I was a founding member."

"Thanks for today," I say, and reach across the emergency brake to give her an awkward hug. Her arms come up to squeeze me close, then we let go and I climb out of the car. She waits in the driveway until I unlock the door, then waves and drives off.

I've been thinking all day about writing a letter to Corey. I don't know if enough time has passed, but it's been a week and I want to sort out my feelings. If the letter turns into too much of a mess, I don't have to send it.

Dear Corey,

I'm writing to tell you again that I'm sorry. I think you know this, but I've never dated anyone, and before Sunday, I'd never kissed anyone. The first time I realized that I might not be straight was when I developed a big crush on my friend Liz. At first, I didn't tell you because I thought it made me seem desperate, and then as we got to know each other, I realized that I had a crush on you too. I'm sorry that you came to visit without knowing everything. And I honestly never thought there was a chance that Liz was interested.

I've always thought of myself as kind of . . . not exactly unloveable, but definitely uncrushable. Do you remember that girl Heather from the party? Well, she made me realize that being fat doesn't automatically mean that a person isn't desirable. She just, like, exudes sexuality. I've been thinking lately that maybe the fat isn't the issue, maybe it's my own belief that no one would like me.

I have this bowl of marbles that used to belong to my grandpa, and I've been thinking about them a lot lately. Remember when we talked about how messy science can be when it involves living creatures? Sometimes I think we're all like loose marbles on a table, running around and bumping and sending each other off in all sorts of directions. Sometimes we hit each other hard and chip the other marbles, or just send them careening off in a direction they didn't see coming. I never thought of myself having an effect on any of the other marbles, though. I always thought I was just sitting on the edge watching, not out there bumping things on my own. I kissed Liz back without even thinking about it mattering to anyone. Who could care enough about me to be bothered?

I've been volunteering at the place where my grandma lives, and we made paintings the other day. I tried to put my feelings on the page like we talked about, but I don't know if it really worked. It's like I have too many feelings inside to get them all out at once.

I really hope that your drive home wasn't too awful, and that your mom isn't mad at you for missing the bridal shower. I hope we can be friends again. I think you're a really cool, thoughtful, interesting person, and I feel lucky that you let me into your life. I hope I haven't screwed things up too bad to get let back in.

We've moved out of my grandma's house, so I'll put the new address and phone number at the bottom of the letter. Call or write anytime, okay?

Hannah

I re-read the letter, then fold it up and put it in an envelope, addressing the front from memory. I feel raw and delicate, like I told secret inner things I've only thought about before. In elementary school, we did this art project once where we dipped string in sugar water, then wrapped it around a balloon, and once the string dried, we popped the balloons and were left with these round cages. They looked pretty solid, but you could poke them and move them out of shape. I feel like my ribcage is made out of the same substance. Just sugar and string, and that's supposed to protect my heart?

50

In the morning, I wake up to the smell of pancakes. I climb out of bed, and find Mom in the kitchen, smiling to herself as she slides a full plate into the oven to stay warm.

"I was wondering when you were going to get up," she says, turning at the sound of my footsteps. When she sees me, she stops short. "What did you do to your hair?"

My hand goes up to my head, and I feel hair sticking up in every direction. I took a shower before bed and fell asleep with it wet.

"Aunt Marion took me," I say, then immediately regret tattling. Mom sighs.

"I should have known I couldn't count on her to just bring you home like I asked."

"She went in and visited Gran too."

She looks into my face, searching like I have a secret.

"She did?"

I nod, and shuffle over to the table and sit. Mom turns to pull the warm plate out of the oven and brings it over to the table. She goes back to the stove and pours another circle of batter into the pan.

"How did you get her to go in?" she asks, turning to look at me.

"I think she felt silly because I was okay going in there, and I'm just a kid."

"You are much more than just a kid."

"A demon kid," I joke, but she frowns at me.

"You're a wonderful young lady, Hannah. I'm really proud of you for helping her go see her mom."

I roll my eyes. "Does that mean I'm done with my punishment?"

"Leticia did say you've been a big help."

"I can keep going," I say. "After school a few days a week maybe. But can I have my phone privileges back? It's been kind of a long week without any friends. If I even still have any."

She slides the last pancake onto a new plate and hands it to me, getting another out of the cabinet for herself. I squeeze syrup onto my pancake and cut off a bite while Mom joins me at the table and takes some pancakes from the stack for herself.

"I need to be able to trust you again," she says.

"You can. I don't think I have any secrets left."

She reaches over and smooths my hair down, then says, "Then maybe I should tell you one. I was on a date last night."

"With Ernesto?"

"How did you know?" She looks surprised.

"Uh, Mom, it was kind of obvious from how you were staring at him at sing-along day."

She blushes, and I stand, holding a fake guitar and swinging my hips like he did during his grand finale.

"You ain't nothing but a hound dog," I sing, and her blush deepens.

"How long has this been going on?" I ask, wondering for a second if maybe that condom wrapper I found was hers after all. I suppress a shudder.

"That was our first date."

Thank God.

"He seems nice," I say. "Kind of short, though, isn't he?"

Mom shakes her head. "You're always lecturing me on how fashion magazines give unrealistic expectations of beauty, and you're going to dismiss someone for being short?"

I take a minute for that to sink in, then admit, "Good point."

She looks pleased with herself.

We eat in silence for a few minutes, then she says, "You seem like you're feeling a little less upset than you were last weekend."

"Yeah, I'm okay."

"Do you think things are going to turn out okay with your friend Corey?"

"Maybe eventually," I say. "I don't really know how to handle someone liking me. It feels so surprising that someone cool would even want to spend time with me."

"You've always had a lot of friends."

"Yeah, I guess sometimes I'm not sure if people really want to be around me, or if I'm just someone to hang out with so they're not alone. I mean, my own father didn't even want to be around me."

"What do you mean by that?"

"Well, it's supposed to be his job to stick around, right? And he couldn't do that. I wasn't good enough."

"Oh, Hannah, that wasn't because of you." She stands and walks over to the roll-top desk in the living room. She rummages around in the bottom drawer, and finally pulls out a thin envelope. I bite my lip, holding back my argument.

"I was never sure when I should give this to you." She hands the envelope to me. It's addressed to her in scratchy ballpoint pen, and my dad's name is in the upper left corner, with an address in New Mexico. I open the envelope and pull out a short note written on a piece of faded notebook paper. It's dated November 7, 1985. I was five, and it was four years after he'd left.

Dear Georgia,

I'm sending a check. I'll send more when I can, but I hope this helps a little. I've been working at a garage in Albuquerque for the past month. It's a steady job, and it feels right to do something with my hands. I might finally be getting on my feet. It's good being in a new town, starting over with new people. And the sun is great, I don't miss the Oregon weather at all. I never realized how much the weather affects my moods. I've been a lot happier here, and I'm sorry that you knew me when I was in such a dark place.

Tell Hannah that I love her. I know that she's better off with you. You were always so good with kids and bills and making decisions. Much better than I ever was. The two of you will have a great time together. I miss her and think about her every day, but I know this is for the best. Most people are better off without me around. I cause trouble, and you need less of that in your life.

Take good care,

Will

I don't realize I'm crying until a tear falls on his name, wrinkling up the paper and making the letters swell.

"He thought I was better off without him?" I look up at my mom, who's biting her lip like she might start crying too.

"That's what depressed people think," she says. "He thought he wasn't good enough to be your dad. It really didn't have anything to do with you."

That seems like it should make me feel sad, like I should want it to be about me, but it just makes me feel bad for him. I've never really thought about my dad having his own needs and feelings, being a person on his own. He was always just my father, someone who was supposed to be there for me but wasn't. This mythical creature that other girls have and I never did.

I understand feeling like people would be better off without me around. I've thought it plenty of times. Not like I think about killing myself, but I've definitely felt like my friends' lives would be easier if they didn't have to deal with me. And I've never thought about whether they would miss me; I assumed that they would feel relieved. I wonder if he thought I would feel relieved to be rid of him.

"Sometimes you remind me of him," she says. I look up at her again. "You get so upset about things and I don't know what to say.

I never knew what to say to him, either."

"I don't know if there's anything to say."

"I think some people feel things more than others."

"What do you mean?"

She gazes into space for a moment, then says, "Things would happen when we were together that would affect your dad so much more than me. You're the same. You get it from him."

"I always thought I got everything from you. Like how no one can tell us apart on the phone."

"No one gets everything from one parent. Aren't they teaching you anything in that genetics class?" She chuckles at her joke. "You get your beautiful phone voice from me, and your tender heart from your dad."

"I wonder what I get from Gran."

"Her sweetness. You think about other people like she always did."

"That's nice of you," I say. I look down at the letter, still in my hands, a little soggier now than when we started. "Can I keep this?"

"Of course. I'm sorry I didn't give it to you earlier. I didn't know you were so bothered by all of this. I should have known." She shakes her head.

"It's okay. I know I don't always talk about things."

"Well you can talk to me. And please know that I won't ever leave you, no matter what. You're stuck with me for life"

My eyes fill up again, and I blink to clear them. "Even if I like girls?"

"Even if you like girls," she agrees. "It's going to take me a while to get used to it, but I'm trying. Just be patient with me, okay?"

"Okay."

"Now let's eat before everything gets cold," she says, gesturing to the plate of pancakes between us. I pick my fork up and dig in, realizing suddenly that I'm starving.

51

I'm out of practice riding my bike after my week of getting driven around, and I get to school late on Monday. I can tell Liz has already been to the locker. I'm not looking forward to seeing her, but we need to talk. If she tried calling during spring break, Mom didn't tell me.

I go through the motions of all my morning classes. A few people tell me that they like my new haircut, and I get the distinct impression that Liz's track friends are more interested in me than usual. Some of them probably saw us kissing, but I can't remember and honestly don't care.

When I leave Spanish, I'm surprised to see Philip waiting outside the door.

"Do you have a second?"

"Sure." I follow him to the same empty hallway as before.

"Joey and Spencer are protesting outside the school district office this week." He's speaking quietly again, and I have to lean down to hear him. "They're going there on Thursday instead of the meeting. They asked me to ask you to come."

"Are you going?"

I expect him to shake his head immediately, but he starts to squirm a little.

"I'm thinking about it."

"Really? I thought you'd be a definite no."

He looks at the floor and shoves his hands into the pockets of his khakis.

"So the school is still saying they can't have a GSA?" I ask.

"Right. They decided that they need to step things up."

"Do you know how many people are going?"

He squints. "Not many."

"What does that mean, like five?"

"Hopefully more than that. Joey said he was writing a press release, but he doesn't always follow through on things."

"So, we'd probably stand out."

"Yes."

"I want to go," I say, "but I have to figure out my schedule at my new volunteer job. And I might still be grounded."

His eyebrows shoot up, and I shrug. I wonder if I look tough, like I get in trouble all the time.

"Are you going for real?" I ask.

"I don't know. My dad goes out of town tomorrow for work, and my mom works on the other side of town, so she wouldn't know."

"If you go, I can figure it out and go too."

"Really?"

"If you can give me a ride."

"I can."

"Do you want to start a GSA here or something? Why is this so important to you? It's not even our school."

"I just . . . it's not right. And Joey was so hopeful that more people would want to protest."

"Oh, it's a Joey thing."

His cheeks flush and he doesn't meet my eye.

"Don't you ever get tired of doing what people expect?" he asks after a moment.

"Yeah, all the time. But I didn't think you did."

"Spencer was so sure I wouldn't come. I get tired of people thinking they know everything about me and acting like I'm just some boring nerd."

I'm pretty sure I've used that exact phrase to complain about him to Paula and Liz.

"Look, Philip, I'm sorry I was such a jerk to you."

"Don't worry about it. Let's meet in the parking lot after school on Thursday."

I nod, and we split up to go to our lockers. I have to smile to myself as I walk. Who would have thought? Hannah and Philip, taking it to the streets.

52

I buy a slice of cheese pizza from the ladies in the Commons, and am almost to our usual lunch table when Liz's laughter stops me short. She and Paula have their heads together, and Liz is covering her mouth with her hand, like that will prevent the sound from ricocheting around the room. I'm debating asking Philip if I can eat with him when Paula sees me.

"Hannah! The warden finally let you out?" A few people turn to look at me when she calls, and I feel my face burn. I walk toward the table slowly, like it's full of executioners and not my best friends.

"Hey babe!" Paula stands to hug me when I set my tray on the table, then ruffles up my hair. "Cute new style!"

"Thanks. Hey everybody." I return her hug, then nod at the boys. I look down at Liz, but her eyes are on her turkey sandwich. Colin and Brian lift their chins at me, and Colin gives a little smile. I smile back.

"So, what's the story?" Paula asks as soon as I sit. "We called, but your aunt said you moved out of your grandma's house and that you weren't allowed to use the phone."

"Did you try calling the house?" I ask, a little like a challenge. Paula's acting like she missed me, but how hard did she really try?

She has the decency to look away.

"Okay, so I wasn't exactly thrilled to get shot down by your mom, especially after . . . Did she tell you how she found us?"

"Yeah."

"Yeah," she repeats, and gives me a half smile. "She was not impressed."

"Especially when we didn't know where you were," Liz interjects.

I look over at her, surprised to see her glaring at me. *She's* mad at *me*?

"You just bailed on us. She was demanding answers and we didn't know anything!" Liz continues.

"I never should have let you throw that stupid party in the first place," I say, but she rolls her eyes.

"Oh, come on, Miss Goody Two-Shoes, you were excited to break the rules. Admit it. Doing something you weren't supposed to do, for once. You love having us around to be bad influences, so you can pretend to be a badass and then act all innocent because it wasn't your idea."

"How can you be mad at me?" I can't believe it. "I just spent all of spring break grounded, totally by myself. And where were all of you? My mom said she didn't even tell your parents. You probably just snuck back into your houses and everything was fine."

That shuts them up, and I can tell it's true.

Josh Cramer chooses that moment to walk by on his way to throw away his lunch sack.

"Hannah, nice haircut!" he calls. "You're really going full lesbo, huh? When are you getting yours done, Liz?"

"Oh, fuck off, Cramer!" Paula yells loud enough to make people turn and look. "When are you going to figure out that nobody gives a shit about what you have to say?"

"Plenty of people care about what I have to say about that party," he laughs. He waves his hand between me and Liz. "And about the evening's entertainment."

At this, Brian shoves his chair back and stands, with Colin following his lead. Brian is no tough guy, but Colin is one of the biggest guys in our year, and he can be intimidating with his all-black clothes and glowering silence.

"Just drop it, Cramer," Brian says calmly. "No one invited you to the party, and no one cares what you saw."

Even Josh knows he's not going to win a physical confrontation with Brian and Colin, not to mention Paula, so he just sneers at us, shakes his head, and turns back the way he came.

"And you could have recycled that bag, dipshit!" Paula yells after him. She flops back in her chair with a moan. "I can't *believe* I have to sit next to him next period."

I find this funny for some reason, and I start to giggle. Maybe it's the adrenaline leaving my body. Paula starts laughing too, and Brian and Colin look at each other like we're hopeless. I glance to my other side to look at Liz, but there's just an empty chair.

53

I'm the first person out the door of my history classroom when the final bell rings, so I beat Liz to the locker. She strolls up as the hallway is starting to clear, French book in hand.

"Bonjour Hannah," she says as she reaches around me to stuff her book into the locker.

"Liz, can we talk?"

"Yeah." She straightens up and looks at me expectantly.

I glance at all the people around and say, "Outside?"

She takes her time choosing what to put in her bag and what to leave, then she follows me out the front door. We cut through the line of cars waiting to exit the parking lot and I lead her into the empty football stadium. Neither of us speaks as we walk, far enough apart that our hands don't have a chance of brushing against each other. In the stadium, we both drop to sit on the concrete bleachers.

I decide to just own up to what she was mad about, so I start with, "Look, I'm sorry."

"Oh yeah? For totally bailing on me on my birthday? Or for leaving me to deal with your pissed-off mom?"

"For both, I guess. But I wasn't the only one who screwed up," I say.

She looks at me like I'm crazy.

"You think I did something?" she asks, and anger flares inside of me.

"Yeah, you kissed me!" I can't believe I said it, but once it's out, it's like a living thing, a third member of our conversation. "You knew I liked Corey, and then you kissed me in front of her!"

"So what?" she says, and I'm surprised to feel my heart break a little bit. "I kiss everyone. I'm a slut, haven't you read the wall in the bathroom in the locker room?"

"There's nothing written on the bathroom wall about you," I protest, but I never use the bathroom in the locker room if I can help it. The doors don't lock.

"Well, it's there. Liz Palmer is a slut. Liz Palmer has nothing to offer anyone other than her body. Not even her best friend, apparently."

"That's not how I feel."

"Well you never tell me how you feel, so how am I supposed to know?"

"Do you want to know how I feel? I've been in love with you since middle school!"

"Well, you have a funny way of showing it." She's not looking at me, and her voice is dry. Brittle, like she could break in half any second. I feel so frustrated. How can she see things so differently?

"What does that mean?"

"Jesus, Hannah! You always act like I'm not good enough. I'm always late and I'm not feminist enough and I care too much about stuff that you think is stupid. You think *I'm* stupid."

"I don't think you're stupid. I'm jealous of you all the time. You're talented and cool and everyone loves you. Nobody even notices me."

"It's not like you try to get people to notice you. You always have your face buried in a book. You just focus on how you're so different and weird."

"People treat me like I'm weird! I'm too fat and too nerdy and don't wear the right clothes. That's what I like about you." I feel like I might start crying. "You always acted like my weirdness was . . . endearing."

"It is endearing." She starts to smile a little, then her face darkens to a scowl. "Or, it was, until you started getting mad at me all the time for not going along with you. I like people to like me. I know you don't care about that, but I do. I don't want to be different all the time."

"But everyone likes you."

"Not Joel."

"He did for a while."

"Yeah." She snorts a laugh. "Until he got to know me."

"Oh come on, Liz. He's the first guy who's ever dumped you. Most of the guys you've dated have been super into you, and you're the one who loses interest."

She lifts one shoulder in a shrug. "Well, it sucks when the one that you really like doesn't like you back."

My anger flares up again, crackling through me like lightning, and I push myself to standing. She looks up at me, surprised. She's acting like that's some revelation I've never thought of.

"What?" she asks.

"That's just it. That's my whole life. It sucks to like someone who doesn't like you back. That's me and you."

"So, what? That's why you've been such a bitch to me lately? Because I'm into guys?"

"I don't give a shit if you're into guys. It's because you're not into *me*."

She takes a moment to reply, and when she does, her voice is quiet.

"Well, it's not like you asked and I turned you down. You never told me *anything*. You let me think you really cared about me, when the whole time you just wanted to fuck me."

At that, I start crying. I sit back down and push my hair out of my face. "How can you say that I never really cared about you? You're the most important person in my life. I just wanted to feel that important to you. And I started to get sick of being constantly reminded how I wasn't!"

"If you're my best friend, you should want me to be happy."

"I do," I say, wiping my tears away roughly. "But if you being happy means not hanging out with me, then we're not even friends."

"I just want to hang out with other people some of the time.

You've always been this constant in my life, Han, like even when my boyfriends get boring, you're there for me. And then suddenly, you're all mad about it."

"That's not fair to expect me to wait around until you're bored with other people."

She shakes her head. "I'm not saying it right."

"So try again. Because it sounds like you've just been taking for granted that I'll always be there for you, no matter how you treat me."

"Like you haven't done the same thing! You expect me to listen all about how bad my taste in guys is, or how I like stupid music, and then turn around and treat you like you're so special." She sniffles, then goes on, "You were always the most important person in my life, but you've just been so mad at me lately. And then you decided to tell this huge thing about yourself to Paula and not me. . ."

She covers her face with her hands, and when she pulls them away, I see that she's crying. Something inside of me shifts, and I can't help but want to wrap my arms around her and comfort her. Instead, I sit and watch her until she looks up and meets my gaze.

"Maybe we've both been taking each other for granted," I offer, and she shrugs, then nods. I continue, "It's not fair to be mad at you for not liking me back."

"You can feel how you feel," she answers. "But it's not fair to be a jerk to me about it."

I smile. "That's true. Wise, even."

She rolls her eyes. She's slumped down, elbows on her knees, looking kind of broken.

"I'm so sick of fighting. I just want us to be friends again," she says, her voice wobbly.

"I want us to be friends again too. That's all I want. I don't expect anything else, you know?"

She smiles weakly, but doesn't speak, so I go on, aware that I'm rambling.

"I think getting a crush on someone else really made me realize that I just wanted to be friends with you."

She looks up. "What happened with that other girl?"

"She was pretty mad after she saw us. We haven't really talked since then."

"What does she have to be mad about? Did you guys . . . do anything?" She's trying to act cool, but I can tell she feels nervous.

"No, but we both kind of thought we were going to." I take another deep breath before I ask the next question. "Why did you kiss me?"

She's the one who stands up this time, wiping her hands on her jeans and stepping down onto the row of seats below us. She speaks to the field.

"You were just *looking* at me. No one has ever looked at me like that."

I feel my face heat up. I reach up and comb my hair over my eyes with my fingers.

"And it's not like you're the only one who's ever thought about it," she continues.

"Excuse me?" Her words feel like a bucket of ice water dumped on my head. I shove my hair back and look at her, but her back is still to me. When she finally turns around, her eyebrows are furrowed and she almost looks scared.

"Don't worry about it. Forget I said anything."

"That's not something I can just forget."

She rakes her fingers back through her hair and takes a deep breath.

"Look, Hannah, I can't deal with this right now, okay? I just want us to go back to being friends, and I want everything to be normal."

"This is normal. People have feelings, Liz, and you have to deal with them."

"No, I don't. I'm sick of not having a best friend, and I'm sick of people being mad at me, so can you please stop?"

Suddenly, I feel a kind of tenderness toward her that I haven't felt in months, and I realize that it doesn't matter to me anymore if she thinks I'm the most important person in her life. It's true that I want to be just friends. It might take a little while to figure out a new kind of friendship, but we can do it. Maybe she does like me, or maybe she's liked other girls, but she's clearly not ready to deal with that. It's a lot, especially in a world that's always looking for another way to tell us that we're wrong.

I think about Philip, how he freaked out when I tried to talk to him about Rainbow Youth in class. He could talk about it when we were alone, though. I almost pity Liz, who's back on the bench a few feet away from me, tapping her hands on her thighs like it's all she can do to keep from running away. I remember what Corey said about how you can't change people. You can just change how you react.

"Okay," I say. She looks up, eyes red.

"Okay what?"

"We don't have to talk about that. I want to be friends again."

She exhales like she's been holding the breath in for a while.

"But if you want to talk, Liz, you know that I'm here, right?"

"I know. Thanks. So, now what?" she asks, and I shake my head.

"Why are you asking me? I never know anything."

"What are you talking about? You're the smartest person in our year. You know everything."

I laugh. "That's definitely not true, but I appreciate your support."

"Do you want to come over and hear this new song I've been working on? The Loyola is doing a battle of the bands this summer, and Susan B. is going to enter."

I remember that I've been wanting to talk to her about the band name, but I don't want to open up a whole new argument.

Plus, I kind of want to ask Philip about it first.

"Not today," I tell her. "I'm volunteering at Silver Wells." I don't say this, but I might need a little more time, too. Time to sort things out and get used to being friends with her in a new way, without my old expectations and hopes. I think she understands, because she doesn't press it or suggest that I come over another day. Maybe she'll start to change her expectations of me, too. I don't want to be just an audience for her exciting life anymore. I want an exciting life of my own, and a friend who will support me through it. Maybe I can have it.

"Let's go back," I tell her, and she nods. We walk back through the empty parking lot together, the silence between us feeling different, but still okay.

54

In genetics on Thursday, Philip produces a small notebook from his shoulder bag. I realize that the bag is similar to the briefcase I remember him carrying in elementary school, but a few degrees cooler. He writes in the notebook briefly, then passes it across the table to me.

"Olivia called and asked if we would mind if we didn't meet in the church today," the page says. "Are you still in?"

"Is everyone going to the protest?" I write back.

He nods, then scribbles, "She thinks the superintendent is close to letting them meet. There was an emergency school board meeting last night."

I write back two letters: OK. He nods, and we go back to taking notes in our own notebooks for the rest of class.

"Have you noticed Josh Cramer staring at you this week? What's up with him?" Philip asks while we're sitting in his car, in line to get out of the parking lot. He has a sedan without room for my bike, so he agreed to drop me back off at school after we go downtown.

"I can't believe you haven't heard," I groan. "He's been telling everyone who will listen."

"I don't hear a lot of gossip."

Oh yeah, I guess you have to have friends who go to parties to hear stories about them. I give him a quick rundown of the party, trying to minimize my lifelong desperate crush on Liz. I tell him she was drunk and kissed me, that Josh saw and got excited.

"I always wondered about the two of you," he says when I'm done.

I laugh. "Apparently, you haven't been the only one." I remember what Liz said, how she might not be totally straight, but isn't ready to deal with it. I look over at Philip, his hands positioned at 10 and 2 on the wheel. I guess we're all at different places of being ready to deal with it.

"So you're totally out now?" he asks, and I shrug. He, of course, is focused on the road and doesn't see me, so I speak.

"I guess so. I told my mom, and she's mostly okay with it."

"That's great."

"Yeah. . . I'm just hoping my pen pal will get less mad at me."

"Was this the first time you met her in person?"

"Yeah. Some first impression, right?" I try to laugh, but it comes out kind of strangled, and he glances over at me.

"Maybe she needs some time and then she'll reach out."

"I'm hoping." I'm quiet for a second, then I change the subject. "Did you know that Susan B. Anthony was racist?"

His forehead wrinkles, but he keeps his eyes on the road.

"Are you asking me because I'm black?"

"No," I say immediately, then take a second. "Maybe."

He snorts out a little laugh.

"I mean," I rush out, "she just focused on white women getting to vote, she thought that black women should wait and that including them would weaken her message."

"Not surprising," he says.

"And I suggested Susan B. Dangerous as the name for Liz's band, you know? And now I wonder if I should ask her to change it."

"Would she?"

"I'm not sure. They already have shirts and tapes and everything."

"What do you want from me? Permission to use the name, so no one has to make new shirts?"

I have to think about this one for a second before I admit, "I don't know."

"Why haven't you talked to her about it?"

"It never seems like the right time. Like bringing it up will make a fun conversation all serious."

"You brought it up with me."

"Yeah, but . . ." I trail off. I don't say that, since he's black, he can't exactly ignore talking about racism like I can. He smirks at me like he knows what I'm thinking, though, and I vow to bring it up next time I talk to Liz. Maybe they can make a statement at their next show or in their liner notes that they don't agree with everything that the real Susan B. said, or at least define Susan B. Dangerous as a different entity, separate from her namesake.

We turn onto the street of the school district office, and my mouth drops open when I see how crowded the sidewalks are. I count three news vans. There's the Salem newspaper, but also two vans with logos for the TV stations that we get from Portland. People holding homemade signs crowd on the sidewalks and the lawn of the district office. I see a few with Bible verses, but most of the signs are in favor of the GSA.

"GSA = Great!"

"We're here! We're queer! Get used to it!"

"Gay kids need love too."

"Holy shit," I say, turning to Philip. His eyes are wide and I watch his mouth slowly form a smile.

"This is amazing!" he says, and I grin back at him. I unhook my seatbelt and am about to climb out of the car when he grabs my arm.

"What?"

"About the band name," he says, and I nod. "It seems like you and your friend should talk about it and figure out what to do. I'm not some voice of all black people who can give you the official seal of approval."

"I didn't mean to -" I start, but he waves his hand at me.

"I know you didn't mean to, but think about how things come out, regardless of your intent, okay?"

"Okay. I'm sorry."

"It's fine. Black people already know about racism, though, and we don't need to be taught by white people who just found out about it."

"I'm sorry," I repeat.

"It's okay. Let's go do this." He nods toward the crowd. "I'm going to stay on the edge as an observer. Is that okay with you?"

"Totally. Do whatever you need to do, Philip. I appreciate you even coming."

"Are you going to go into the middle? I'm sure they have an extra sign you can wave around."

"I guess I might as well," I say, and we get out of the car.

55

Olivia sees us first. She's dressed up, in dark jeans and a light blue button-up shirt, her blonde hair out of its usual ponytail. She's holding a sign that says "Salem schools shouldn't teach hate." She runs up to us, a huge grin on her face.

"Hey! I'm so glad you made it!" She hugs Philip, then me.

"I'm just here to observe," Philip says, and she nods and looks at me expectantly.

"I'll do whatever," I say, and she punches the air in triumph and hands me her sign.

"I wanted to get the megaphone back anyway!" She runs back into the crowd, where I see Spencer hand her a megaphone.

"We want our clubs back!" she yells into it, and the crowd starts chanting along. It's not the catchiest phrase, but I join in, waving my sign. Philip retreats to stand near the handful of people who are watching from the sidewalk. I'm surprised to see someone I recognize - Michael Jarvis, Liz's ex and the editor of the school paper. He sees Philip and makes a beeline for him. Philip smiles and the two talk for a second, then Michael heads to me.

"Hannah, can I get a comment?" he asks. He sticks a black tape recorder in my face.

"What kind of comment?"

"I'm planning a piece about the protest for the next issue of the school paper. Why did you decide to come today? "

"I . . . um, I just think this is really important. It's important for kids to have a place to go. Like, a place where they won't be judged. And canceling all clubs just because you don't like one is stupid."

"Is this a *personal* issue for you?" He has a glint in his eye, and I know what he's asking. I don't really see any point in hiding it, so I nod.

"Yeah. As a member of the GLBT community, I know how like, essential it is to have other people to talk to. People who know what you've been through."

"Do you intend to start a GSA at East?"

"Maybe. Why not?"

"We could end up with all of our clubs canceled."

"I already said that's stupid. That's why we're protesting, and why people who aren't even part of the GSA at South are here. Because it's not fair to punish everyone instead of letting a few gay and bi kids get together once a week."

He clicks his tape recorder off. "Great, thanks, that's plenty. Can I take a picture?" He shoves the tape recorder into one pocket and pulls a camera from another.

"Uh, sure."

He steps back, pointing the camera. I hold my sign, then see a head of blonde curly hair zooming toward me.

"Did someone say 'picture'?" Joey asks with a grin, wrapping his arm around my shoulder and turning his face to Michael. I laugh and reach my arm around his waist. We hold our signs and stare into the camera triumphantly. Michael asks Joey's name for the caption, then whips his tape recorder out again once he learns that Joey helped organize the protest. I see Spencer smiling at us from behind them, and am on my way over to him when the energy of the crowd changes. Everyone gets quiet and turns toward the office, where I see the door open and the superintendent step out. He's wearing a suit and looks tired of all of this.

"Can I please have your attention!" he calls, even though everyone is already getting quiet. The reporters, including Michael, rush over to him. Olivia comes to join Spencer, Joey, and me, megaphone held loosely at her side.

"This better be good," she mutters.

"The district appreciates your interest in our process, and we also appreciate that our students are showing so much passion."

"Get on with it! What about the GSA?" Joey yells, and the crowd murmurs agreement.

The superintendent holds his hands out to quiet everyone, then speaks. "After careful consideration, we've decided to continue to cancel all clubs at South Salem High for the rest of the year. We will host listening sessions over the summer to get more input on how parents feel about the clubs, and make a final decision before the fall semester begins."

The crowd erupts in groans and yells. Joey and I exchange looks of disgust. They're doing nothing? Just waiting?

"That's just fine!" I'm surprised to hear Spencer's voice magnified. He must have gotten the megaphone back from Olivia. "Summer is almost here, and we'll have nothing but time. We can stand out here all day!"

The crowd cheers at this, and the superintendent blanches. He seems like he thought this would make us happy.

"Perhaps," he says, "we can begin listening sessions before the school year ends."

"Yeah, *perhaps*!" Spencer yells back, and the two stare at each other. The superintendent breaks the stare first, then opens the door and steps back into the safety of the building.

"We can't stop now!" Spencer calls into the megaphone. "GSAs are good for students! GSAs are good for students!" We all start chanting along with him, and I even catch Philip's lips moving from the sidelines.

56

On Monday, the local newspaper reports that listening sessions will begin next week to gather feedback from the community on whether GSAs should be allowed in Salem schools. I wonder if Philip's dad will be there to speak in opposition. I hope not.

I cut the article out and tape it up on my bedroom wall. We only get the paper on Sundays, but Silver Wells gets it every day, and Leticia didn't mind me bringing a page home. Mom agreed that I can have my phone and friend privileges back, but I wanted to keep going to Silver Wells. Until summer starts, we agreed that I'll volunteer for a few hours after school on Mondays, Wednesdays, and Fridays. I help Leticia with setup and cleanup, but mostly I sit with Gran and do the day's activities with her. Since I'm there to help, and because I told her that I enjoyed it, Leticia has added a second painting time each week, on Friday afternoons. She really is a nice lady, like Mom said. And based on Mom's constant grins and the fact that she's out with him again tonight, Leticia's brother seems pretty nice, too.

I fold up the rest of the newsprint sheet to take to the recycling, then pick up the handful of brochures that I got from the school guidance counselor during our appointment at lunch. Several college brochures, plus one about the Driver's Ed class that I can start taking this summer. I might as well get on with it. The other brochures are for schools with strong science programs, which I'll need if I want to apply to veterinary school after college. I could also start with a year or two at the community college, to save money and stay close to Gran for a little longer, then transfer. I'll be better able to decide that in the fall, once I start taking math there and get a feel for the campus.

The phone rings and I drop the brochures, go to the living

room, and pick up the receiver.

"Hello?"

"Hannah?" The familiar husky voice stops me in my tracks, and I sit on the couch.

"Yeah. How are you, Corey?"

"I'm doing all right. How about you?"

"I'm good. I'm so glad that you called."

"Thanks. I actually have some news I wanted to tell you."

"Oh yeah?"

"Yeah. My parents just sent my deposit in to Reed. So I'm moving to Portland at the end of the summer."

"That's great!" I say. "Congratulations!"

"Thanks."

"Wait a second. Are you calling to like, warn me? Like that you're coming to the state so we need to set boundaries to keep us from running into each other by accident?"

"Oh my God, Hannah. Of course not," Corey says, and I swear that Valley Girl inflection never came out of her mouth when we first started talking. "I was hoping we could try again at being friends."

"Does that mean you're not mad at me anymore?"

"I was never that mad. I just felt so stupid, you know? I knew I was overreacting, but I couldn't stop."

I lean back into the couch cushions and nod. "I definitely understand feeling stupid."

She chuckles, and I smile at the warm sound.

"I'm moving up in August, so we should get together sometime after that. And if you want, you can, you know, bring Liz or whoever you're dating."

I can't help but laugh at that. "That's not going to happen. Not Liz anyway."

"No? I wasn't sure if the party was the start of something for you two."

"No." I hope I sound as definite as I feel. "We talked, and she was just drunk and swept up in the moment or whatever, you know? I think we'll always be friends, but that's it."

"Oh. Cool." Does she sound hopeful, or am I imagining things? Normally, I would be sure I was just imagining it, but I need to start giving myself more credit.

"So," I say, "I can come up when you move up to Portland. Or you can come down to Salem if you need a break from school."

"Yeah. That would be great. And can you still write something for my new zine? I want to put it out this summer."

"I totally can!" I'd almost forgotten about that. But I think I actually have more to say now than I did when she first asked.

"That's great. Send it to me when you can, okay?"

"Yeah, I'll start working on it tonight."

"Thanks so much."

"Of course!"

We're both quiet for a second, then the words start spilling out of me.

"I miss you. It's so weird how you became one of my best friends so quickly, but I really started to count on you."

"Yeah, I know what you mean. It's funny how it can be easier to get to know someone through the mail."

"Totally. And so much has happened since we talked, too. I ended up going to the protest about the GSA, and I was even interviewed about it for the school paper."

"That's great!"

"And I got a super gay new haircut."

She laughs. "I can't wait to see it."

"Yeah, I can send you a picture."

"Perfect."

"How are things with your mom?" I ask. "Like with you missing the bridal shower?"

"They're actually going okay. We had a really long talk about it after I got home. I guess she mentioned it to my brother's fiancée at the shower, something about how I was being so ridiculous and stubborn, and Stephanie said that she doesn't want me to be uncomfortable."

"That's awesome!"

"Yeah, she said I can wear the same thing as the groomsmen."

I imagine Corey dressed in a suit, and feel a flush creep up my neck.

"I'm sure you'll look incredible," I say, trying to keep my thoughts out of my voice, but it comes out too formal, and she laughs.

"Yeah, I'll send you a picture."

"Thanks."

"Hey, listen, I actually have to go. I told my mom I'd come to the restaurant and help with closing because one of the other waitresses had to go home early. But I've been thinking about calling you for a few days, and finally just decided to do it."

"No problem," I say. "Thank you so much for calling. I'm really glad that you did."

"You're welcome. Thank you for writing. I'll talk to you soon, okay?"

"Yeah, that would be great."

"Yeah."

We hang up, and I go into my room and dig my notebook out of my backpack. I turn to a fresh page in the middle, one that looks like it's just waiting for me to use it to sort things out. I don't know what I'm going to say yet. Something about slow grief, about holding on and letting go, about the way relationships change and you just have to change with them. About how no one is perfect, not even historical heroes or wise girls who make zines and think about the meaning of life. Not even shining golden musicians who everyone loves.

Maybe the real purpose is to create a little pocket of kindness in the world like Gran did. To be confident like Heather, outspoken like Paula, smart like Philip, brave like Joey and Spencer. I don't have everything figured out yet, but maybe that's okay.

Acknowledgements

First and foremost, thank you to Sage Adderley-Knox, my self-publishing mentor. I could not have come nearly this far on my own, and your encouragement and gentle challenges have been invaluable. If anyone reading this is thinking about self-publishing a book, I can't recommend working with Sage highly enough. Check out her website at www.sageadderleyknox.com.

Thank you to Amber Smith for being my best friend and ally through my own trials of high school; Sarah Berkowitz and Rebecca Berkowitz for being my most long-lasting zine pen pals; Gillian and Theresa Beck Van Heemstra for being my first real-world zinester friends; and Katy McElwain for helping me find my place in the world and being the best sister I could have hoped to chance upon. You've all made me feel a lot less alone in the world.

Thank you to my first readers: Becky Morton, Beth Bray, Beth Caldwell, Hilary Browning-Craig, Jack Salt, John Bennett, and Lisa Wilson. Your feedback improved the story tenfold, and your encouragement throughout this process has meant so much to me. I seriously couldn't have done this without you. You're also some of my best friends, and I appreciate the way you help shape the way I look at books and the world.

Thank you to Amy M. Long, GNP, for meeting with me to talk about your experience working with people with dementia, and to Myriah J. Day and Sara White for messaging with me about fruit fly labs. Any mistakes about either subject are mine.

Thank you to my parents, Pam Burt and Karl Pearson. Both for your genes and for your love and unwavering support of me and my projects. Thank you to my grandparents, Jim and Rosalie Pearson, for being constant inspirations to read, write, and self-publish.

Thank you to Marty and Benny for being the worst writing assistants and best cuddlers in history, and to Mary Dinsdale for standing by me through all my weird ideas, feelings, and impulsive decisions. You're a wonderful partner and your calm nature is a great balance to my tendency toward the dramatic.

Thank you to all leaders and members of Rainbow Youth, past and present. The members of the group in this book are all fictional, but Rainbow Youth is a real group serving LGBTQIA+ youth in the Salem, Oregon area. Connect with them at www.rainbowyouth.org.

Finally, thanks especially to zinesters, queers, fatties, and other weirdos everywhere. You're my favorite people in the whole word, and I am constantly inspired by your insistence on being yourself in a world that wants you to be anything but.

CPSIA information can be obtained
at www.ICGtesting.com
Printed in the USA
FFOW02n1526110718
47398696-50543FF